The author started out not intending to be a writer of novels, but more a hobby script writer, getting the writing bug and imagination back in 1993. Indeed, this novel started life as a pen-script around that time. As for income, working in the education system pays the bills, as writing for a living was seen as a pipe-dream. For the author, recent changes in first-time writers' work being considered by publishers was monumental in switching to novel writing and hope!

I dedicate this book to my parents, who, sadly, have passed away and cannot share my great joy in the publication of this novel.

Nisar Hussain

LUKE WOAM – THE MISSING LINK

AUSTIN MACAULEY PUBLISHERS™

LONDON * CAMBRIDGE * NEW YORK * SHARJAH

A CIP catalogue record for this title is available from the British Library.

ISBN 9781398449695 (Paperback)
ISBN 9781398449701 (ePub e-book)

www.austinmacauley.com

First Published 2023
Austin Macauley Publishers Ltd®
1 Canada Square
Canary Wharf
London
E14 5AA

I would like to thank my publishers for having faith in my second offering and all the people who have continually been asking me about my books, that, in itself, is a kind of encouragement. It inspires you to no end. Also, my nephew Faisal Hussain, for again being the designer of the front cover.

Chapter 1
The Invasion

Luke Woam is standing ready at the beach, on the Kent coast, in southern England with a slightly rusty looking but nevertheless majestic sword in hand, looking far out into the sea, eagerly scouting the straight featureless horizon for any signs of the enemy. It is late summer in the year 55 BC and word from the muddy cart tracks of Gaul is that a mighty Roman general is about to invade Briton or Britannia to the Romans. Now, this general is none other than the all-conquering Julius Caesar himself, one of history's first great fiction writers and storytellers (with bits of non-fiction woven in to further embellish the written accounts).

Luke is not alone at the beach, far from it, for around him are lots of his fellow Britons, most of whom he knows, many from his and surrounding villages. None came here out of a sense of loyalty though, for when the local chieftains and their henchmen enter your village looking for able-bodied men to fight, you 'volunteer' your services. If you survive a battle, well, that counts as a bonus or just plain lucky. You live to fight another day—or die another day!

"I can't see them, maybe they're not coming," said Luke to all around him. "Maybe the big general guy heard about all us bad boy Britons and got scared. We have won without any of us even fighting, whadya' think lads?"

"Somehow I doubt it. This guy, the Roman general, I hear he is looking to become the top dog in Rome and needs military victories to support his challenge to become Consul or king. We are part of his plan to become the leader. So, I very much doubt he has been scared off, I mean, what have we got for him to be scared of, Eogan's pitch fork, my dangerous looking broom, Cynwrig's thoroughly worn out sickle? Or maybe our famous inclement weather, the rain, the cold, the wind? It's only a pity it's a rather a good weather day today, good fighting weather," replied another man, looking quite intelligent amongst the rag-tag motley crew.

"The Romans could always sail a lot farther up the coast into the forbidden lands and attack the Picts way up north. Those wild, red-haired, bushy-bearded, painted cut-throats—the likes of which the Druid gods cannot even tame," said another group member.

"Doubt it!" came the whole group reply.

"Not even the bloodthirsty Romans are that crazy mad," replied the intelligent one again.

"Listen guys, whilst we are waiting around, how about you all taste my new food creation," said an Asian guy in the group. "Might be the last meal we ever have."

He begins to hand out some spicy chicken chunks to everyone near him. They all accept the much appreciated snack tit-bit.

"Hmm—this is really good mate, just a little on the burning hot side though, could use it as a weapon to poison the Romans. Who told you about this recipe—Morg the sorcerer? Is it meant to fire us up for the battle?" asked Luke.

"No! It wasn't him. Funny enough, it was this passing stranger who came into our village about two weeks ago, he was one of those crazy people who believed in just one god, he said he had just come from Jerusalem or something like that. Anyway, he had travelled a great distance in lands to the east of the Roman Empire and brought back with him many spices to garnish food with. He let me have some of these spices and I have roasted this chicken meat with them, using some metal skewers he gave me, over a flaming fire. What do you lot think of it?" replied the Asian guy.

"Delicious! Best chicken ever!" rang out from all.

"You got a name for this fiery chicken?" asked Luke.

"I've been thinking of a name these last few days. The traveller from the east was called Masala, the skewers he called Tikkas and since I am using chicken meat, I came up with the name of 'Chicken Tikka Masala', kind of honouring him. What do you think?"

"Chicken Tikka Masala? Definitely catchy, got a ring to it, I must agree," admitted Luke.

"It is a most excellent name for your creation. You deserve to survive this battle and make it big with this chicken recipe idea," said the intelligent one.

"Thanks, friend. This is jolly good news. I am thinking the same. I have this dream that my chicken tikka Masala will become the most favourite food in Briton, loved by everyone, especially after you Britons have drunken too much mead on a night-time. Who knows, maybe even the dreaded Romans will like it too? I mean, the Romans are rubbish with food, aren't they, I've heard about what they eat, stuffed dormice covered in garum, everybody's favourite rotting fish sauce?" announced the Asian one.

"Nonsense! My food will become the best in Briton," burst in a Chinese guy from the group, he is standing right next to the Asian guy. "I have also been creating tasty new foods. Now you taste mine."

He too begins handing out snack sized chunks of poultry. As before, nobody resists this welcome treat and begin eating this new snack with relish.

"Not bad at all, Lin Chun. What is it, it isn't chicken, I know that looks like chicken?" asked Luke.

"No! Not chicken. It is duck. Caught fresh early this morning. I cook it myself from my recipe, no help from strangers," replied Lin Chun.

"What you calling your creation then, Lin," asked the intelligent one.

"Oh—I have name. When I was cooking in pot, I used the whole duck, the head still on. When my wife look in pot, she said duck was looking straight at her, in creepy way. She no eat it now. So I call this peeking duck!"

"Peeking duck, eh? Sounds good to me, sounds kind of funny too, easy to remember though," said Luke.

"Yes, that is why my duck will be best food in Briton, not chicken tikkle Masilly," proudly boasted Lin. "Everybody will buy peeking duck in Briton. It is my first dish so I will call it number one, the peeking duck."

"No way, Emperor Ming! Your reeking duck is good but my chicken tikka is way better. It has way more spices—it's just—better!" back came the Asian guy.

The two start a low key verbal battle that no one makes any attempt to stop. Waiting there on the beach is boring and now some entertainment has come their way.

Then, out of the blue, a grilled chicken leg stuck on the end of a short sword is thrust in between the Asian and Chinese guy's head. They both stop the verbal sparring and stare at this charcoaled chicken leg in the middle of their two faces.

"There is no point in you two arguing a losing battle man that will happen soon enough when the rotting fish flavoured stuffed dormice munchers get here!

Say hello to the winner. This is my creation, this is going to take over Briton. Not the Romans but my chicken dish," said an African man in the group.

"Ah—you are the Nubian guy I heard about, you just arrived a few weeks ago, were you escaping the Romans?" asked the intelligent guy.

"Nubian! Why do you all white men think every black guy is Nubian? I am not from Nubia. Never lived there, just passed through it! I blame those bloody Egyptians. I am from the great forest lands, which is far south of Nubian lands," replied the African with some annoyance.

"Sorry, I stand corrected, my friend from the great forested lands. Now, what amazing culinary delight have you cooked up?" said the intelligent one.

"I too cooked this chicken leg with no help, it is all my own work, I use my very own secret sauce."

He swings his sword with the chicken leg stuck on the end around until it comes very close to a fat man's face, it is so close in fact to his mouth he takes a bite out of the chicken leg and immediately begins chomping away.

"Hmm—it is good fellas. It is most deliciously good. Different to the other two," acknowledged the fat man.

The African moves the sword and chicken leg around so others can tear bits of meat off the leg with their mouths, they all eat it with the same satisfying feeling as the fat man. They all agree with the fat man that it is very tasty.

"And that's a strike! This is good as well. Guys, we've got to survive this battle, if only to go home to eat some more of these foods," said a happy Luke.

"Same question to you, sir. What are you labelling your amazing culinary delight?" asked the intelligent one.

"He's already told us mate, it's a chicken leg dish, not coolinary, whatever that is you keep calling it?" burst in Luke. All the others agree with Luke and wondered why the intelligent one did not hear the African tell everyone that it was a chicken leg.

"Well—I don't k know yet, still thinking about it. If I was to name it after what I was doing at the time of cooking, I probably would have to call it jerk chicken!"

On hearing that everyone makes a revolting expression on their faces and some begin spitting out some semi-chewed chicken out if their mouths. They are all thinking of something but no one actually says what.

"This secret sauce, it's not white and sticky and comes as a result of a certain pleasuring action you were doing at the time—alone?" asked Luke.

"No batty man! My sauce is made from spices I brought with me from the mother land," replied the African.

"Why jerk chicken then and I must admit I don't really know if I want to know the answer to that one?" asked the intelligent guy.

"Because, at the time I felt sudden twinges in both my arm muscles and that made me jerk my arm and the raw chicken leg I was holding dropped into the spice pot I use for only the vegetables. Anyway, I decided to leave the spices on the chicken leg and I cooked it. This is how I discovered my creation—jerk chicken—you see?"

Everyone present now felt a sense of relief and regret at spitting out the lovely chicken.

Another voice sounds from the crowd. "Can I just say that I am Egyptian and I certainly do not think all black men are from Nubia." The voice came from a man clearly identifiable as an Egyptian. He was looking at the African when he said it.

"Thank you, Egyptian. It is a pity more of your people are not as knowledgeable and understanding as you are. They just see us as slaves or cheap labour," replied the African.

"Hey! Were you a prince back home in Egypt? Were you born of a high status, royal even," asked the intelligent one.

"Prince? What the heck are you doing here in soggy Briton about to fight the Romans who are friends of your people, the Egyptians?" asked Luke.

"The Romans are friends of no people. They just rob you of all your resources and then enslave you to serve them until you die. We are treated like second class citizens in our own country. I realised that but most of my people haven't yet," replied the Egyptian.

"Us Britons will never do that to anyone if we had an Empire!" burst in Luke.

"Is that what brought you here, to Briton? The only place free of Romans, so far, well, for this morning at least?" asked the intelligent one.

"No! I just did not agree with Egyptian culture anymore. Well not some of it anyway, to be honest, most of it. I think we Egyptians need to evolve, modernise. We are stuck in a time warp which began more than two and a half thousand years ago and still dictates how we live our lives to this day. I just did not feel it was right to marry my own sister or get mummified when I die.

I mean, who wants some lowly servant to scoop out your brains through your nose, pull out all your guts and things and put them in a pot. Then cut out your heart and put that in a separate pot. Then, rub all your body in salt until you look like a shrivelled dried prune. After all that, wrap you up in bandages and shove you away in a mountain side, in a cold and unwelcoming tomb that no one will ever visit apart from the most daring tomb-raiders. Plus, I got sick of eating sandy, gritty bread. Bloody sand in everything."

"Yeah man, I can see why you're here. Why can't your people just toss the body into the bog or river like we do here? And having your sister as a wife? That totally sucks!" said Luke.

"Have you got new foods for us to try, Egyptian?" asked the fat man as he moves next to the Egyptian.

"Not really! As I said, you wouldn't want Egyptian food, not unless you like the taste of bloody sand! I hate standing here at the beach where all I can see is sand everywhere. I thought I had left it behind. Anyway, I only bring this with me." He pulls out a very flat piece of a papyrus sheet, all so very dry, thin and stained brown.

"You eat that, you're right, nobody would want to eat that, it looks all dry and tasteless! Is it made of sand?" remarked the fat one. He quickly breaks a small piece from the papyrus sheet and puts it into his mouth. "Ergh! I'd rather eat pig dung!"

"Nah! We wouldn't eat that either!" said all in the group except the intelligent one, he is looking out at sea.

"Look sharp people 'cause lunchtime is over, our uninvited guests have just appeared on the horizon," shouted the intelligent one as they are all digesting what the Egyptian gave them, the information that is, not the papyrus sheet.

Indeed, on the horizon appeared many Roman ships as tiny dots, all heading for the coast at a good speed. Soon they are past the horizon and in plain sight for all the watching Britons to see and fear. The tiny dots have enlarged to scary looking big war ships.

"There are so many ships I've never seen such big ships, if we had ships that big, we could catch loads of fish," stated another man in the group.

"Show him a boat and all he thinks of is fishing. He's just a simple fisherman true and true, isn't he?" said Lin Chun the Chinese guy.

"They are kind of fishing, just they're here to catch us, our land, our wealth, not forgetting our freedom," said the intelligent one.

"Well, they're not going to get it easy, all those things, I can tell you. I'm fighting them all the way," boasted Luke brandishing his sword.

"Hey, Luke. Where did you get that expensive looking sword, if I'm not mistaken, it looks like a Chieftains' sword? How can you afford to buy such quality? You're just a corn miller's apprentice—a bad one at that!" asked the Asian one.

"I—got it. Got it from the Sacred Lake," Luke proudly boasted.

"The Sacred Lake!" replied everyone in unison, with great shock like surprise, not forgetting the sudden quiet that followed after the shock revelation.

"Yes, the Sacred Lake. It was thrown in a couple of weeks ago. So it's still all mostly shiny and that so, I just rubbed some dirt into it to make it look a little older."

"Then it is a Chieftains' sword. Luke, if the Druids find out about what you did, they will certainly see to it that you're the next human sacrifice. Probably get tortured first," informed the intelligent one.

"Yeah well, the dead Chieftain doesn't need it anymore. And I am using it to defend the new Chieftain's kingdom, he should be grateful. So, the Druids can kiss my bony arse. Besides, like I said, none of us are going to survive today. The Romans are a professional fighting machine, the strength of a hundred dragons. Not even the Druids can stop them."

"You better not let the Druids hear you say that. Nicking sacred objects and then bad-mouthing the Druids, maybe you're better off not surviving today," advised the intelligent one.

"They are getting closer, brothers. Time to shut up and fight!" shouted the African one. "I know how they operate, so be alert."

The Roman fleet stops short of beaching. Then there is hesitation on the part of the Romans, not one soldier is storming the beach.

"What are they waiting for? Why don't they attack? I know the Romans as well, too well, they are not scared of anyone," wondered the Egyptian.

"I don't know, it's a mystery. They should be half way up the beach by now, using our fallen dead bodies as a red carpet," replied the intelligent one.

"Got it! Like I said before, they're scared of us Brits. They have heard about us and now, they see us for the first time out here in our hundreds and thousands and they are shitting it. They're scared to fight us, my Egyptian and African forest friends!" shouted Luke.

"I don't know, it could be a tactical move, part of their plan," mused the intelligent one.

"Nah! You would say something like that. They've plain bottled it. I've got an idea. I'll show them some Brit grit. Watch me, lads. (On saying that, Luke runs fast down the beach, past the conscripted men and even past the proper soldiers at the front. He eventually stops right at the waterfront). Come and fight me if you think you're hard enough. (He waves his sword around like he knows what he is doing). Otherwise go back to Gaul and keep your stupid dangly frog legs, we don't want them or eat them here, we've got enough tasty foods of our own!" Some native Briton chiefs stare and point at the sword Luke is waving around and comment to each other about it.

There is some activity from the Romans just at that moment. A Roman standard bearer suddenly jumps into the water, waist deep and runs towards the beach. This triggers a mass storming of the entire beach from everyone Roman soldier on every ship. Suddenly, there is a two football pitch sized carpet of Roman soldiers fast approaching en-masse towards the shoreline, yelling to high heaven, headed by this brave solo standard bearer at the front.

Luke sees this horror sight up close and almost personal, since he is the furthest Briton out. If he does not scarper from there in the next second or two, he will have the dubious honour of being the first Briton to be killed by the Romans in open battle on mainland Britannia. Now, Luke is not that loyal a patriot. Sure, he is here and taking part, surrounded by approximately ten thousand other men, where his plan was to hang about mainly near the back.

It has been established already that if he had not come here today of his own free will, then the Druids would indeed have had their next human sacrifice victim all served up, on a plate. Cowardice is not permitted in this Celtic society—it displeases the elemental gods and the harvests would fail!

Luke about turns and runs like the clappers back towards the safety of the many. He gets some real nasty looks from the frontline proper fighting men but he just ignores them, he eventually stops near his group of friends at the back.

"The hero returns! Well done, Luke, you've terrified them to bits. And at the same time showed them that we are utter pansies!" muttered the intelligent one.

"I don't need a big brain like yours to figure out that I'd rather be a live coward than a dead hero. Besides, I'm irreplaceable to my village, I'm the miller, we all need bread!" replied Luke.

The first battle of Briton begins. Eight thousand well equipped, battle-hardened and seasoned professional Roman soldiers engage the rag tag Britons who number no more than a couple of thousand semi-professional soldiers amongst maybe seven or eight thousand farmers and labourers.

A typical Roman slaughter is on the cards then. Luke was along the right lines when he predicted none shall walk away from this battle or very few will. On paper and most likely, for real, there will only be one winner today. For a while, Briton will scorn to yield, but inevitably, it will yield to Roman sword and shield.

To the credit of the native Britons, they are fighting like real brave men. If only they had been trained in combat sword fighting instead of ploughing and sowing, it would not be such a one-sided encounter. Even though the Romans are a little fewer in number, their skill and experience is telling. They are cutting down the Britons, like the Britons cut down the wheat on a good (human sacrificed, Druid pleasing) harvest season.

Luke, standing at the back, finds that the protection and safety in numbers of the men in front of him is now disappearing fast. His fellow Britons are not so much standing in front of him as laying in front of him—dead. Luckily, his cohort of friends is still around him, mainly behind him. He stares hard at the grim sight in front of him.

"Guys! This is definitely not going to plan or it is going as planned, depends how you look at it, but it is not panning out the way the Druids said it would go. Pity really, enough good goats were sacrificed and a couple of old ugly women and for what, this slaughter? I think it's time to do the right thing and leg it, while we've still got legs attached to our bodies. Whadya' say, guys?" Luke turns and looks behind him to see no one near him, all his friends are running away, leaving him by himself. "What the hell?"

A huge, fat mountain of a Roman soldier charges towards Luke. Luke turns back around to the front again to see this barn door sized Roman swing his sword at him. Fortunately, Luke manages to swing his recently 'acquired' dead Chieftain's sword just in time. Both swords clash and make a noise like thunder clapping. Both swords then fling free of the two men holding them and fly off in different directions, the Roman's sword breaks into two. After all, it is only a standard issue Roman army sword with many miles on the clock.

Luke and the massive Roman are now unarmed, so now it comes down to good old fashioned man to man combat—no weapons. Again, the advantage is clearly with the Roman, Luke must be a third or a quarter of his mass. Just like the battle, it is a no-contest or a one-sided contest, depends which way you prefer to describe it. The massive Roman lunges for Luke before he has a chance to scarper. All the bulk of the Roman falls on Luke and both fall to the ground hard, needless to say, Luke is underneath the Roman, poor chap!

In the kitchen, Luke's mum, Jean, is preparing a traditional full English breakfast late in the morning. The Woam household love breakfast, the first meal of the day. For this reason, they have a full English a few times a week. This is one of those days. Maybe explains why Jean has a somewhat rotund body shape, a lover of good food! Anyway, most of the breakfast food was plated up, except the bacon rashers, four of which she is pan frying now. When they are done, she moves the pan closer to the plates to put the slices in each of the two plates containing the other items already. She looks at the rashers in the pan.

"Oh, that's a big piece, I'll have that one."

Using her flat spatula, she tries to push the biggest rasher into her plate from the pan. Unfortunately, she is not too careful and the choice slice falls to the floor.

"Oh—sugar!" Jean said in annoyance and proceeds to pick it up.

Now, standing nearby is the family dog, Patch, a small West Highland terrier. It sees its chance for some breakfast of its own and in a flash darts for the bacon rasher. The family pet gets to it first, its jaws clamp down firmly on one end of the rasher. However, mum Jean also makes quick moves of her own. She manages to grab the other end of the bacon rasher. What follows is a tug of war between human and beast connected by a bacon rasher. Both fight for dear life for this tasty, juicy bit of freshly sizzled bacon.

"Patch! You silly mutt! Let go of it, now!"

The battle of the bacon rasher does not last long. Jean pulls with more force and lifts the rasher and the dog into the air a few inches, the dog's grip loosens and he falls down to the floor, thus freeing the slice. True, a bit of the other end is missing and it did lay on the not so clean kitchen floor. Jean looks at the bacon rasher with one end of it all ragged.

"Pity, it was the biggest one, but never mind. Can't waste it. Expensive! (She puts the hard fought over rasher on the plate—one intended for Luke, along with another one). There! Breakfast sorted. Now to take it to that good for nothing slob son of mine."

Jean takes this plate, complete with knife and fork and a white envelope and leaves the kitchen and heads upstairs.

Jean enters Luke's room without knocking and hears Luke making noises and moving in jerky movements. She guesses he is having a nightmare. She puts the plate and letter down on top of a side chest draw and goes over and sits right next to her son whereupon she starts prodding him many times with force in an effort to wake him.

Suddenly, Luke shouts out loud. "Get off me you big fat smelly bastard!" After that delightful burst, he fully awakes and is alert.

"Oh charming! Nice way to greet your poor old mum in the morning. I'll just take the full English back down and save it for myself as lunch."

"Mum! Sorry, did I just say something not very nice? Something I should not have said?"

"Yes, son, you did."

"I was having this dream, I singled-handily stopped the Roman invasion of Britain. I was just about to kill the last sorry ass one of them when you woke me up. I was about to clobber that Julius Caesar and his legions. I reckon if I had been there back then, our great island would have stayed spaghetti and pizza free for a good while longer. I would have been remembered as a hero, who saved Briton."

"Yes, it sounded like it. Did the Romans really try to invade Blighty? I didn't know that. What on earth for? Do they like the rain?"

Luke looks at his mum. "Never mind mum. (Luke clocks the full English on the chest draw top). Is that for me, you're the best, mum? Pass it over, will ya' please."

Jean passes him the plate and a second or two later, puts down the letter next to him on the bed. Luke looks at it totally not knowing what it could be. He does not fuss about it either.

"Eat your breakfast, hero. And there's nothing wrong with spaghetti and pizza!"

Luke, still totally ignoring the letter, pays more interest to the plate of lovely food in front of him with the added bonus of it being breakfast in bed as well.

"You never bring me my brekky to bed, normally you shout so loud from downstairs, the whole street can probably hear it. We haven't won the Post Code lottery have we?" asked Luke as he hooks the raggedy bacon rasher with his fork and looks hard at it wondering what had happened to it then puts it down again.

"Nope! We should be so lucky, only people on the adverts on telly win."

Chapter 2
The Letter

Mum Jean lets Luke devour the breakfast for a few minutes before saying something. "There's a letter there for you son, aren't you going to open it? It could be important, certainly looks it, see what it is."

"Doubt it! Probably the Christmas bonus from the jobcentre people. A measly ten pounds, ten pounds for a year's worth of hard work signing on."

"Bonus, yeah for being their best customer, year on year!"

"Or, it could be a bill, just leave it unopened and toss it across the room like they do in movies."

"I'll toss you across the room, cheeky sod, you make bills, you don't pay 'em! They don't even come in your name."

Luke picks up the letter. "Fair point mum. Now, let's see what this letter is about. Can't be an overdue library book fine as I always use Sam's membership, he would get the fine. (He opens it and skim reads it). Hmmm."

"Well, what is it?"

Luke smiles. "Mum, I've got a job, it seems."

"Great! When do you start?"

"Day after tomorrow! A long morning shift, it says here."

"Then it's a great day today. My son has got his first job after all this time."

"Wait a minute! I never applied for this job! I've never applied for any job ever!"

"I did! Well, not me, your brother did. He filled in the application form for you."

"Sam! That squirt! But he's only fourteen years old!"

"I know, I wanted it to look professional. I can hardly do it, can I?"

"That's just brilliant, ain't it? A spotty teenager got me a job—you two got me a job. No wonder you haven't ask me what kind of a job it is or where it is."

"You should be grateful. Working in a bakery, baking bread and stuff, it'll make a change from being the bone idle, good for nothing, couch potato that you are and have been since leaving school."

"Mum, you do know how to say the nicest things about your own flesh and blood son."

"They're not my words, son. That's what the vicar said to me this Sunday gone. That's why he says you've never ever step foot in the house of God."

"The vicar! Good job he's a vicar or else—"

"Or else what?" mum interrupted.

"Or—else it he could have been the dole officer, then I would really be in the bumboclaats—in deep shit, as our local vocal vicar would think but not say."

"You're already in deep shit with them. You've been sanctioned more times than the Russian Olympic team."

"Mum, these application forms require a signature at the bottom. I remember doing some in school. I never signed the one you sent off."

"I told you, Sam sorted it out. He signed it for you."

"But I've got a really hard to copy, super stylish signature. It's uncopiable."

"Yeah, it did take him two goes to perfect it. Besides, no point having such a fancy signature if you only use it at the dole office. The only thing they care about is when you don't need to sign on anymore. Well, now you don't need to. That'll make 'em happy for once when they see you next."

"Me—working? Blimey, things have just gotten heavy. Me a baker, I mean, what do I know about baking bread? I know how to eat it, all toasted and spreaded."

"Again that's all sorted out. This job needs no skills or any experience nor brains whatsoever, perfect for you. It says the job is ideal for a school leaver. They just need workers fast for the busy Christmas period coming up. They are hiring people just from what it says on the application form, so I told young Sam to fill it out so you actually knew something."

"But I'm not a school leaver. I am twenty-three years old."

"They've hired you, haven't they? Job done, I'd say. (Mutters to herself very quietly). Probably no school leavers applied for it, a bit beneath them."

"Well, I suppose so, I'm gonna be a working man."

"Finish your breakfast, son. And don't be going back to sleep afterwards. (She starts walking to the door, then turns back around to face Luke). You won't have time to dream from now on. (She turns back towards the door and starts

21

walking out, muttering to herself again). I don't know, dreaming about fighting Julie Christie and her legions, shame on you. Who would want to hurt her, she was ever so nice in Mary Poppins."

Much later in the day, Luke is sitting next to his girlfriend, Tina Simpson. She is one year younger than him, so twenty-two and they have known each other from their school days, although they only became an item way after leaving school. Now, Tina is no oil painting. She is plumy to put it kindly, definitely below average in the looks department, to put it kindly again and would be more hindrance than help in a Trivial Pursuit board game. But Luke, who is skinny to medium in body shape, sees past the outer shell and really likes Tina, who really likes him, you could say the force is strong between these two, kind of a like for like in personality thing.

However, most unlike Luke, Tina has had a range of temporary jobs throughout her time after leaving school but presently and for the last year and half, has not had a job. The two are sitting at an outdoor cafe table drinking lattes from one of those over-sized coffee cups, they tend to serve these types of fancy named coffees in. Even though it is nearly mid-November, the weather is unusually mild today and so the cafe tables are out and so the customers get to enjoy the continental cafe experience for today anyway. There is a tree next to their table and sitting up on a high branch are two pretty love birds chirping away to each other.

"So, you see Tina my love, I have now got a job, I have got a career. OK, it's a temporary job and a temporary career but they could keep me on after the Crimbo season and I reckon they will. I am the Bolton baker. Yes, the impossible has now become the possible. What I'm saying is—now we can afford the better things in life—eventually—when I get paid.

We could holiday in Blackpool, staying more than just the day—stay overnight in a hotel. We can order the special at the chippie, each, one for you and one for me. We can buy some top branded food stuff in the supermarket. Buy a house in the near future, to live in or maybe rent out like the Asians do. Crazy stuff eh? (Luke reaches out across the table and clasps Tina's right hand in his). Life will never be the same again. I will treat you like the beauty queen you are. I can give you proper things now, no discount store stuff."

"Can't wait. So far, in all the years we've been together, the only thing you've given me generously is the cold and flu virus. Then you have the cheek to borrow money off me to buy me winter remedies!"

Luke laughs a little. "I'm not even gonna argue that one, guilty as charged, me lady."

Tina, with her left hand, takes a big bite out of a chocolate Éclair and chews on it with her mouth open. After a few seconds, she speaks. "I still can't believe it, you having a job. What does it feel like?"

"I won't know until I actually do the job. I start day after tomorrow."

"My man a baker. Hey! I've just thought of something really funny. (She giggles). What if we have a bakers' dozen children? Is that twelve, same as an ordinary dozen?"

"No way, man—lass. But I'll tell you something for nothing though, with a beautiful girl like you, we'll just have a bakers' dozen practice every night!" Luke has a lecherous smile on his face.

"Luke! Don't be so crude, you gorgeous hunk. We are outside, there are people around us who might hear us."

"Who cares? Let them hear. They are only jealous of us. Some might even be envious now that things are finally happening for me—us. You know, I'm as happy as a sex-starved gay man given a life sentence without the chance of parole."

"Luke, what shall we do tonight?"

"Well—funny you should ask—"

Up with the two actual love birds again, the male bird has mounted the female bird and doing what the birds and the bees are good at doing.

Back with the two human lovebirds, Tina gets a tiny bit serious.

"Luke, don't spoil this godsend of a chance, like your friend Toady did with his first job."

Luke bursts out laughing. "Tina, you make me laugh. I don't think I've earned many points with God at the moment, more like the Almighty's wrath. His earthly henchman, the local Vicar, is displeased with me at the moment. And as for Toady, the firm shouldn't have hired a pot head like him on the restoration work for that old Georgian house. It's their fault he put a double glazing PVC window in. How was he to know? Nobody in their right minds will let a smack-head like Toady anywhere near a building site, he could burn down an igloo with a single safety match without its box."

"Isn't he the one who also drives his banger BMW backwards in snowy icy conditions, to turn it into a front-wheel drive mode so it won't slip on the road?" asked Tina.

"No! That's his older brother, Gumpy. They're a good laugh that lot, I meet the whole family every time I sign on down the dole office. Funny enough, they're always straight in and out of that place, they never get interrogated by the job-centre Gestapo about what they've been doing to find a job."

After their celebratory cafe treat (and it is a treat to those not flush with disposable cash who cannot afford coffee shop/cafe prices) Luke and Tina get up and head for their car. When they lazily get to it, one thing strikes you (like a prized boxer's punch) about it, the next owner of this vehicle will a scrap-yard merchant. It is an old banger Nissan Micra that even the local takeaways would probably reject. Many panels are of a different colour (not counting the colour of rust) each riddled with the aforementioned iron oxide in every crevice. This certainly is a car of a long term unemployed person.

"Back to our passion wagon, Tina my love. Our very own love mobile," raved Luke like he sees something in his car nobody else does.

"Yes! Our sweet chariot," replied Tina, equally blissfully ignorant of what is actually in front of them.

They both get in and Luke turns the key and starts the engine. Suddenly there is a big bang from the exhaust followed by blackish smoke. Unfortunately, just at that time a mum, pushing a pram with a toddler inside, are walking by on the pavement right next to them. The bang makes her jump and the toddler starts to cry. Luke drives off regardless of what his passion wagon has just done. The mum shouts something of scorn to Luke as he is slowly driving off.

Luke winds down his window and pops his head out.

"Sorry, lady. Didn't do it on purpose, sorry about the little one. But I've got a job now and soon I will have a brand new car, I'll part exchange it with this one!"

To that he speeds off. Now, Luke gets one or two things wrong in his thinking. Firstly, he absolutely will not be able to afford a brand new car, more likely, a slightly newer model than this sorry excuse of a car and secondly, absolutely no one in their right mind will part exchange anything for this wreck on wheels! Unless the exchange is his car for about twenty-pounds tops, as scrap metal fodder.

As the two are driving, Luke looks all around the inside of his car. "I'll miss this car, Tina. It has served me well, what with the very low running costs."

"You're right there, babes. It has low running costs because most of the time it isn't actually running per se! It just sits outside your house all broken and that.

It only gets fixed up when you come into big money like when the dole office send you the annual ten-pound Christmas bonus. By the way, have they sent you that yet, I haven't got mine yet and you don't want to miss that now you've found a job?" There is no comment from Luke.

Chapter 3
The Job

Luke is sat in a comfy but well-worn office sofa in a small office manned by a secretary sat at her desk. Luke is reading a standard coffee table magazine about cars and seems totally engrossed by whatever he is reading. The secretary is on the phone and clearly talking to someone nothing to do with company business. It is one of those personal calls that employees make at the expense of the company—naughty but nice if you can get away with it, rather like doing your personal printing and photocopying at the workplace.

The secretary gives a quick look at Luke and figures he is oblivious to her chatter by his body language/posture, so she turns back to almost cuddling the phone in an effort to make it even more secretive. "Oh darling, my baby, I've been long enough on the blower, the boss might get suspicious. I'm sure I'm gonna get caught one of these days making these calls to you. What shall it be then—Indian, Chinese, Italian, fish and chips, KFC?"

Just then a light of her multi-function office phone lights up and the secretary has to get back to doing her job or even just start doing her job today.

"Have to go darling, duty calls, ring you later." She presses a button and has a short conversation with someone other than her beau for once. After ending the conversation, she puts the phone down and turns to Luke. "Excuse me, Mr Woam, you can go straight through to see the supervising manager, Mr Sloane. He called for you just now. It's right through this door over here." She pronounces Luke's surname correctly. It pleases Luke.

Luke puts the magazine down and gets up and starts to walk towards the door of the supervisor by way of the secretary. "Excellent and thank you—Miss Secretary."

"No problem, happy to be of help."

As Luke reaches right opposite the secretary, he stops.

"Plain old fish and chips any day, I'd say. (The secretary is startled and looks up at Luke a little annoyingly). Support the local economy love—eat British!" Luke smiles after he had said that but the dagger stare from the secretary for ear-wigging her private banter makes him stop and hurry towards the supervisor's door.

Luke knocks and enters when he hears a voice from the other side say, "Come in." He enters and makes his way to the chair opposite Mr Sloane, the supervisor; naturally, a desk separates them. Luke looks quickly around the room and figures rightly it is a down to earth working type of office room, not plush with fixtures and fittings like a city centre office. They shake hands and Luke sits down. Mr Sloane, in keeping in style of the office is not in managerial attire but a battered warehouse coat. A proper working boss!

"Hello, I'm Jack Sloane, the Chief Supervisor round here on this side of the site, mainly the bread baking end. You must be Luke—Luke Woam?"

"Yes sir, Mr Sloane. I'm Luke Woam."

"Luke Woam! Your parents had a sense of humour had they?"

"Yeah, something like that. Trouble is, when parents do that, the unfortunate child is too young to do anything about it, after that you can't be bothered to change it in adulthood. You just get used to it. I'm a nobody really, not famous, so I don't get much stick about it."

"Lucky you, spare a thought for celebs like Minnie Driver or Tina Beans. Then there's Zowie Bowie. But he's changed his to a more normal one now though, I think. You haven't got any siblings have you?"

"Yes, a brother. Younger than me."

"They've not named him Richard have they?"

"Richard? (Luke is initially bewildered by the suggestion of an ordinary name but has a little think about it then he gets it). Oh I see where you're going with that. No, he's called Sam. Lucky for him my parents lost their sense of humour soon after I was born."

"Anyway, let's get down to business. I've been looking at your application form and it is impressive, I must say. Impressive in experience and the way it's filled out. You should see the presentation of some of the ones I get, you'd think the pet dog had filled it in for them or their much younger siblings."

"Who would do a silly thing like that? But thank you, I aim to please and do a good job in everything I do, like application forms, kid stuff literally. I'm happy my quality and ex—well, just good quality has struck out."

"Your work history has all been in the baking industry I see, so plenty of experience we could and will need here. I'm sure you have a wealth of skills to offer us."

"That's—that's what it says. In fact, in all my years in the bakery business, there's really only one thing I still need to know."

Mr Sloane looks at Luke with intrigue and says, "Oh yeah, what?"

"Everything!" replied Luke and puts on a smile.

Mr Sloane half laughs and says, "That's kinda funny, young Luke. Looks like you've gained the humour your parents lost. You know what, we could do with some fun and jokes in this place. I'm not supposed to say this but the foreign contingent and that's practically all the workforce, lack humour. The only time they show some kind of emotion is when I'm unable to give them overtime in low season. It's another string to your bow, isn't it?"

"Yes! I suppose it is," agreed Luke smugly. Little did Mr Sloane know that young Luke was totally not joking when he said, "everything." Does Luke deserve credit though for being honest?

"Now, let me put you in the picture. Leading up to the Christmas period, we always get very busy but this year our new Christmas product lines seem to have hit the G-spot of the consuming public. We're busier than at any time in our company's history. We've dispensed with the drawn out interview process and decided to hire quality staff based purely on the application forms.

That's why you are here now, ready to start work ASAP, once we get all the new starter induction stuff out of the way in maybe less than an hour. I know you're an experienced hand in this game but some rules can't be broken so you'll be starting at the bottom, erm entry level. That OK with you?"

"Oh OK, that's totally fine with me, just treat me like a beginner, I prefer it that way if I'm being honest. Treat me like I know nothing."

"Good. Now let's begin with the fast-track induction. I'll show you to the locker rooms, then a quick site safety tour plus briefing and then to your area of work."

Mr Sloane gets up and so does Luke. Both head for the door and as they walk and talk; thus, begins the fast-track induction.

"Excellent. Can't wait to just get going and do the job," replied Luke.

"That's what I like to hear. Luke Woam, you know I like my night time herbal tea lukewarm. Helps me go to sleep on a night."

"Nice to know!"

"Don't worry Luke, if you're a dab hand in the bakery business world as your application forms says and I know you will be, with a bit of hard work you'll become head of your team and maybe the whole section in no time. I'm sure of it. As you will know when you applied, the job starts as a seasonal temp post, but we usually retain the good ones on a permanent basis."

"Sound good to me. With all my skills and tons of experience and—other helpful attributes, I always knew I'd get to the top sooner rather than later."

"It's far simpler than that son, so far you're the only one who can speak fluent English down in the primary production level. You're the only one that's white and native English in fact."

"Really? How strange?"

Mr Sloane looks a bit puzzled.

"What bakery factories have you worked at? The EDL Eccles Cake Bakers or the NF Muffin Factory? (Luke looks bemused). Only kidding son. The only skill you really need to exceed above your wildest dreams here is the ability to understand simple instructions given to you by the supervisors in simple plain Queen's English. You know, we got people down there with degrees in bloody this and bloody that but ask them to put some racks in the proofing room and you've got a real headache on ya' hands."

Luke makes a slight perplexed face and says to himself, "Great stuff."

Chapter 4
Stack 'Em, Pack 'Em and Rack 'Em

Luke, together with Mr Sloane are on the factory floor, standing at the end of a very long machine that is traying-up raw dough blobs that will, eventually, become bread cakes. There are three other workers present, all sub-continental Asians. Two are on one side of the two-metre wide constantly moving conveyor belt with one on Luke's side. All four workers are kitted out in overalls, trousers and work boots, hair caps (one even has a beard snood on)—all supplied by the company.

"Let me get this right, Mr Sloane. My task is to wait until this machine fills out a tray with twenty-four dough balls after which I put the full tray onto this tall racking trolley. Just like these guys are doing now?"

"Spot on, my son. I knew you were going to be just right for this job, you sure are a quick learner," replied Mr Sloane, oblivious to the sarcastic tone in which Luke had said it in.

"Oh, I'm Einstein me, it's all those years of bakery experience."

"But only put the tray in the proofing rack if all the dough balls are of the correct shape and size and of course, there are twenty-four of them on the tray. Anything else just leave the tray aside and change the defective ones to complete the tray."

"No sweat, I can do that."

"Well, that completes the intensive training and induction. These guys that I have already introduced you to, they will be on your shift till the end. They will remind you of breaks and stuff, so make friends with them. This beast of a machine only takes a breather when new dough mix is put in at the other end, otherwise it doesn't stop and the trays just keep spitting out.

Oh, maybe I shouldn't use the word spit in a food factory. Anyway, just keep up to speed, the full racks will be taken away to the proofing room over that way.

I'll be saying good bye for now, see you later, don't forget to clock out." Mr Sloane then heads off.

Luke looks at the machine and the three working guys and ponders for a second or two. "Great! Stacking trays for the next ten hours."

Three hours have passed and Luke and the other three have been at it none stop. Luke looks at the man next to him and the man looks at him. "Hi, this is fun, isn't it?" It was the first conversation in all that time.

"What, repeat please?" replied the man.

"I said this is great fun, isn't it?"

"What, repeat please?" came the same reply.

Luke hesitates for a second then says it again but slower and simpler. "This— fun!"

"What, repeat please?" came the same reply for a third time.

Luke looks at one of the men opposite him. "He can't speak English, can he?"

"What, repeat please?" came the exact same reply from this guy too.

A despondent Luke tries for a final time. "He (points at the guy next to him) doesn't speak English, does he?"

"Sorry, what? Repeat please."

"Oh never mind—I give up!" sighed Luke.

"They no speak English!" said the third of the threesome, opposite Luke.

"Oh good, someone with a vocabulary greater than three or four words. Hi, I'm Luke as you may or may not remember, I was just saying this is great fun, stacking trays for the next umpteen hours in a large chilly room."

The man looks at Luke without any facial expressions other than serious. "This work, this not fun. This fun for you?"

Before Luke can say anything more the guy tells the other two in Punjabi that this 'gorah' (means white man in Punjabi/Urdu) thinks this job is fun. They all half smile and look at Luke in a weird way.

After another hour passes, four new guys (all Asian) come up to them. They all speak in Punjabi with each other and then the original three start to walk off. The one who knows a little English beckons Luke to follow them. "Come, come, gorah saab."

"Ah at last, break time. I could murder a cup of tea and a bacon butty! (Luke faces the four newcomers). See you guys in a bit, us lot have to flowcha!"

As the four co-workers walk towards the break area, Luke wants to start a conversion so as to really bond with his small team. "Hey, guys, I've got a very simple joke, but I don't know if you'll understand it but let's give it a go. It's to do with what we make. Why do bees (Luke speaks slow and clearly and makes a buzzing bee sound to aid understanding) really like bread? Because bread has flour power! Get it? (Only the one with little English, Zahoor, smiles).

How about this one then, what is odd about prisons? They are the only places that chuck you out early because of good behaviour! (The three just look at him without reaction, dead-pan look). No! Obviously not, not even you Zahoor, not as funny as you three and half the workers in this factory officially stating their birthday as January 1st from what Mr Sloane told me! If I only knew about a very cheap six-bedroom house for sale with a possibility for extension or the latest UK pound to Rupee rate and how to send money abroad, you'll all become champion Conversationalists no matter what language, even in Swahili, wouldn't you?"

Inside a long porta-cabin room that passes off as a break room, Luke and his three co-workers plus many others are all sat at tables. So it is quite busy and many are eating their own food stuff brought with them from home.

"So, you're all Muslims. Even if there was a canteen, it probably wouldn't be selling a nice juicy bacon butty due to zero demand, eh guys?" laments Luke as he looks around none too happy.

"Not all Muslim. Have other gorah saabs here, other side work. Some Polish, some Roma, not Muslim. Also many Afreekay, some of them Muslims like us," said Zahoor, the English speaking one from Luke's team.

"Are you saying that I am the only gorah saab that is from England, you know, born and bred here, proper English English?" Luke asked.

"I think yes, not hundred percent sure," replied Zahoor. "You are only English gorah saab worker on our site. But! The manaaygers, they are also English. (He says something to all around him about Luke being the only English white guy worker on the site and everyone has a chuckle. Luke guesses the laugh is about him and his situation). Tell me Luk saab, why you work here, you not finding job anywhere else?"

Luke thinks about his answer. He could tell them the same made up work history he, sorry, Sam (his younger but much wiser brother) wrote on the application form but Luke thinks why bother. Besides, he cannot remember what Sam had written anyway. "Yeah, something like that."

"I work in bakery, my three younger brothers are taxi drivers and my elder brother is a chef in big restaurant, he cooks for hundreds of people every day."

"That's nice. I can boil an egg, bang something in the microwave oven, but that's about all. Me mum takes care of all that, bless her. Cooking for hundreds? He must have done a cooking—cheffing course—in college like, that teach you how to prepare food for hundreds of people in real fast time, then?"

"Oh no, he learning those skills at home."

Luke laughs. "Oh, I see, of course, extended families and that."

"You want some food, Luk saab?"

Luke looks at all the tempting Asian food all around him and his face lights up. "Oh I wouldn't say no to that, I can live without the tempting Satan's butty for the time being." Luke had not brought any packed lunch with him.

"Good, good. You see that table over there, the company puts food there for us, go on, go get all you want, all free!" said Zahoor.

Luke looks disappointed but the immediate thought of free food makes it short lived. "You mean that is all for us, no pay?"

"No pay, free," replied Zahoor.

"Then I'm gonna check it out pronto, it'll be rude not to. After that I'm gonna go to the John—erm—khazi. That's toilet to you guys. Well, I'm going to flowcha! Laters!"

Luke gets up and walks towards the table containing several large trays full of all sorts of baked goods from bread cakes/rolls to buns and pastries like Danish whirls. He wastes no time reaching the tables, then picks a Danish and devours it in no time. He makes short work on a good few more. Eventually, he has had enough. He turns around and remembers he needs to go the toilet. He looks at the nearest guy to him. It is a middle-eastern looking man, happily eating a kebab. "Excuse me, John, where's the loo around here?"

"What, repeat please?" replied the middle-eastern man.

"Oh forget it! I'll find it myself," exclaimed Luke in annoyance.

Chapter 5
Bread

Luke and his three colleagues have been labouring away on their repeating routine of picking and stacking trays for many hours now. The buzzer goes off nearby.

"Ah! Home time. Have four hours gone by in a jiffy, didn't even notice," said Luke in great relief but with much sarcasm too.

"Sorry, repeat please," said one of the two non-English speakers.

"It's nothing, go home Wordsworth. We all go home now."

"We clock card on machine, Luk saab," informed Zahoor.

"Oh yeah, I've got me card in my pocket. I'm more used to signing in rather than clocking in. (Luke chuckles). It's Luke by the way—but you can call me Luk if you want to."

Four different guys appear on the scene and they take over Luke's crew on the machine that rarely stops. Luke and his chums set off for the locker changing rooms, but enroute the three Asian men go a different way. Luke follows but he knows it is the wrong way.

"Isn't this the wrong way, mate. I know that much already, even though I'm new here and only a dippy gorah?"

"We always go this way, you will see, you will see, Luk saab," replied Zahoor.

The four stop by another section of the same building complex where the packing of the bread cakes into various sized packs happens. Zahoor speaks and greets other workers responsible for packing, must know them well.

"We here, Luk. We get, for home," said Zahoor.

"Get? Get what?"

"These! (He points to a twelve pack bread cake bundle. He picks one up (as did the other two) and stuffs it under his company overall. All three pat down the bulge until it is fairly flattish and normal looking). You get one Luk, take home!"

Luke does not know what to do, but with the three looking at him to follow suit, he too does the same. There are now four less packs for the lorries to transport.

In the locker rooms all four get back into their home clothes, which basically means removing the company outer layers like the overalls and boots. Luke looks at the slightly flat twelve pack, then he looks at his jacket. It would be a much harder job to stuff the bread cake pack under that without raising suspicion.

"Listen Zahoor, I'm guessing this little enterprising caper, this escapade is not quite sanctioned by the bosses—"

"Sanctioned? Not understanding. Sanctioned—oh yes, when you no get paid by dole people because you late—but this is not dole—totally different thing. This is taking bread home. Plus, we are not escaping—we are working here—and just going home."

"It doesn't look good for me though, does it? It's my first day at work and I'm already on the take, I could lose my first ever job over a bloody twelve pack! (Luke has a think about what he just said). I mean my first job in over—let's see now, a month at most!"

"If you not want, give me."

Luke moves the pack closer to Zahoor. Luke looks hard at the nice soft, still warmish but most of all, still smelling of that freshly baked bread aroma, he has second thoughts. He withdraws his arm and therefore the pack.

"I think I'll keep it, as they say in the business—when in Rome." He stuffs it under his zipped up jacket and pats it down a bit more.

Luke and many others walk past other employees in the bakery yard on their way out. Some inevitably are men in charge. Luke is especially nervous but the others are OK with it. They get to near the exit gate which is deserted.

"You know Luk saab, none of us took bread home on our first day—you lucky—no?" remarked Zahoor.

"Looks like it—not quite something for Sam to write on my next application form though!"

Luke, his mum and little brother Sam are sat around the dining table eating the evening meal, a plain meal consisting of chips, veg and fish fingers.

"You two boys can make a chip butty with the bread cakes you got today," suggested mum.

"Yeah," came the reply from both.

"'Ere, I hope they pay you proper money for your work son, not pay you with bread cakes instead?" quipped mum.

"I don't think the company knows much about these bread cakes, let alone pay them as money substitute, mum," informed Sam.

"Paying workers with food instead of money? You know mum, this isn't the medieval times we're living in or even nineteenth or early twentieth century for that matter. You don't get a bit of stale bread infected with fungus and plague after working for fourteen hard hours for the local evil landowner Baron or factory owner," replied Luke.

"What was it then, first day present?" carried on mum.

"Kind of—more like a reward they give us every day, if we want it," Luke answered.

"Good! Come in handy that will. It's nice to have a working person in the house, you're the first Woam man to have a proper job in a long time," mum said.

"Didn't dad ever work when you two were together, mum? Not even a sniff of a job—cash in hand type stuff," asked Sam.

"Fat chance! You must be joking, young 'un; your dad suffered from a sticky arse, didn't he? And together? You could say that was the problem. We were always together, he never bloody left the house. His only contribution to this family was eating and hogging the telly.

Mealtimes was the only time he came to life, his working tools were his knife, fork and spoon. He just slobbed on that armchair in front of the telly all day and night; drinking and eating and the other thing—involving the toilet. Honestly, he was more useless than those big round half litre tubs of ointment the doctor gives you for skin conditions. Both of them never worked."

"Together but apart, eh mum?" chipped in Luke.

"Yeah! Ever since we got married, son. Lord knows how you two came along!"

"I'm not the only one from a single parent family in school, there are loads of us. I think we are more numerous than the normal two parent families these days," informed Sam.

"Sadly, that's the modern way, innit. Marriage is only until both members of the couple get tired of each other and then the inevitable separation happens. Trouble is, between the marrying and the divorcing some babies get made. Hard on them.

We're the real victims in all this, the kids. Both the parents get their end away with somebody new and fresh and we kids have to deal with the consequences," said Luke to slightly turn the mood a bit serious, which nobody wanted.

"Anyway, half the kids in any class of mine don't have their exercise books on them because they've left them either at their mum's or dad's. Don't half annoy the teachers," joked Sam.

"I wonder if dad is still with that slapper?" said Luke.

"I doubt it, son. She'll have kicked him out by now. He's a lazy eating machine and sluts like her are always looking to parasite off other people's easy money. He has none. Even slags have their limits," mum said in no cotton wrapped words.

"True, true, then I wonder where he is right now?" asked Luke.

"Not thinking of finding him are ya'? Going looking for him just because now you've got a job and its Christmas as well? He'll have all your money off ya'," mum said strongly.

"Give over mum, Luke couldn't even find a job by himself!" quipped Sam.

"No! God no. Besides, what do I know about finding missing people?" Luke replied. "Although, the end of my boot could well find the backside of Sam if he's not careful."

Just then, Patch enters the fray and barks to let everyone know he's part of the family too, probably wanting any left overs to gobble—no chance of that.

"Hello Patch, you cheeky rascal you," said mum.

Sam looks at the dog. "I just thought, Patch will be glad you got a job too, we won't need to treat him with black magic lotions and potions and witchcraft conjured up by that old toothless lag, Madame Friedel, for when he gets ill like. Or, rely on dodgy internet advice from crackpots and self-styled miracle healers. We can take him to a real proper vet from now on."

"Give over, Sam. He's alive, ain't he? There's nothing wrong with dear old Madame Friedel, saved us a fair few bob over the years. You know, it costs more to treat a poorly dog than a poorly human," replied mum.

Luke adds to the discussions and looks at Sam. "You mean take him to that Dr Finn 'The Quack' Hiller's Vet and Pet practice? Never, not even if he was the last Doctor Dolittle in the land! I'd take him to a vet, a proper vet. I've always been suspicious about that guy. I mean, what kind of a vet surgery doubles up as a pet shop—a one-stop shop?

Have you ever noticed an awful lot of animals, sick or not, meet their maker under his supposedly quality care? A customer goes in with 'Old Yeller' and comes out with 'Puppy Love!', strange, very strange. People don't call him 'Hiller the Killer' for nowt, you know."

"Could be worse, it could have been 'Dr Finn Hiller's Vet and Kebab Practice'. It would take care of the problem of disposing of the dead bodies nicely," joked Sam. "Although I don't think the local council business planning board might agree."

Mum and Luke wince on hearing that as does Sam himself.

"Give over, Sam! All I can say is, I'm glad it's fish fingers tonight," said a relieved mum.

Luke looks at Patch. "You hear that Patch, behave yourself or else we'll book you into the totally loopy 'Dr Kebab and the Petta Breeds' clinic. Go in alive and kicking, leave as a donor kebab in chilli sauce!"

Patch sees that Luke is talking to him and responds by a joyous bark and excited movements. Oh, if only he understood!

"If Patch ever gets famous, his b-i-t-c-h fans can literally have a piece of him," further added Luke.

Both Luke and Sam laugh, eventually joined by their mum.

"Your wages can also pay for a dog trainer, train him not to pee on my bed of roses in the garden," proposed mum.

Luke laughs at this and looks at Patch. "Oh yeah! Bad doggy, Patch, very naughty of you. I thought our roses stopped smelling of roses for some time."

"You can bloody laugh. He learnt that off you, you silly bugger. The neighbours are constantly on at me about it, they see you, drunk on a night, relieving yourself," voiced mum.

"That's because the neighbours worry about small things, very small things," chipped in Sam.

Luke flicks a small piece of fish finger at Sam, who ducks and the food fragment falls on the floor whereupon Patch makes short work of eating it up. Being Patient has paid off.

"Cross my heart, I never do that! I don't know what you're on about, mum."

"I know, we can send Luke to this dog training school as well. This time he might actually learn summat in class, from the other dogs in his class," continued Sam with his put-downs.

"I'm warning you, you annoying oink. No pocket money for you if you carry on. Why don't you go and do something momentous and ground-breaking like trying to get past level one on all your computer games?" said Luke with a sort of satisfaction at a brill come back.

"Oh no! No more pocket money, I'll starve to death!" replied Sam in proper sarcastic mode, ignoring the computer game dig. "Besides, it's not charity, I deserve a cut of your monthly wages, for services rendered, not be content with some measly pocket money."

"Stop it you two! I want to eat in peace, act like brothers that you are," ordered mum.

With that, everyone gets on with the rest of their evening meal in relative peace.

Chapter 6
It's Good to Talk

Some weeks have now passed in the job and Luke, along with most of his crew are doing what they know best—stacking and packing. None are in conversation.

Zahoor looks at this watch. "Ah good, break will be in ten minutes."

"Inshallah! My brothers," uttered Luke much to the surprise of his three co-workers. They laugh and make comments in Punjabi to each other.

"Wah-wah, inshallah indeed, Luk saab," said Zahoor.

"Inshallah!" said the other two, in smiles.

"Don't be surprised, my Asian friends, I've been here a good few weeks now and I've picked up one or two words of your lingo. None of the Asian lads at school spoke it much or if they did, it was only swear words. To tell you the truth, I already had heard and learnt of inshallah back then.

As long as it was not science, maths, French, geography or most school subjects apart from history, I was OK with it in school. Now, history is the only one I passed. Got a grade A in it in fact, fellas and the A doesn't stand for absent neither. In fact, everyone got an A in it that year, it was so bloody easy. History— bahort hatcha hai."

Zahoor and the other two are well entertained with Luke's prowess in their language. The buzzer for the break sounds and four guys show up soon after and they swap places.

"Break—canteen jaldi, time for some bubbling balti!" ordered Luke, still showing off some of the words he had learnt. They all go off.

In the portacabin canteen, everyone on that break rota are as usual tucking into their break time food which as usual consisted of home stuff and what the company provided them gratis from its production lines.

Luke too, has brought his own food in the form of sandwiches. Although he is always careful not to bring in his favourite, ham and cheese, so as not to offend his Muslim friends. The sweet course, he gets from the free stock in the bread trays as does everyone else.

There is a good cluster of people around one area, one of which is also Luke. To his nice surprise, there are a lot more who can speak English in today's collective. One even has a local accent and is youngish, sort of student age and Asian. Luke looks at him.

"You speak good English, mate. I'm guessing you were born here, right?" asked Luke.

"Yeah! How did you guess? My name's Umar. I already know your name, Luke, right?"

"Yes, I don't exactly blend into the background around here. So, I'll start first, you're working here so what's your sob story, 'cause apparently, you need one if you end up in this place, what with you being born and bred in England and speaking good English?"

"I just finished a degree course, in Criminology. I just got this bakery job, whilst I find a job related to my area of expertise, they're a bit hard to get. Now you?"

"Well, I've got hardly any qualifications to write home about and I just got this job because—I had no job and wasn't likely to find one any time soon because I've got no experience—in having a job or doing it. It's a good sob story and totally true."

Luke smiles a little for two reasons, one because what he said was funny but mainly to lighten the mood. He knew no one would pay much attention to the fact he just mentioned he had not had a job before this one.

"Blimey, I see what you mean, Luke mate, we're making it sound like this is the place of last resort, if you're doomed in life, you end up here. It's all relative though, to your personal situation. There are a lot of Asians here, as you've found out by now. Most of them are Pakistanis and nearly all of them are immigrant Pakistanis, came here by way of a marriage visa.

This is their first stop job, in the promised land, land of milk and honey so to speak. To them, getting into England legally, well it's heaven on earth stuff innit. They love it here, the foreign contingent, you have to drag them kicking and screaming out of the UK. It's only the native white British who hate and moan about Britain. To the immigrants, this is a place of opportunity, not dead-end," replied Umar.

"I knew this Pakistani guy once who said that any baby born a Pakistani, must have been bad in a previous life, God's punishment like."

"True, so very true, but he must be a British Pakistani, born here in England. Such a soft, cotton-wrapped life, compared to where the immigrants come from, the life they have left behind. I understand your friend's view point though.

You don't know what it's like living within the British Pakistani community here. It's just one long round of stress, heart-ache, rows, bad-mouthing, backstabbing, double-standards, evil relatives, long-term major fall-outs, etc. I can really see what made this man say that, I am in total agreement, this is normal, everyday life for us. Hardly heaven on earth, for us British Asians."

"It's nice to have a cheerful conversation in full on English with someone here for a change. (Both Luke and Umar laugh). It's nice that I'll be able to use complex words, My English has dropped down to primary school level for the last few weeks. Having said that, don't be using any degree level words on me, Umar my brother."

"I won't. If I go on to further train as a criminal solicitor, most of the people I'll be dealing with, will only have a word bank of a thousand words or so and most of them will be offensive or expletives. A lot of Criminologists end up in the prison service too."

"Yeah, I can imagine. Hey, if you work part-time as a solicitor and prison officer, you'll see your client before and after the sentence, in court and in prison. With you being their legal rep, they'll get an after-care package thrown in," joked Luke. Both chuckle.

"You're funny, Luke. But I can add to that. With the two jobs, I'll be in bar and behind bars."

"Nice one but I'm not done yet, get this, if you become corrupt and get caught, you will be de-barred and barred."

Umar looks at Luke and says, "OK, let's quit, whilst we're ahead, shall we."

"Good idea, let's."

So, Luke has at last found Umar and a few others with a good command of English to converse in during the breaks. He looks at his newest cohort of friends.

"Hey guys, we are in the busy Christmas period, you or most of you are Muslims so do you celebrate Christmas, the Christmas spirit, it's on Wednesday 25th of December?" asked Luke.

"Of course we do, Englishman, it's hard not to, we believing the same God and we are living in England. But it might not be Wednesday for us, we have to wait until after prayers on Tuesday 24th of December for our Mosque's Imam to confirm it, Christmas could be on the 25th or it could be on the 26th, we just have to wait and see," said someone from the gathering. Most of the group are in raptures.

"What! Christmas is on the 25th, it can't be any other date, that's just daft. No one can change it! It's been like that for two thousand years," gasped Luke. There is a chorus of loud laughs from all the Asian contingent even more now.

"They're just messing with you, Luke. It's an in-joke in our community, you won't get it," said Umar.

"The hell I don't! Don't count me out too quick. I do get it, it's coming to me now. It's because you Muslims never know the exact date of your Eid because you follow the lunar calendar but mainly it's because each group of Mosques act as rivals to each other, something to do with different branches of Islam and they don't or never agree, proper chalk and cheese stuff. Right or am I right, Umar bhai?"

There is sort of silence around the mob, especially from the ones who can understand him properly. Luke is all proud of himself.

"You are right, gorah bhai, you are a clever man. Tell me, how you know such thing?" asked an Asian guy in the gathering.

"Simple, I am from Bolton, born and bred, like you lot said, it's hard not to know. I had many Muslim friends in school and come every Eid time this debate would be hotly discussed. Mainly by the teachers because they wanted to know on what day more than four-fifth of the students won't be turning up to school."

There are applauds from the gathered Asian men. Luke has won their respect even more now. For the first time in his life he is achieving things—strange but true.

"Yeah guys, I'm not intending to stay as a dumbass, good-for-nothing, zero-future, dog's body baker all my life. I'm going places!" Luke exclaimed to all, little realising he had just offended nearly everyone gathered there.

"Where are you going, saab?" asked Zahoor. Others looks at him too. Luckily for Luke, no one fully understood or gave a thought that Luke's words were actually condescending, derogatory and disrespectful to all of them and to all the workers in the factory.

"Oh, it's just an old English saying, my Asian friends. My fellow English gorah bhais say it, forget it, not important."

"So you stay, not leave!" asked Zahoor.

"Yes, I stay. Somewhere out there is an opportunity waiting for me but it hasn't found me yet, so I stay. Come on guys, break is up just about, let's flowcha!" said Luke.

As they all walk out of the cabin canteen, Zahoor asks Luke, "Luk bhai, what is meaning of floochai? I am not hearing it before?"

Luke laughs a little before answering. "It's flowcha! It means 'to go', you say it when you have to leave! You know—go with the flow—moving. Flowcha!"

"Flowcha! I am understanding now."

"Excellent bud. We'll make a brown-skinned Englishman out of you yet. Hang with me and you'll be the master of English in no time. I'll teach you everything I know—granted that's not much but it's better than nothing. And nothing, is what most of you seem to have. You could say, it'll be the blind leading the blind."

Chapter 7
Freedom, Not Independence

Back to the production line it was for all of them. Luke sometimes wondered if there were enough people in the world to consume all the bread products they were churning out. The simple answer is yes! He had time to think rather than talk whilst at his post, as meaningful conversation was a little less common on the line. This was partly because of the background noise including that of the operating machines, but also because no one could think of anything to talk about—anything new. Complex topics were off bounds due to the nature of his three fellow workers and the culture difference this resulted in. So, for long periods of time, Luke just let his thoughts and imagination occupy his time.

Walking towards Luke's crew is a white guy. Luke sees him heading towards them. "Hey! Look, another gorah. One of the Polish contingent, no doubt."

The other three look at this approaching white guy. His hair cap conceals a large amount of hair and his beard snood snares a proud beard.

Zahoor laughs. "He no Polish. He is Dylan, he is hippy. He has long hair like girl because he says he is a happy hippy. Him English, like you."

"English! You said there were no English floor workers, that I was the only one. You said all the foot soldiers, the ground troops, were all foreign, that I had the honour of being the only pork chop munching, ham and cheese eating English infidel in this place."

"You are the only one and Dylan saab too. He work in different building, not ours. Him English. Some people call him dummy Dylan."

As Dylan, the hippy, comes real close, Zahoor speaks to him. "Hello, Dylan saab. This Luk here, he is Englishman just like you." All four crew members work as they talk.

Dylan stops and looks at Luke. "Why hello, Luke dude. How ya' doing man? Nice to have a fellow countryman on the premises. We are a rare species at the very bottom level you know."

"Hello Dylan, Nice to meet you. I know why I'm here, at the bottom level as you put it, what circumstances got you here?" A popular question with Luke it appears.

"I fundamentally disagree with the system man, the authorities aren't educating us, they're brainwashing us working class folk. Don't matter what you colour or creed is, they are doing it to all of us. I rebelled, I saw through it. I realised what the government was doing and still doing. Subjugating the people's free will and ability to think for ourselves."

"You're saying that you ended up as a lowly bakery operative because you were—are fighting against the regime, rage against the machine just like that naff record that was a Christmas number one a good while back?" asked Luke a little in jest.

"Spot on Spartacus! The slaves shall rebel against the oppressive empire. And some might also say because I failed all my exams at school as well, but it's definitely the former explanation that keeps me down and forced to work here."

"Where are you going, at this time, it is not time for break? This is not your area of work also," asked Zahoor.

"Oh, the regime we call management want to see me, I think they're angry with me. Something about putting 20kg of baking powder into the mixing machine instead of flour. I mean, anyone can mix those two up, they look very similar. If you ask me, this company is in league with the government to conspire against me, in fact, everyone has got it in for poor old Dylan Rutherford! It's not fair."

"Rutherford! Your second name's Rutherford?" asked Luke in mild excitement.

"Yeah man, what's the big deal?"

Luke laughs out loud and the other Asian guys' looks at him a bit confused as is Dylan. The three Asian guys start to smile a little too but not too convincingly, just copying Luke or smiling at him rather than with him.

One of the non-English speaking guys says in Punjabi, "What are we laughing at?"

The second non-speaker replies, also in Punjabi, "I don't know. Zahoor, what is so funny here, why is your white friend laughing?"

"Luke saab, what you finding funny?" asked Zahoor to clarify the issue.

"Rutherford. It's the name of a very famous scientist professor, very intelligent. He made amazing discoveries about atoms. If I remember rightly, something about there being lots of space inside these tiny atoms. In fact, he stated rightly that most of the atom is nothing but vast empty space, ages before we had modern equipment."

"Atoms! Yes, I learn about atoms in school too, metric level science in Pakistan," exclaimed Zahoor. He proceeds to explain all this to his two friends in Punjabi. One of them says something and all three start laughing.

"What? Let us in on it too," begged Luke.

"He said, that our friend Mr Rutherford here is indeed connected to your famous Professor Rutherford," informed Zahoor.

Both Luke and Dylan look confused. Luke gasps, "Connected? Give over. You're not suggesting that the most revered Professor Rutherford might be some sort of a great, great—granddad to this fella here? Our Dylan a descendent? That would be spectacular, that would—have the professor turn in his grave no doubt."

"That's heavy man, how come no one in my family ever told me about this?" wondered Dylan.

"No, no, no. You two are not understanding. My friend here is making joke. He said our hippy friend Dylan has an atom sized brain with lots of empty space in his head too. You see, he is connecting with Professor Rutherford," informed Zahoor.

All the group of men laugh out loud, strangely, the loudest is Dylan's.

"Hey, that's funny is that, man. You did have me going though, for a second or two, I thought I might be related to this brainy cat professor. What's his name again?" asked Dylan in disbelief to Luke.

"I think it might be Professor Rutherford, Dylan," replied Luke.

"Oh yes, that's the geezer. Anyway guys, I'm off to the office. You never know, they might be calling me in for something else like making me a supervisor—instead of the other thing. Of course, I'll immediately turn it down on principle, they can't bribe me or pay me to shut up. Anyways, see you around bothers. Stay brainwash free now, you hear me, don't let the bastards grind you down," said Dylan and went off.

Luke looks at his three co-workers, then Zahoor. "What I can't figure out is why on earth have the company put him on mixing? He's the last person I would put on that job."

"Oh, he's not on mixing, he is the cleaner. But I am thinking he is best friends with a Polish guy who is mixer. His Polish friend takes many secret breaks to smoke cigarette. Maybe—" Luke interrupts as he can figure out the rest.

"This polish guy asked Dylan to stand in for him whilst he went on a secret fag break. That fits."

"That is what I am thinking," said Zahoor.

Mr Sloane appears on the scene, with him is an African worker, very young, of student age.

"Hello, guys. (They all reply back). Listen Zahoor, I'm needing to borrow you for a short while so I've brought this young chap with me to replace you, his name is Yusaf."

"What is it about, Mr Sloane, Have I done something wrong?" queried Zahoor.

"Oh God, no! The head of the North of England division is here and he just wants to ask a random selection of workers about how they feel about working here, that's all."

"Oh, I am liking it here, boss. I am happy."

"I know, that's why your name has appeared on my totally random chosen list. So, I'll leave the totally capable Yusaf here with you guys for a while, come on Zahoor, let's get this over with."

The two go off as Yusaf, the replacement, now completes the four-man team.

"So, my friend, whereabouts in the world are you from?" asked Luke.

"I am from Chad," replied Yusaf in an African accent.

"Chad? Where on earth is that, there's no such country, are you sure you're from Chad?" an unsure Luke asked.

"I am very sure, Chad is in Africa."

"I've never heard of it? Chad? Is it newly discovered?"

"It is an old country my friend, but not many English people I speak to have heard of it either."

"Well, now I know that there is a country called Chad and it's in Africa. That is amazing. So Yusaf, what are you doing here in England, studying?"

"That is right, but mainly looking for someone to marry, I need to find wife so I can stay in England permanently."

Luke laughs out loud. "Like 'Coming to America' but only to England."

His three co-workers just look at him, no reaction.

In Mr Sloane's office, the big boss, Mr Miles, has finished with Zahoor. Mr Sloane is waiting outside.

"Thank you, Mr Khan. Nice to know the workers are very happy working here. It pleases me very much. Thank you for taking the time to come up here to see me," said Mr Miles.

"No problem, Mr Miles. If that is all, I am going to flowcha now!" replied Zahoor.

"I'm sorry, what was that, you're going to—flowcha? I'm afraid my Indian language is not even at a basic level, non-existent would probably best describe it. Apart from food related words in Indian restaurants."

"Yes, Mr Miles. I am needing to flowcha, so I can continue my happy work. It is not Urdu or Indian language word but it is an English word, the language we are speaking. I am learning it from Luk saab." To that, Zahoor goes off.

Mr Sloane and Zahoor approach Luke and his crew. Yusaf and Zahoor swap places again.

"Thank you again Zahoor, Mr Miles seemed happy, another year sorted. Good, good. I'll be off now, well both of us. See you fellas." To that, Mr Sloane and Yusaf go off.

"You're a lucky man, Zahoor. It's nearly break time again. One break followed by another," informed Luke a little jealously.

Zahoor has a big smile on his face. The other two immediately question him about how his meeting with the big boss went.

Back in the canteen hut, Luke and many others are tucking into their food stuffs and talking. Luke looks at all the delicious foods spread out on the table. By now they had a system where everyone contributed a food item or two and they all shared the collective, like a fuddle or buffet.

"As the great religious men of Judaism, Christianity and Islam once said and we still say at mealtimes to this day, come on fellas, dig in, let's eat to the beat, rub a dub dub, thanks for the grub!" Luke wasted no time 'digging in' to mostly other people's exotic foods. He contributed egg and cress sarnies and packets of crisps. Some in the 'congregation' had a slight look of scorn at Luke and his modernist take on the thanksgiving meal prayer.

Suddenly, from nearby there is a loud serious statement, said in a British Asian accent.

"Hey, we don't get many English guys working here."

Luke turns around and sees an early twenty-something aged Asian guy looking straight at him, one he had not seen before.

"Yep, I'm English. I said to them, listen I'm proper bona fide White English man, can't you just let me become a manager straight away. They didn't," Luke said and laughs, his reply is an attempt to humour this new guy. He did not know how it would be received.

"They'll probably make you manager in quarter the time it will take us," replied this Asian guy.

"Come on, anyone who works hard, gets promoted. It's all about how hard you work nowadays. It's what you can give the company. If you can make your employers money, then it doesn't matter what ethnicity you are. Money talks my friend."

"Think you know everything, how about answering me this—"

"I don't think I know everything," Luke quickly interrupted, the Asian guy just carried on.

"When all the European countries left their illegally occupied colony countries, finally left, especially in Britain's case, did those occupied countries gain their freedom or gain independence?"

"Before I answer, I'm Luke by the way, to whom am I talking to?"

"I'm Sid."

"Sid? Isn't that a tad British sounding—or maybe Spanish if you consider El Cid?"

"That's a nick name! My Muslim name and proud of it is Syeed. Sid for short. Now answer me what I asked."

"OK, I will convey to you my opinion. Independence or freedom? I would opt for—freedom myself. Although I have an idea about why all the powerful European countries called the leaving process Independence."

Sid looks a little gobsmacked at first like he had had a hard hitting counter-attacking speech/answer all ready to unleash but now could not because Luke unexpectedly gave the 'wrong' answer to him—sort of the right answer but wrong for Sid.

After a few seconds he says, "Yes! My thoughts exactly. You—you surprised me a bit with your answer. I am taken aback. I didn't think you, an Englishman, would agree with me. I didn't think you would say that."

"I like to think of myself as unpredictable, mate. Or Sid should I say?"

Sid looks at all around him.

"You see people, brothers. This white man knows the wrong that has been done. History has been written by the rich and powerful and the white. In most cases this means, it was written by the conquering armies and people from Europe, the Westerners. When India was overrun by hostile foreign forces a few hundred years ago, mainly by the sausage and bacon eating British, India became an illegally occupied country. The Indians lost their sovereignty and their freedom to these foreign aggressive outsiders.

The British were not native to India and the Indians were and are native to the land, indigenous is the word. So, I ask every one of you here, when these foreigners left, how can it be called independence? We did not come from them, they weren't our fathers and mothers. They had nothing to do with our biological heritage. They were just our captors—our enslavers. When they finally went home, we simply regained our freedom."

"Just where are you going with this, Sid my mate? What's the end goal?" Luke asked.

"It's not an end goal, more a start, start of my campaign to get historical events written or labelled correctly. I want India to stop celebrating Independence Day and replace it with a National Freedom Day or better still, just a holiday. I want Pakistan not to even have an Independence Day celebration, replace it with an Anniversary of Creation Day, I also think the Commonwealth is an insult to the occupied countries. Why be in a stupid club that celebrate the fact that you were criminally taken over by Britain?

I mean, Pakistan has never been taken over in its short history, why on earth is it in the shameful Commonwealth club? I also disagree with the fact that Gandhi has been called the Father of India. I totally respect the guy but Father of India, how can he be? India is over seventy thousand years old, way, way older than even its future and last occupier, Britain.

He was a great freedom campaigner—not independence campaigner. He is up there with other stand out modern age notable Indian figures. India did not spring into existence in 1947. Like I said, it has been around for thousands of years. Complex civilisation existed in India when Britain was a collection of mud huts. Even the Saxons, who would become the English, were a bunch of savages just a mere twelve hundred years ago.

At the same time as these barbaric Saxons, in India, the great Mughal Empire ruled. The world must stop the use of the word independence and replace it with the more accurate word freedom. That is my lifelong mission."

"And good luck with that, Sid, that does sound like an important lifelong mission. I certainly wouldn't want to get in your way. And—working in a bread factory is a great place to start your mission! We are all with you my brother from another mother, remember what we honorary Asians say, 'don't worry, eat curry'!" bellowed Luke. Just then everyone laughs, even ones who had suspect English, including Sid.

Chapter 8
Money to Spend

Luke, his mum and Sam are at the breakfast table in the kitchen, busy eating breakfast which is not a full English for once, today it is a mix of toast and cereals. All around are bread or cake products, all nicked from the company. Why so many? Well, once the habit starts, it becomes instinctive, even when there is no need to do it. There were a few days here and there when Luke did not smuggle any products home; but when everyone is doing it religiously around you, it's hard to—well, not to.

"It's nice to not to be at work for once," Luke said happily, enjoying a day off work, that he had booked, he has not done a 'sickie'.

"It's nice to have you awake and eating breakfast with us after a good few weeks now. Work has really been good for you, us," chipped in mum.

"Four weeks of getting up early, breaking my back, well, legs and arms, just standing there stacking trays. I—I told them that I can speak English you know, fluent English, something that's a real commodity in that baking factory, worth at least five GCSEs, the boss said I would be promoted in no time just on the strength of knowing the Queen's lingo," complained Luke.

"That's gold, that is? You get a job which you didn't even apply for, have zero experience in and you expect to get promoted in that job in record time, to a flippin' manager. You don't expect much do you, bruv," chipped in Sam this time.

"But it's true, I mean what I say, in this place you just need to be able to have a good command of English and you're sorted or should be sorted. Even one GCSE in English would make you king of the castle in that place, pity I haven't got one in English but it's still true," answered back Luke.

"A good command of English? Explains why you are still at the bottom," joked Sam.

"Shut up, twerp!" fired back Luke.

"I used to like bread cakes, Danish, croissants, rolls, etc. Now I'm just plain sick of them. Why don't you leave and get a job in a sweet factory, I'm willing to write you another award-winning application form no sweat? I could go maybe a year before I get sick of sweets," suggested Sam.

"Both of you be quiet. It's better than paying for them. Anyway, it's your day off, Luke, what ya' doing with yourself, something nice?" asked Mum.

"See Tina, I haven't had that much time for her these past four weeks so I'm seeing her for some quality catch-up time. Go up town, eat in a fancy restaurant, drink expensive beverages, stuff like that."

"Good on ya', son," said a happy mum.

Luke cleans out his cereal bowl and two toasts (as always) and says, "Right, I'm off. I'll have my phone on me, now that I have a new working phone with not a single crack in the screen, a contract phone, you can ring me if need to and more importantly, I can ring you back, using my monthly minutes allowance."

"Enjoy yourselves, you two. Say hello to Tina for me, son. Bye," said mum as Luke picks up his jacket and car keys and leaves the house.

Later, Luke and Tina are in their car in traffic lights. In front is a mounted policeman (on a police horse).

"It's beautiful, real majestic looking," said Tina, looking admiringly at the horse in front.

"Yeah, does look good. Thoroughbreds are real nice looking horses. They're the ones they use for racing, all over the world."

"So big! Looks scary sitting way up there."

As they both wait for the lights and continue admiring the horse, the horse starts taking a dump, some of the manure is propelled onto Luke's car bonnet. Both Luke and Tina make murmurs of disgust. Eventually, Luke winds down his window and yells at the policeman.

"Hey, excuse me, Mr Policeman. Your horse has just taken a dump on my car!"

The policeman looks around and shrugs his shoulders and turns back around, he could not care less.

"Great! If I make a big deal of it, he'll just arrest me for disturbing the peace. So there's no point complaining to him about it," said Luke in anger.

"Probably right, Luke. Best leave it," agreed Tina. She winds down her window also to let the air circulate better in the car.

A gang of youths are leaning or sitting on a small wall lining the pavement nearest Tina. They had seen all this and found it all amusing.

One of the youths laughs and says to the rest, "Look what we got here guys, shit on shit!" Clearly a reference to Luke's pride and joy car.

Another one says, "Maybe the fresh shit will make the old shit on wheels look and smell better?"

A different teenager says to another in the group, "Check out his meat sack of a bird, I wouldn't be seen dead with that. He's surrounded by shit!"

All the youths' chatter is loud enough for Luke and Tina to hear as their car windows are down.

"Get out of here you dope heads, even better, go learn to read and write!" Luke scolded at them. The youth gang laugh loudly as they go off. With a copper in front of Luke, he decides it would not be wise to retaliate further against 'children', even though most were as big as Luke.

The lights turn to amber then green at last. The policeman's horse trots off. Luke has a smile on his face.

"Right, disturbing the peace? Why not?"

Luke puts the pedal to the metal and his car makes the usual bangs and noises as it accelerates off. His car goes to one side of the horse still making these noises and the horse is startled and becomes uncontrollable for a few seconds. Luke speeds up but not so as to break the speed limit. He looks out of his rear view mirror and gives a satisfying smile.

"You're a right 'un, aren't ya'?" remarked Tina.

"Oh yes! Having a job and thus being a proper working-class guy has made me right crazy!"

They both laugh loudly as they head into town.

For most the rest of the day Luke and Tina spent money on having a good time. Highlights included expensive coffee shops and buying branded clothes. Finally, they ended up in a posh city centre restaurant. They have been there a while now.

Luke is slicing/cutting and chopping away at a big juicy steak without putting any of it in his mouth. Tina is looking at him but Luke does not notice.

"Have you established the cause of death yet, Dr Quincy? My professional opinion would be it took place in a slaughter house and the perpetrator being a big hench butcher armed with an even bigger knife, who most likely isn't on the Christmas card list of the local RSPCA!" joked Tina.

"What? Did you just mention Dr Quincy?" answered Luke with a question.

"Are you eating that steak or doing an autopsy on it?" asked Tina.

"Oh yeah! I see what you mean. I was just wondering what I'm getting for twenty-six pounds a head, that's all. Is this steak from a cow that lived in the stables on the grounds of Buckingham Palace I wonder?"

"Or the chef could be one of those Michelin star rated ones. I very much doubt it but he or she could be. We are in a posh restaurant Luke darling, not the usual greasy fry-up in back street Bolton. And no one comes in here to order a health conscience five leaf mix bean salad, or a bleeding donor kebab."

Both of them laugh as they continue eating their pricey treat steak dinner.

"Talking of Quincy, have you ever wondered how he and his side kick Sam never ever have a single blood stain on them after the autopsies?" asked Luke after a short while.

"Yeah, but that's the television world for you, innit. No one ever goes to toilet much or eats much on telly. The hero never has any family to worry about in an apocalypse, well maybe just his wife and kids that's all, the nuclear family. Heroes never has to worry about their cousins, nieces, nephews, uncles, aunties, grandparents, when they have to flee a horde of zombies or other world disasters."

"Keeps things simple, doesn't it, I suppose. If you think about it, instead of the hero finding a fast getaway four-seater car, if it was like reality, he'd have to find himself a bloody coach to escape the impending disaster, to fit in all the extended family in."

The two laugh again as they tuck away at the gourmet food.

Much later the two are walking the beat on the night time city streets in a leisurely way, both drinking cola from a can. Both are holding small bags in the other hand. "It's been a lovely today, Luke. Having money does bring happiness," confessed Tina.

"It does. Only people who misuse it or don't have any say it brings sadness. We've proved today that money can buy happiness if used—spent sensibly, wisely."

"Well said grasshopper. Let's be getting off home, I'm a bit jiggered, I need to rest and digest the banquet of a dinner we had. It is bit different to having a burger either at home or from the local takeaway when we're usually together. (A few seconds later). Luke, why do they always say grasshopper on TV and in some films, are grasshoppers really intelligent for insects or summat?"

"I don't really know myself, but I have heard it in films too, comedy films especially, many times. I think you might be right, grasshoppers might be really intelligent for insects, considering their size and that, have big brains."

"Anyway, I have enjoyed this day—just what the doctor ordered. Not Dr Quincy of course, as he only deals with dead bodies and the only thing he orders is a coroners' inquest, after getting angry and shouting at everyone because the office coffee is lousy." They both laugh out loud at this.

Luke announces proudly. "Get used to it, Tina my lovely. This is how we are going to be spending our time together from now on. When I get promoted soon then—it's going to get even better! Drink up, babes, time to quicken the pace, time to flowcha!"

It is well into the night now in the city and the two lovebirds are steadily walking in the suburbs. The scenery has changed from bright lights and fancy glass towers to back alleys and industrial red brick warehouses and small workshops set around litter strewn streets in need of repair.

"You got money now, Luke, why did you still park way out here, what's wrong with the city centre?" asked an annoyed Tina.

"That may be darling, but do you know how much it would have cost me in parking charges to park in centre of town for the whole day and into night?"

"I know, maybe when you get promoted. Well, at least it's not raining."

"Even finding these very few free parking spaces outside town is hard, they all get taken up pretty quickly too."

"My legs are aching, how far is the car now?"

"Will you get mad if I say it's just around the corner?"

"Yes! People who know things are far away always say that, now tell me the truth!"

"The truth is, it's really isn't too far now, down that street and then down the next and it's there."

"Two streets, I can handle that."

"Nice one, we'll be there in no time, it's not far away now, just around the corner."

The street in which the two are in now has a group of drunken lads hanging about, all in their early twenties, at the other end. Luke and Tina see them from their end but it is too late to change direction so they carry on towards them. Hopefully, there will be no altercation.

As the two get real close, the drunken lads, five in number, take a worrying interest in them, their body language is the clue. This concerns Luke and Tina but they steadfastly stick to their task of walking down this street hoping nothing will happen. They, well Luke, is now about two metres from them and getting closer. Luke is in front of Tina as she is lagging behind about three metres due to her aching legs. Being together would have been way better but it is not so.

"Hey! Mate, aren't ya' gonna wait for your pet gorilla? Why don't ya' wave a banana at her to catch up," said one of the goons, quite loudly so Tina could hear as well.

Luke stops and looks at the goon, who stops smirking now and looks like he is bracing for some sort of a physical reaction from Luke.

"Luke! Luke! Just carry on walking. Ignore them. It's not worth it. Just keep on walking," shouted Tina from behind, doing her best to avoid a confrontation.

"That's it—Luke mate, carry on walking like a coward. The guy doesn't even have the decency nor stomach to defend his pet," continued the first goon. The other four and him, laugh. Luke stands there, looking back and waiting for Tina to catch up.

"Just ignore them, they are just drunken jerks," advised Tina.

"Jerks! Listen coward, teach your lard arse gorilla some obedience, train it to respect humans and what comes out of its mouth or we will!" said the lead goon spokesman. So far the others just laugh and drink from their cans and bottles.

"Right! I'm here now. (Tina grabs Luke's arm). Let's get out of here. They are all talk and no action, harmless drunken cretins."

Tina instantly regrets saying what she just said. Like showing a red flag to a bull in one of those olden day cartoons.

"Harmless cretins! I'll show you who's harmless love!" said the lead mouthy goon and punches Luke in the belly real hard. Luke is floored as his attention had been on Tina so was not looking at the goon. The shopping bags fall to the floor.

Tina yells in panic and the main yob punches her in the belly too and she also falls to the floor along with her bags also.

"Oh man! I thought you never hit girls?" asked one of the other goons.

"I don't, I've not hit a girl! (They all find his comment hilarious). Besides, I hit the bitch in the lard-arsed belly and she fell on her lard-arsed bum. Probably didn't feel a thing either way, but—we felt an earthquake." They all laugh again.

The yobs decide to move on, after all, they had just committed a criminal offence. Even drunken yobs know when they can get their collar felt by the local police force or be seen by CCTV, so best to scarper.

"Check this out guys," said the main goon. He kicks Luke in the private area once and then he kicks Tina on her bottom. "Now we can go. Those two won't be bothering us again!"

Sometime later, Luke pulls up and stops outside Tina's house.

"And so the day ends," said Tina rather sombrely.

"Yeah, what a day, eh?" replied Luke equally sombrely.

"Despite the last part, it's been great otherwise, I mean that."

"Thank you, pet. Thank you for sharing this mostly brill day with me."

They both have a quiet giggle and a hug.

"Luke, I'm the one thanking you, you don't need to. You heard those—waste of spaces. No one—no boy has ever given me a first look, never mind a second look. No boys ever look at me in any other way except like those boys at the traffic lights and these yobbos tonight. You're different, you like me for me, what you see is what you get. And you're happy with that."

"No, no, no, no. I get a whole lot more than what I see. You are the most loving, kindest, warmest, gentlest—good natured—can't think of any more at this time of the night—person I've ever met. When God made you, he made a mistake. (This last remark gets an immediate and unfavourable reaction from Tina and Luke sees this and so carries on with the rest of his comment very quickly).

You see, Tina my love, God accidently gave you the beauty of five girls. There are right now four other girls walking around in the world plain butt ugly, well maybe some of them sleeping actually right now at this time of night."

Tina smiles after hearing these well-meaning and comforting words. "You're so sweet, Luke. But sometimes I wish I could travel back sixty-five million years in time and take with me a nuclear rocket bomb. I would blow up that meteor that destroyed the dinosaurs, while it's still out in space, before it ever reaches earth.

Humans have treated each other and earth so lousy that maybe the dinosaurs' descendants would have been better owning it. (She looks at Luke, who is listening affectionately to her). Oh listen to me, ranting on, it's too late in the night for a deep meaningful lecture and I'm shagged out. Want to come in for a cup of tea or coffee or painkillers?" They both giggle again after the very short serious bit.

"I'm gonna have to say no to that as I've got to get up for work at five in the bloody morning, back to the grind!"

"Oh yeah, I keep forgetting."

"I'll walk you right up to your door though."

"OK, my lovely."

They both exit and stand on the pavement next to the car. Luke suddenly grabs Tina and hugs her then plants a kiss on her cheek. This makes Tina drop her bags onto the floor, a second time today.

"Luke! My family could be watching or even worse, the nosey neighbours."

"Let them, the ruddy insomniacs. You are no longer dating a jobless good for nothing fella. Before you say anything, that's probably what everyone thinks of—thought of me as. I know my mum does—did, even the parish padre."

"No they d—" Tina is cut up by an old lady sounding voice.

"You two young and pretty lovebirds want to buy a lucky charm necklace?"

Luke and Tina are startled and turn to see a little old lady dressed in clothing not too dissimilar to something Gypsy Rosie Lee or other sea side fortune telling practitioners would wear.

"Excuse me, what did you say?" asked Luke.

"Would you two like to buy a lucky charm necklace? It will bring you much good luck, my pretties," the old lady replied.

"Sorry, it looks like your luck is out tonight. Come to think of it—so was ours right at the end. You need to buy that lucky charm off yourself because we're not interested in buying," Luke said firmly.

"Wait, hang on a second, Luke. Can we see it, please?" asked Tina. Luke did not say anything.

"Of course, you may, sweetheart. It'll improve your chances to win the lottery." The old lady hands the charm necklace to Tina.

"I suppose you've won the lottery many times, have you? And you're just hawking this lucky charm trinket around in the middle of the night just for fun, right?" Luke asked in sarcastic tone.

"I'll take it, how much?" Tina asked.

"Only five pounds to you, miss."

"Five pounds?" Luke sounded off.

Tina gets five pound out in coins and pays the old lady.

"Thank you, young lady. May it repay you with much luck and bring joy and happiness to others around you. Goodbye, young lovers."

To that, she walks off into the night like a person half her age.

Tina puts the necklace around her neck. "What do you think?"

Luke looks at Tina and the necklace around her. "Hmm, you look great as usual. Shame about the expensive to buy but cheaply made tacky necklace though."

Tina hits Luke with a soft playful slap on his shoulder. "Get into the mood of it—it's all about the feel good factor. How it makes you feel—I know it's not a bringer of good luck really, but it does let you hope and dream."

"I'll tell you what makes me feel good, continuing where we left off, after we were unlucky enough to be interrupted by Widow Twankey and her fake-luck charm." Luke once again embraces Tina and plants another kiss, this time on her lips but slightly longer this time.

"You're wrong, sweetheart, I think the lucky charm necklace is working already," Tina mumbled a second after the event.

Chapter 9
The Bake Off

Luke as usual is on the stacking and racking operation along with his three colleagues. The buzzer goes signifying his team had completed their last shift of the day and are due to be replaced any moment now.

"Boy! I'm glad to finish today," Luke said to the others.

"You are glad to finish every day, Luk bhai. I not hearing you say anything else all time you be here," replied Zahoor.

Luke laughs. "That's true, but I was out on the razzle dazzle, on the sauce yesterday night, got in late so I'm very tired today."

"You speak strangely my friend, I am not understanding but I think I know what you are meaning. You goray—English people always spending your money as quickly as you are earning it. You should be like us Asians. Earn money, spend little, save money to buy houses and put on rent. Very good life rules."

"I know the Asian way, I grew up with Asians in this town don't forget, half of Bolton belongs to your fellow countrymen now, you lot have bought up everything going, four-bedroomed houses are like gold dust in Bolton. Nor would anyone have trouble finding a house to rent either. What you really need to do is a mix between English and Asian ways. Have fun and also have some investment assets to show for working your butt off all your life. I'm not one for mixing myself, it was just mainly drinking like a very dry sponge—or like sand in the Sahara Desert and the only thing I got is the ass in asset."

"I not go out and throw good money into gutter. I am not smoking or drinking and not betting money on horses. This is how I save money for when I am retiring."

"Zahoor, mera Asian bhai, by the time you retire, you will own all the cash in England and you'll probably croak it when this money mountain falls down on you. Anyway, besides counting your stash every day and internet searching the latest Pakistani Rupee exchange rate or house for sale, what do you do for fun, how do you entertain yourself?"

"Oh, I am watching television, on satellite dish—Sky TV Asian channels."

"Oh yeah? And what in particular do you watch on the Asian network, Currynation street, Balti Towers, Always Open All Hours or maybe, Married with 'Eight' Children or just Chapatti westerns?"

Zahoor (or the other two) does not understand Luke's humour, a humour that most definitely could be labelled as mildly racist in these modern times. As a result, he just says, "I am this moment, watching a Pakistani police programme where they are fighting criminals and corruption and bribes. In each part, the police are solving crimes and locking up big, ugly gangsters."

"Pakistani police solving crimes, arresting bad guys, busting back-handers and tackling corruption—hmm—must definitely be a fiction drama then," Luke said and then laughs.

"What are you finding funny, Luk saab? You are saying something funny, no?"

"No mate, it's nothing really. Just a private joke, meh bahort bifqoof hai."

The three Indian-subcontinental fellas smile with admiration yet again at Luke, the gorah, for knowing Urdu words. Luke basks for a few seconds with this praise. Learning was never this easy at school when it mattered. What he just said in Urdu translate as, 'I am a big buffoon'—now he is definitely in non-fiction mode—factual comments!

"We'll make a Pakistani out of you yet, my friend," said Zahoor.

"Doubt it, matey. I spend money—on fun and wasteful things. That rules me out of being a proper honorary Pakistani even though I think of myself as one in this place, don't it? No investing for me, I've never had money to invest. But talking of money, where do you lot keep your money—the cash, I've heard you lot don't keep it in banks in case it can be tracked, for benefit purposes?" asked Luke but wondered if he had or had not offended his Asian friend.

"Oh I keep my money in a safe in my house. I have hidden the safe under a pile of old clothes so it cannot be easily spotted."

"Safe? Nowadays, burglars look everywhere, no hiding places left, they even empty rubbish bins inside the house, they're mighty sneaky these days. But, if I had a safe, then I would not hide it—more, I would have it in plain sight, I would put a bottle of champagne on top of it, with some drinking glasses. However, I'll open the bottle first and dissolve a shit load of sedatives in the drink, then cork up the bottle again."

Zahoor looks at Luke all puzzled, who can blame him?

"What are you meaning by all this, bhai? I am not understanding."

"You will, buddy. You see, when the burglars break open the safe and find the loot—the cash, they'll be so happy, they'll be wanting to celebrate. There just happens to be a nice expensive bottle of the bubbly and conveniently placed glasses in front of them. They won't be able to resist and drink up, probably most of the bottle, since it won't be a big bottle. And hey presto, they are knocked-out for the count because of the sedatives in the bottle, the knock out drug. When they wake up, they won't be seeing stars, they'll be seeing bars."

"That is wonderful idea, Luk saab," agreed Zahoor, now that it has been explained.

"Buy yourself a bottle of the good stuff, it's an excellent security plan."

"Oh, no can do my friend, I am a Muslim, alcohol is not allowed for us. It is banned, it makes people who drink it go mad and behave very nasty and silly and start fighting. Many people in my community call it 'urine'. No, I cannot even go near it, very bad, very bad."

"Think of all the money in there that it might keep safe, enough money to buy your next renting house."

"You are right my friend, I'll buy a bottle after work, there will not be many people in the shop at that time to see me buying it!"

"You'll have to explain to the Mrs, of course, about why you have Satan's urine in the house."

"Oh yes, she will understand once I am explaining to her why I bought it."

"Silly question this, but you do have just the one wife, don't you?"

"Yes, yes, I am having just one wife."

"That's nice, you're a modern type of fella I can tell, some traditions are best left forgotten, kind of modernise a bit."

"It is illegal to have more than one wife in England."

"What ya' saying, if you could have more than one wife, you would?"

"Tohbah, tohbah, Allah maafi deh! (Zahoor pinches/touches both his ear lobes, one at a time, with his right hand thumb and index finger). Oh no, Luke saab. I would not be liking two wives."

"Why not, double snogging time, gives a man choice, don't it? That's why you lot have many wives, otherwise—no point, unless you like being nagged at."

"Two wives mean two mothers-in-law. Why would you want to punish yourselves every day?" Both Luke and Zahoor laugh. The other two just smile, as they have no idea about what has been said.

"Also, many wives mean many children. The average Asian fella would need a car with ten doors to get his children to school on time!" joked Luke, but this time he did feel guiltier straight away about what he had just said. He now wished that Zahoor did not understand English either like the other two. Luke need not have worried though, Zahoor did not register the definite racist undertone to Luke's joke. Phew, Luke gets away with it!

They crew are in the changing rooms. Many are, as usual, are stuffing bread product packets up their coats. A lot are eating some of them.

"Blimey! Can't they wait until they get home," asked Luke to Zahoor.

"No Luke, these ones are different. We make these for Waitrose. They are made with very expensive flour and real butter and others expensive ingredients. They taste much better. Here, taste one."

Zahoor gives a bread cake to Luke who consumes it fairly quickly.

"Hey, that's not bad. You can tell where the extra money goes."

"I know you not take bread cakes home sometimes but I have one packet for you, these special Waitrose ones. You want?"

"I want, I'll 'curry' one of those about my persons! Thanks old buddy. I will take it home with pleasure. If it's good enough for posh Waitrose shoppers, then it's good enough for the Woam household."

Luke stuffs the six pack up his coat and follows everyone else out of the building.

Outside on the company yard area Luke is lazily walking towards the exit gate. He sees supervisor Jack Sloane up ahead looking over the workers as they walk past him. Luke thinks he could have done without him being there today but he is there so would have to walk by him. In no time at all he gets to him.

"Good day, Luke. Finished your shift then?" asked supervisor Jack.

"Yep! Ready for home sweet home, Mr Sloane, time to flowcha! What you doing out here?"

"Just checking."

"Checking! Checking for what?"

"You see Luke, there's a slight discrepancy between the numbers of bread cake unit packs being produced to pack units being shipped out. The computerised system is detecting a small but distinct shortfall somewhere."

"You should really update your computer systems. Those ZX Spectrums are not fit for purpose anymore." Luke laughs, Jack smiles.

"It's not our computers, they've been checked. The problem is elsewhere."

"Well, I'm all out of suggestions, I'll be off now, see you tomorrow." As Luke is about to set off, someone from behind bumps into him and Luke almost falls over. This unfortunately loosens the wedged bread cake pack and it slips out from under his jacket and falls to the floor in full view of Mr Sloane.

Luke looks at the floored six pack and then at Mr Sloane. "Holi boli and I'll be a monkey's uncle! How did that get up there?"

"There's nothing holy or even Christian about it son, so why don't I enlighten you instead, you put it up there! Even an aging ZX Spectrum that's on the blink will be able to work that one out."

"Me? I can't remember doing that, why would I, who risks their job over some poxy bread cakes? Plus it's an Indian Hindu Holi, not Christian holy."

"Whatever, I'm just bothered about the great big 'holey' in our shipment numbers, so see if you remember this, tomorrow, see me first thing, in my office."

Luke smiles and says "You should have been a comedian in life. But I'll try my best, what with my diagnosed medical short term memory loss condition and my impulsive taking off things medical condition I suffer from, I'll aim to be there. But let me assure you again boss, I did not take this bread cake pack." Luke starts to walk off but not before he picks up the bread cake packet.

"I'll take that, if you don't mind." Mr Sloane snatches the bread cake packet from Luke's grasp and looks at it. "You're not daft are you? Taste for the premium stuff."

"Sorry, there goes my medical condition again. I take things without thinking about it. Make sure you take that into account tomorrow morning, Mr Sloane," pleaded Luke as he is walking away.

"Bring me a genuine signed doctor's note and I might!"

A very short distance away, Luke stops and looks at Mr Sloane and with a raised voice says, "Got it! I was reversed-mugged, sort of reversed pick-pocketed. Whoever smuggled it out, saw you, panicked and purposefully bumped into me and planted it on me. You saw that yourself just now when I nearly fell over. I would have only found out at home if you weren't here today, thank you for that, Mr Sloane, you saved me a lot of heart-felt anguish."

"With a good spun yarn like that, you should be working in the mills, only the last one in this area closed about fifty years ago. I'm not a comedian or a 'thou shalt forgive' type, so office, tomorrow."

"You're a hard man, Mr Sloane, picking on innocent young workers. This is the reason why we had those factory reform laws they teach you in history at school, I know 'cause I got an 'A' in it," said Luke as he walks off slowly again.

"I'm not your father, Luke, I'm not a forgiver, remember. So 'dough' be late, you hear me, master Luke?" said Mr Sloane in a raised voice too and in a definite comedic tone and smirks. Then he says much quieter, "Although people say to me that I can be a funny man!"

Luke is a little distance away and shows no reaction to his comments and Mr Sloane thinks his genial 'comedy' might have been wasted. Never mind!

The next morning, a bit after the starting time of 5 o'clock, Luke finds himself outside of the admin office. He knocks and goes in and sees the secretary he had done on his interview day sitting at her desk, talking on the phone, just as he had seen on that day as well.

"Hi, I'm Luke Woam, I'm here to see Mr Sloane. Might be about the promotion he's promised me."

Luke said this without really waiting for the secretary to focus her attention on him. As Luke goes further in, the secretary puts the phone down and looks at him.

"I remember you, you're the guy who came for an interview some time ago and had a funny name."

"Well remembered, miss. And what's even funnier, I still got it. I'm Luke Woam, Mr Sloane wants to see me about promotion or something."

"Luke Woam! That's how I like my hot chocolate." It was said in dead pan mode so Luke could not figure out if it was said for mocking purpose or genuine. He let it slide anyway, she probably meant it as a genuine comment Luke concluded.

"You can sit down over there, I'll inform Mr Sloane."

Luke sits down in the same place as all those weeks ago. It is fairly quiet, so he can hear Mr Sloane's raised voice from his office. "Is Mr Sloane talking to the head honcho in there?" Luke asked.

"If he is then it's on the phone. The owner won't be in today."

"This company, it's still owned by the same family that started it, isn't it?"

"Yes, it was founded by Mr Haversham Sr, he retired years ago and his son has been running it ever since. Mr Haversham Jr won't be in today like I said, so he won't be handling the promotion you're after."

"Why not? His Rolls Royce or Bentley broken down?"

"No, you see these walls aren't the best for secrecy you see, so from what I can gather, Mr Haversham's daughter has done a runner, run away I think. I've never heard of any crisis before in their family. This is the first."

"Daughter gone missing, runaway, eh? The granddaughter of the main man I presume?"

"Yes."

"How old is she?"

"I think she's about fifteen, not too young but not too old either."

"Fifteen. Right age to do something like this, to rebel against the old guard."

"Yeah, but it's still really sad."

"Must be. Here, what they doing about it, have they called the police or summat? Did you manage to earwig that through the wall or door?"

"I don't think I heard the police being mentioned so far. Besides, the police don't do anything for a couple of days anyways."

"Oh yeah! That's true. Nothing more you know then?"

"There is one more thing I know, the boss has asked Mr Sloane about hiring a private investigator to try and find his daughter. I've heard Mr Sloane mention a figure of £5000, some even higher."

"£5000! Bloody hell fire, that's a lot of dough, an awful lot of bread, if you excuse the pun. £5000 for just finding a missing spotty, angsty teenager. That's—easy money. Easy money for someone to make."

"It is, if you find the missing person, otherwise you only get daily expenses money. Haven't you seen stuff like that on the telly? The big money—is only if you complete the job. Just like anywhere else really."

"Where could a rich, spoilt teenage girl go to in two-bit boring Bolton? Just search the usual places like the local park, the shopping arcade, a junkie dig or try her best friend's large back garden and viola, you've found the two smoking pot and drinking alcopops and puking up behind a big bush and thus, say hello to a cool 5000 smackeroonees."

"She might be rich but she isn't stupid. My guess is she'll have gone to London. I've often heard the boss talking to Mr Sloane about how all the family really enjoyed their stays in London. He said many times that his children loved it down there. It is the number one destination for all first timer runaways. I got that from the telly too."

"London! Of course. I bet she'll have planned this way ahead and that means she'll have pugged away enough money over time to last down there."

"That's what I would do too."

"Listen, Miss Secretary, this Haversham family, they are local to this town, aren't they?"

"Yeah! They have stayed loyal to their birth place."

"So, they will have their mansion local too?"

"Oh yes! You can't miss it, it sits on top of the hill overlooking the whole town."

"Oh—that's their place, I've seen it all my life but I've never bothered to know anything about it. It's a mega place."

"I wouldn't move away either if I lived there."

Luke is quiet for second, deep in fast thinking mode.

"Listen, something important has come up for me and I have to like flowcha like right now. Tell Mr Sloane, that I can't accept the promotion this time around and that I might even have to love and leave you lot. I will come back for my redundancy pay in the near future though!"

To that Luke makes a quick exit, he did not really wait to hear the secretary's reply, which she does anyway as Luke is scurrying away.

"Redundancy? I thought you were here for a promotion," replied the secretary but more to herself than to Luke who had disappeared by now.

Just then, Mr Sloane comes into the secretary's office. "No Luke Woam yet, I could do without this hassle right now to tell you the truth."

Which hassle he meant—Luke's or Mr Haversham's, who knows?

"Oh he was here, sir, but he had to 'flowcha', that's what he said. I think it means he had to go 'cause he flew off straight after. Something urgent I think," replied the secretary.

"Oh well, if he's gone, he's gone. Hopefully off site for good, I'll check a bit later. But he'll be back, those sorts always do, cap in hand, saying it was all a misunderstanding and they'll never do it again."

"Oh, he said he'll be back, I just remembered, sir. To discuss his redundancy pay and not the other thing—the thing he came for—promotion."

Mr Sloane reacts like he has been zapped by a dozen police tasers, then he laughs to himself.

"Promotion? Redundancy pay? And what kind of a word is 'flowcha' anyway? What a joker, he's out of his mind! It must be all the stolen bread cake diet he's been on, it's made his tiny brain go stale!"

The secretary takes a second to get it and laughs. "Stale! Very witty, Mr Sloane. Very witty."

Chapter 10
Lost One, Gained One

Luke is a bit out of breath, he is standing outside a small printing shop. The name on the boarding reads, 'Gold Star Printers'. He goes in.

Luke goes over to the Chinese male proprietor. The business is a small affair operation ideal for printing things like wedding invitation cards or leaflets or what Luke came here for—business cards.

"Hello, sir. My name is Mr Smith and I'm interested in business cards but only a small sample quantity. Can you tell me your prices?" asked Luke, not one to waste time with idle chit chat.

"Hello to you too sir. I will get out my price list," replied the Chinese owner and gets out his price list from under the counter. He opens the book to the right place. "Let's see, for 1000 top quality cards it is £50, for 500 it is £30. For medium quality cards, it is £40 for a 1000 and £25 for 500."

"No! I want only a sample, so I'm talking about five or ten tops, no, just five in fact and in the lowest quality possible also."

The Chinese printer looks dumbfounded and stares straight into Luke's eyes without saying anything. "What is your business, a paper round? (He laughs for a second). Five? I don't do such small quantities. I do bulk printing. And my cheapest quality card is the non-glossy, mono-chrome, recycled card ones."

"None cheaper than that one?"

"Cheaper still? I got some crayons and some empty cereal boxes in the back, if you want even cheaper ones." The Chinese printer lets another short laugh break out, satisfied at his own joke.

Luke does some more fast thinking again, ignoring the printer's joke. "Listen, my boss, Mr Woam, said get some samples and if he likes them then he would order like—five thousand or thereabouts. So, for a potentially really lucrative contract, will you just do a sample for me in your—recycled paper—card, please?"

The Chinese man is quiet for a few seconds. The news of a big lucrative contract must be ringing in his grey matter.

"OK, tell me what you want and I will make a test card and I will send picture to your phone. If you like, then I can make five by tomorrow afternoon."

"Oh no, sir. I—my boss needs them now. I need like five cards in about an hour's time, ready to take away. Now, how much will that be?"

"You need now, as soon as possible?"

"Yes sir, I do."

"That will cost more, more urgent work."

"You haven't even told me the price and already it's gone up, marvellous!"

"I cannot tell you price for this, this is not how I work. I will work hard and finish five cards in recycled card quality and then I work out price."

Luke makes a screwed up face but says nothing, he is at the printer's mercy and the printer knows this. "Oh—OK. But know this, I only have very limited funds."

"It will take me about forty minutes, you wait or you come back?"

"I wait. Ain't got anywhere better to go or do."

Luke conveys all the required details to the Chinese man quickly like name, contacts, business name, how he would like the layout and design to be, then he makes himself comfortable on the waiting area settee. The printer gets to work.

After about thirty minutes, the printer had made the sample cards.

"Mr Smith, please come, cards ready. (Luke goes over to the desk). Luke Woam, hmm, your boss has funny name. You know, that is how I like my noodle soup! (Luke grimaces). I finished, you like?"

Luke holds one up and looks hard at it. He is no expert on business cards but it is mostly how he had described it and wanted it to look like.

"Yeah! I like. So, how much for five very cheap, very non-glossy, very recycled cards?"

Luke's triple mention of the word 'very' was a deliberate ploy.

The Chinese printer man picks up a pen and paper and starts to write something down. Luke thinks that is all for show to make it look like he is costing the job professionally through legit means, when all he is really doing is trying (and failing in Luke's eyes) to justify a higher price.

"The total cost for this extra fast work will be ten pounds."

"Ten pounds! For five poxy cards in the cheapest format ever possible? Should have gone for the crayon and cornflake box option."

"Yes! That is reasonable price. That is cheap price for fast work."

Luke needs the cards quick time so decides to pay the printer the ten pounds and puts the cards away.

"Thank you, Mr Smith. Tell your boss I do good deal for five thousand cards, very good deal."

"My boss is poor, just like me. You are ripping us off and you know it. You are robbing the poor—you're no Robin Hood, that's for sure."

"No! Not Robin Hood! Robin Yu! I am Robin Yu. (He gets out a 'Golden Star Printers' letter headed piece of paper and on it is written his name, 'Robin Yu'). You see, my name is Robin Yu. Much better than Robin Hood. Robin Yu!"

"How appropriate, Robin Yu. With your prices, you certainly live up to your name!" replied Luke then leaves.

In about half an hour Luke gets to Tina's house. He gets out of his car and goes up to the door and knocks. It is Tina who opens it.

"Luke! Whatya' doing here, at this time, you should be at work right now?"

"Should be. No longer required to though. There are, let's say, irreconcilable differences that have arisen between myself and my employers that can no longer maintain the status quo with regards to my position with them as an invaluable, I repeat, invaluable employee."

"I've no idea what you just said but I take it you are no longer working for them, what's the technical word for it—sacked?"

"To tell you the truth, I don't really understand if it makes any sense either, but to put it in simple terms, I will not be going there again—to work. I might need to go back at some point to sort out some termination stuff though. And just for the record, I have not been sacked. I left of my own accord and I probably will resign before they can sack me."

They both make their way to Tina's bedroom to continue the conversation, they sit down on the bed side by side.

"No work! Oh Luke! Just when things were going great for us. We have plans—had plans, our house—the good nights out—ordering the special at the chippie. All that's gone now."

"Not necessarily, Tina my darling!" said Luke with glee.

"What do you mean? We haven't won the lottery or anything like that, have we? You've been keeping it a secret from me, is that it? The lucky charm?"

"I wish! Unfortunately, it's more down to earth than that. I have had an amazing idea, Tina. I have decided to open my own business. That's why I have left the bakery."

"Own business! What? How? I—well what? What business?"

Some minutes pass, Tina is holding and looking at the business card that Luke had had made earlier.

"I don't believe it! 'Luke Woam. Missing Person Finder'. (Tina bursts into laughter). What is this? Now you're a missing person finder? You don't know anything about finding missing people. One minute you're a baker, the next minute you're a business man, not forgetting the long jobless stint before both of those two."

"Us, both of us, my lovely. Look further down the card, it says, 'Partner—Tina Chapman'. It's written in smaller size font. That was the printer though, not me."

Tina sees her name on it too.

"OK, both of us haven't the foggiest about how to find missing people. Oh Luke, you'd only just about found yourself a job for the first time and you go and lose that already."

"We can learn. Besides, we are only finding a teenage girl who is in London—somewhere—maybe. How hard can it be, all runaways probably go to the same sort of places? There's bound to be a dive down there that doubles up as, I don't know, a runaway and homeless hotspot like a first stop shelter or runaway central. Only, the authorities don't know about it because, just like in that famous film, the first rule is that nobody talks about it."

"Teenage girl? How come you know about her, who is she?"

"I keep my ear to the ground, I hear things. That's why I know we can make a go of this. That is why I have made these cards. All we have to do now is bag the gig—the contract. Only I and the family and a couple of their workers know about it so far."

"Contract—workers? Whose daughter is it?"

"Some rich dude's daughter with a big house. We need to get to him with not a second to lose. In fact, we'd better set off now."

Tina is torn in two minds. Put a stop to this fantastical absurdity or go along with it until Luke's fervent imagination eventually runs out of steam. She decides on the latter because, that way, it will not be her fault when it all comes to a crashing end. She will not have to say, "I told you so!"

"OK, Luke. I'm with you. Let's give it a go and see where we go with this. Let's do this, whatever this is?"

"Yes! I knew you would see the light. It's the right thing to do, sweet heart. In fact, it can't be more righter. You'll see, it'll work our nicely."

"If it doesn't, you go back to the bakery and get your blooming job back! What am I going to do with you Luke? Dogs have better luck than you, at least they are for life, not just for Christmas. Your job was just for a bit of Christmas, never mind life."

"I'm just swapping jobs that's all. The money is there just waiting for us to pass go and collect."

"Most people swap jobs after years, not four or five weeks. It's called holding down a job. You have gone from jobless to baker to—missing person detective or summat like that."

"Yeah, it is a bit of change. Job swapping—you know, that could be quite funny if you think about it. Being trained and experienced in one trade, then suddenly having to do a different job that could lead to all sorts of mishaps, if you think about it."

Tina does have a little think about it. "I see what you mean. For instance, if you are following a nasty character on your latest career venture and he comes at you with a baseball bat, all you can do is bombard him with some stale bread cakes stuffed up your jacket. Or from your bone idle days, you could hope to bore him into submission with your in-depth knowledge of daytime telly programmes, like Kojak and Quincy."

Luke laughs even though it was said at his expense.

"This is unlikely but what about if an ex-abattoir worker or butcher becomes a male gynaecology surgeon and he turns up to work drunk one day?" Both Luke and Tina too hold their crutch area and wince.

Tina has another little think, busy lady!

"What about if an ex-Demolition Derby driver becomes a bus driver and he turns up to work drunk as a skunk?"

"On the day he has to take the old folks on their annual trip to the seaside!" Luke continued. They both laugh out loud.

"Or an ex-shot put champion or discus thrower gets a job as a waiter," said Tina.

"And he turns up drunk to work," said Luke and Tina in unison.

"Ooh, I've got another one," said Tina excitedly. "This isn't a job swap exactly but work with me on this one, what about if a wine taster got trapped in a deep isolated pit or cave and the only things he had with him in the cave were wine bottles? He'd be dead of dehydration in days."

Both Luke and Tina mimic a wine taster's action of supping and spitting out of the sampled wine and then laugh.

"I've got a real good one, Tina. You'll love this one. What about if an ex-poet becomes a suicide prevention telephone counsellor for the Samaritans?" Luke mimics holding a phone.

"Hello, you are through to Paul.

Who's here to save your soul.

Please don't take your precious life.

With that very big kitchen knife.

Or jump of that coastal cliff.

'Cause you'll end up as a smelly wet stiff.

You should be with your family.

Rather than bothering me.

Never consider suicide.

As God will never be on your side."

Luke and Tina loudly cheer and perform a high five. This last one was something else, something special. Spin in your grave Chaucer! Coming soon— 'The Bolton Abbey Tales'.

Tina says after the praising, "Poetry? It'll make me want to top myself even more. Some poor sod of a suicidal university educated librarian might get talked out of it but us Lancashire people are hardy and see a job through, we stick with it, even if it's committing suicide, God forbid. Unless it's a bakery job!"

Luke gives Tina a mean stare but says nothing.

Chapter 11
The Client

Luke and Tina pull up in the large grounds outside the Haversham mansion and park up near some expensive premium cars.

"Nice cars!" exclaimed Luke, looking at the premium metal from his driving seat.

"Yeah! Real high life these people have."

They both get out and make their way to the main door and knock. A teenage boy opens the door. Luke speaks first.

"Oh hello, young boy—young master. I'm here to see the owner, I assume it to be a certain Mr Haversham, your father I'm guessing?"

"Yes, he's my father. Is he expecting you?" replied the young son.

"I forgot to make an appointment on account of me being ever so busy, but I am here now about Mr Haversham's daughter's—your sister's—disappearance."

"Oh that! You'd better come in then, follow me."

Luke looks at Tina who looks at him. This hare-brained scheme of Luke's has just gotten real. Point of no return has been traversed.

They are led into a large grandiose room that must be the communal living room. Inside, there is Mr Haversham and his wife along with now, of course, Luke, Tina and the son.

"Dad, this is some guy who says he's here about Isabelle," said the son.

Mr Haversham looks a bit puzzled. "Thanks, Archie."

"Hello, Mr Haversham, my name is Luke Woam, this here is my partner Tina Chapman. We are missing person finders. This is my card." He hands a card to Mr Haversham who gets it and reads it.

"Luke Woam. Missing Person Finder. Always one step behind."

"Yep, that's me and that's true," said Luke with great pride and a smile to boot.

"Surely it is better to be one step in front or am I not getting it?" asked Mr Haversham.

Luke stops smiling to think about it. Yes, it would make more sense to write, 'Always one step in front' rather than 'behind'. Tina gives a quick, unseen elbow nudge to Luke and also a bit of a scornful look. She had not bothered to read that bit earlier on.

"Too right, but what that means is although the missing person—the runaway, has the advantage over us but we are almost always right behind them—like one step behind." Luke did not sound too convincing but he thought he had managed to dig himself out with merit.

"Oh—well, I suppose so if you put it that way. Anyway, how on earth did you know about our family predicament, good God man, we only found out about it earlier today ourselves?"

"Sir—in our line of business it pays to know what is going on—and more crucially—when it is going on. We are always one very small step behind remember. Our firm has a north of England enviable reputation as being one of the best in the business that other firms can only dream of."

"I've never heard of your—firm. I and my associates have rung around some of them this very morning," stated Mr Haversham.

It is one of those moments again where Luke has to do some fast thinking. How do you bring to life a firm that did not exist only an hour or two ago?

"Mr Haversham, our policy—our first rule is—that we do not talk about our firm—our business—I mean we do not advertise our establishment. Either you know about us or—we contact you in your hour of need. That is what brought us here today."

"I not sure about your publicity mantra—ethos. I am a business man and it sounds a bit—strange to say the least, not the type of business model I would advise anyone. Not advertise the business, that's financial suicide? But never mind all that now, what are your rates?"

Luke's face lights up. "Our rates are in two components. One is the upfront one-off payment of £6000 and the second one is a daily expense rate of £100. If we fail to find the target person, half the upfront fee of £6000 pounds is returned, the daily rate is non-refundable. Mostly, going on our past record, we find the missing person within a couple of days."

"£6000 and a daily rate of £100?" gasped Mr Haversham in a manner that sounded a lot like he had just been broad sided by a Spanish galleon, completely flabbergasted. Mrs Haversham picks up on her husband's reaction.

"Henry darling, it might not be the cheapest quote but we don't want no time wasters or cowboys. They claim to be good and they did find out about us amazingly quick. Time is of the essence right now. We need someone on the case right away. Every second counts, my love," Mrs Haversham pleaded.

"Her ladyship is right, sir, time can be either the saviour or enemy, depending on how you use it," Luke quickly added.

"Don't you worry, Cynthia, I understand fully. (Looks at Luke). Very well, I accept your rates, you have got the job of finding our daughter. Keep us informed at all times."

"Thank you, sir, we will endeavour to find your daughter as quickly as we possibly can," Luke replied.

"If you provide me with your account details I will transfer you the money, the upfront fee, once we have signed the necessary paperwork," insisted Mr Haversham as he looks over the business card again. "Luke Woam! You know, that's how I like my mushroom and asparagus soup for starters at the evening meal." Luke grimaces again upon hearing this but more so because of the mention of paperwork and the signing of it. Time to think quickly again.

"Tina, did you bring the contract papers with you, like I asked you too?" Luke asked Tina but Tina is at a loss for words. What papers? There are no papers!

"I—I—picked—them up but when you—asked me to answer the office phone I must have put them down and left them by the telephone because I don't have them with me right now," replied a slightly worried Tina as she just about manages to wriggle out of the sticky situation. It is what you call superfast on the spot excuse making.

"Oh shucks! That will take time now to fetch them—time that could be used to find—Annabelle—Isabelle. But officialdom is both a formality and a must as signed contracts are the cornerstone of global business since—forever." Luke is rambling hoping a certain person in the room would speak up again. She does, to save the hapless duo from scuttling.

"Henry, the contract paper stuff can be signed later. Let them do their work. I want Isabelle home as soon as possible," said Mrs Haversham, the potential saviour.

"I suppose you're right, Cynthia darling. Listen here Mr Woam, I'm prepared to forgo the contract signing stuff and even the references, for another more convenient time, retrospectively so to speak. Preferably when you've brought back our lovely Isabelle safe and sound, although by then it will only be a formality like you mentioned, is that OK with you?"

"Absolutely dudely alright with us, Mr Haversham. I don't normally work like this but I am more than happy to make an exception," agreed a very happy Luke.

"All our daughter's details are written down on that piece of paper in that envelope over there on the table, included in there is a picture of her but I'm afraid it's not too recent. Our contacts are also in there," informed Cynthia.

"Oh yes, the details, they will certainly be needed, I'll leave my bank details here," said Luke as he picks up the information pack and leaves his account details in its place.

"I can send you more recent pictures of my sister from my phone album, sir. I will need your number," chipped in Archie.

"Good idea, young master. My number is on the business card your father has, feel free to send me the photos whenever it is convenient to you. I thank you humbly," said a grateful Luke.

"If there's nothing else, Mr Woam, Miss Chapman, you can be getting on with your task. Young Archie here will show you out, goodbye. Oh! Mr Woam, I know it's a bit too early but from experience, have you any idea where to begin your search? We have already tried all her friends and her membership clubs."

Luke takes time to answer so it appears like he knows what he is doing.

"In my substantial experience of doing this sort of work, I usually find that once the local known sites have been searched, like her friends and clubs, which you have covered, teenage runaways usually head for the great metropolis that is London. We'll probably find that London is key to finding Isabelle. Also because I happen to know through our primarily groundwork, that Isabelle has a penchant for the big city."

"Why, that is so true, Mr Woam. Isabelle loves London, she never wants to leave when we holiday there. I have a good feeling about you two," exclaimed Mrs Haversham.

"Impressive, Mr Woam, Miss Chapman. I am reassured that I have hired the best money can buy. I wish you good luck and bring back our daughter safe and sound. Good day to you two, Archie, show them out please."

"Don't worry, sir; the next time we meet, we will have your daughter with us, that is our promise. Who would want to leave this splendid mansion home, set in idyllic green gardens, it's so tranquil and peaceful and most of all so quiet here that—you could hear a fish fart!" stated Luke, everyone in the room is taken aback with what he has just said. Archie giggles a little.

"Good bye, Mr and Mrs Haversham," said Tina to rescue the moment. She then quietly whispers to herself, "Fish fart? What a dick!" They both follow the still smirking Archie out of the room and eventually house.

Luke and Tina are in the car driving home.

"You added an extra grand to the fee, you told me you were gonna charge them five big ones," asked Tina.

"I know, it was just a spur of the moment thing. Well, maybe not that spontaneous. It's a fact, that the cheapest quotes are usually by cowboys, conmen, so I decided to up the fee a bit to make us look a bit more professional, a more reliable blue chip outfit, ergo more expensive. Also, when I saw their cars and house up close and personal, I thought, why not?"

"Oh yeah! Clever. But we did get a bit lucky at times even although we managed to blag it. He very nearly caught us with our tail between our legs with him not recognising or knowing anything about us or the paper signing thing."

"Yeah! I sweated a few buckets during some moments in there."

"You know what, it's the lucky charm. The one we got from that creepy gypsy woman. It's bringing us luck."

Luke laughs. "Leave off will ya'! Lucky charm? I got sacked—will get sacked officially—soon. I have lost a job—my job today, end of. And the funny thing is, it was the very next day after buying that supposedly lucky thing from a con woman that this happened."

"Luke, you're not seeing it. Right after losing your job, another opportunity sprung up. I call that super lucky."

"Tina, my gullible, loveable teddy bear, you're not seeing it. I wasn't wearing the so-called lucky charm around my neck when this opportunity 'sprung' into my head. It was all me. I thought of it. That thing was and is around your neck making the seller very lucky. Five pounds lucky."

"You can believe what you want, it was all the work of the lucky charm."

"OK, you can believe that, that's your progative."

Tina laughs. "It's prerogative, not progative."

"Pre—prerogative! Er—that doesn't sound right and that doesn't sound like you at all. Is that charm thing making you clever with words darling?"

"Probably. 'Ere, I just thought, we can still order the special?"

"Of course, how about mushroom and asparagus soup for starters?"

"Why not, as long as it's hot and not lukewarm, if you pardon the pun?" laughed Tina.

"On the topic of other-worldly things, you also firmly believe that we are not alone in the universe, don't ya'?"

"Yeah, that's because we ain't. We cannot be the only ones in the vast universe, we just can't be."

"You should be careful in what you believe in. Look at the dinosaurs you mentioned a while back. All those creatures living on earth sixty-five million years ago, they probably looked up in the night sky and wondered if anything besides twinkling stars was out there.

There was, a great big bloody meteor heading straight for them. Before they could blink it went from being out there to in here. And just like aliens, it probed the nether regions of old mother earth good and hard. You can still see the crater scars to this day!"

They both have a good laugh at this as they drive on towards Tina's house.

When they reach Tina's house, still in the car, Luke gets out his phone.

"Might as well check to see if my bank account can handle numbers bigger than a single digit and on rare occasions, double digits? The bank already sent me anti-fraudulent and money laundering texts about my first—and unfortunately, only wage," said Luke and begins tapping and swiping.

They both wait anxiously until, "Yes, yes, yes, yes! If I was a rich man, da ba da ba da ba dum! A cool £6000 in my account. I bet the bank people personally phone me this time asking, "What the hell! You've put our computer into meltdown! Where did you get the money from, steal it you little thief?" Listen, we've got work to do. You go in and pack one of those small wheelie suit cases for a couple of days stay in a hotel and I'm gonna do the same. I'll come and pick you up in about an hour in a taxi."

"Will do? How we getting down to London?"

"Coach! Why you ask?"

"Coach! Didn't you just look at your bank account, it's the first time it's got proper money in it since—forever practically. I'm not counting your one-time poxy wage from the bakery, the bank people probably thought that was a charity

Christmas gift from one of your grandparents. The fraud squad are probably investigating you as we speak and you want to go to London on a bloody coach!"

"But the train is expensive. What's £25 compared to £120 and that's each?"

"Train!" firmly said Tina.

"Coach!" equally firmly and sticking to his guns replied Luke.

Chapter 12
The Big City

Luke and Tina are on a coach en route to the bright lights of mega city (nearly) London. Tina is by the window seat, Luke in the aisle seat.

"She's a pretty little thing, is Isabelle," remarked Luke as he gazes hard at her picture on his smart phone. He gets no answer from Tina. He turns his head to look at Tina.

"Tina, sweetheart, we need the money for our future. We can't flitter it away on expensive luxurious transport if perfectly adequate and cheaper transport is available. It's not like we are on a roof of a dusty train or wagon like you see on the telly in India and such like."

"I'm sure you enquired about whether we could ride the roof, anything to make it cheaper."

"Listen cupcake, London is one of the most expensive cities in the world. A single cup of coffee down there costs as much as a whole meal for a family up north."

"Have you booked which London park bench we are going to kip on or have you pushed the boat out and got us a place in one of the airport benches?"

"We're in a Travelodge, it might not be the Hilton but it fits the bill. It's quite close to the city centre, there was a cancellation and I rang just at the right time and nabbed it. Anyway, back to business, that son of theirs sent some pictures of this Isabelle, our target. She's a bonny lass. (He shows his phone with a picture of Isabelle on it to Tina, who does look at it). Her being really beautiful is not helpful to us, that's for sure."

"How is what you look like a factor, how does that matter?"

"Come on Tina, use your noggin. Pretty girls anywhere in the world, especially runaways, are in far more danger than fat ugly ones. All the lurid, evil pervs, sex pests, the pimps, sex gang runners, etc., are always scouting the big cities on a daily basis. They know all the places where runaways go. They have a certain type they look out for, big payday types and Isabelle is that type."

"So, what you're saying is if I decided to run away, all those lovely church-going bunch of people you mentioned will not bother me. I'll be safe as the next fat and ugly girl, still camping out on the Kings Cross bench, completely unmolested, completely unapproached."

Luke looks annoyingly at Tina.

"Did I say that? I did not say anything like that. Besides, we've been through all this before. To me and that is what matters, you are the most beautiful, the most attractive, the most—gorgeous, caring, sensitive girl I've ever had the pleasure to meet."

Luke at that moment hears a noise on the seat across the aisle and looks. It is a young teenage boy who is listening in—eavesdropping! He laughs and makes a barfing (retching) action. Luckily, Tina is oblivious to all this. He turns back to Tina.

"Listen Luke, I know you mean that, you've got good intentions, but my concern is that you haven't met any other girls in your life. I am the only girl you've ever met. That is OK in a two-bit woolly back town up north like Bolton, but here we are heading to London. I mean London! It's the UK's city of sin. Pretty women are dime a dozen down there. They wear thousand pound frocks and pay for their pink cocktail drinks with money from a Versace purse snuggled inside a Gucci handbag. All of them real, not fake."

"Look, when those types hit on me down there, I'll fight 'em off with all my might!" Luke joked hoping to reassure Tina.

"You will what? I mean, you will be out of your depth with those man-eaters, Casanova. Just be content with eyeballing them from a distance. What makes you think they'll be interested in your puny peasant ass anyway? I meant you lusting for them, not them lusting after you! Come on, get serious!"

"Well—thanks for that, puny peasant ass! Listen sweetheart, I just thought a little humour—" Luke started replying but was cut up by Tina.

"No, you listen. I might have slightly jealous and suspicious thoughts back in Bolton when you're out by yourself, but not in London. No girl is going to hit on you down there, mind you, no girl's ever really hit on you back in Bolton either apart from me to my knowledge. Anyway, if by some miracle, you do hook up with some stoned out bimbo babe who can't even remember her name, you'd probably take her back to a hotel room on top of the London cab roof just to save a bob or two, you stingy git!"

They both look at each other hard. Then they both burst out laughing. Then they embrace, cuddle and kiss. The young lad opposite stares again but Luke puts his left arm behind his back and puts up his middle finger, whilst still in the embrace.

A short time later, after some non-awkward silence, Luke says to Tina, "At least us going to London isn't a waste of money or time. I mean, I actually did some proper detective work and went to the coach station and the woman on the counter there remembered Isabelle from the day before, buying a single ticket to London. The woman even remembered Isabelle wearing the same top as in one of the pictures on the phone."

"It was me that suggested you check at the coach and rail stations, Sherlock."

"Yeah! Nice one, Tina love. What a partnership, made in heaven, right?"

"Right! Also no point in fritting away money on wild goose chases, if she's not down there."

After what seemed forever, their coach stopped at St. Pancras Coach station, King's Cross, London. They both get off and collect their baggage and walk out of the massive complex.

"What now, hail a taxi—a famous London black cab?" asked Tina.

"Nope, 'cause, you know when I said we got lucky finding a room in the city centre, well we got even luckier in that our accommodation is well within walking distance. We don't need a taxi or the tube," replied Luke expecting a lashing in response.

"Oh, you deserve a medal, you really do! It is a public bench, isn't it? That's where we are going to be sleeping, just tell me now?" Tina is not a happy bunny.

"We are in a hotel, have some faith in me, love. Tonight, we will be sleeping in a nice comfy bed in a proper hotel. We can get to it with just a short walk. Anybody would do the same. Come on, let's get going, I'm ready for a lie down."

Luke walks off and after a few seconds so does Tina but she clearly is not amused, like a certain royal London resident back in the day.

The Farringdon Travelodge is indeed a good brisk walk from the station. They get there, check in and are right outside their room door, Luke is holding the door key.

"Well, Tina, my princess, let us go in to our one room palace. Bagsy with the shower—or a full bath."

"Out of my way, Prince Charming, this lady is hitting the bath first." Tina grabs the key off Luke and thrusts open the door and runs in, followed by Luke.

The room itself is basic but clean and well fitted out in all the decor. How a customer rates a room depends on who you are and what you are accustomed to. For Luke and Tina, it is definitely five stars.

After a couple of hours, the bath has rim marks on it, the shower cubicle is all wet, the main room is messy and Luke and Tina are laying on top of the bed, rapped in towels.

"That was so good! I feel refreshed. So, what's our plan for the rest of the day, whatever is left of it?" asked Tina.

"Plan? I thought we'd stay in, charge up our batteries for tomorrow."

"Stay in! This is London mate, not—Doncaster or Morecombe. The night is when everything comes alive down here. Besides, we need to eat."

"Food is sorted, isn't it? The extra sandwiches we brought with us. Might as well use them. No point wasting good money on expensive food when we have it right here."

Tina becomes a tad angry with yet another example of frugalness from her beau. She picks up a bed pillow and hits him with it.

"Ow! What was that for?"

"You know what for! Alright! This is the last time I go along with your miserliness, we'll eat the bloody sandwiches, only because we've got them and shouldn't be wasted. I am even going to accept staying in tonight. But come tomorrow, darling, you'd better start splashing that £100 a day expenses or I'm on the next stagecoach outta here, understand?"

"Agreed! Agreed! But remember it is expenses and not holiday money. Like you said, London is London, where a £1 thing costs about £3, I think they're called 'Three-pound shops'. Here, they have a mark-up system, we're not all foreign tourists ripe for ripping off."

"I know that, but we're not gonna live like one click above the London homeless either."

Luke laughs. "You'd be surprised? Do you know how much the homeless beggars make in London and other big cities around the world? Thousands of pounds a year. You know, one could say, being homeless and begging in London is the fastest and easiest way to afford a house down here."

Chapter 13
First Day on The Job

The next day Luke and Tina are in the famous King's Cross underground station holding their 'All day' travel passes.

"Ready," asked Luke.

"Ready," replied Tina.

The two had decided to spend the entire day sightseeing and not on the job, looking for Isabelle Haversham can wait another day.

So, with the priority firmly not on the case, the two, over the course of the day went to as many places as time allowed. Trafalgar square, Museum of Natural History, Piccadilly Square, Harrods, London Eye. Of course, they were extreme rush jobs. In Oxford Street, Luke pretended to be a beggar, a Japanese tourist even gave him five pounds and Tina had to suffer a "I told you so" lecture for a while afterwards.

In Soho, Luke, just for a laugh, wanted to go into an adult only venue and was firmly held back by Tina—both laughing. For food, they went into a mid-priced sit down restaurant. It was super enjoyable until the bill came which Luke paid for in cash but then insisted on showing Tina his now empty wallet. Luckily for Tina, Luke did not do a 'Quincy' on his steak this time around. The expensive price is standard down these parts.

It was around half eleven at night when the two fell into their room.

"Oh Boy! What a day it's been," sighed Luke.

"I don't think my feet are still attached to my legs! I'm past the pain part, I think both of my feet must have fallen off somewhere in the city. I've never been so tired in my life," moaned Tina.

"I've never spent so much money in one go in my life before. This city just bleeds—leeches the money out of you. It should be called Leechdon, not

London. Get me to a bank, I need a wallet saving money transfusion," joked Luke.

"If I go anywhere near a bank now, I'll—probably rob it. Not to get rich, rather just to have some money to put a bit of food on the table in this city of sin."

"I'm thinking—bed—sleep for the next—all day tomorrow. We won't bother to get up, like school holidays back in the day. That sound good to you, honey bun?" suggested Luke.

Tina laughs. "Get up! Sounds a bit rude to me since you're asking, what with us lying in bed. Anyways, I'm not even changing, I'm sleeping in these clothes, goodnight, John boy."

"Night, night!" replied Luke as both fell sound asleep.

The next day, it is mid-morning and Luke and Tina are standing in King's Cross railway station this time. When you are used to getting up early most of your life, sleeping in all day is not going to happen easy—old habits die hard.

"This is the place to start the search, they all come here first. I've seen the programmes on the telly, welcome to runaway central. I bet half the people sitting down on the benches right now are either runaways, homeless or just using it as free lodgings, whilst in London," Luke announced.

"So, Luke Woam, the great and mighty missing person finder, what do we do now?" asked Tina.

"I don't really know—I guess—ask around, show people these pictures I've printed out of Isabelle. These commuters come here day in and day out, daily."

"Pass me a picture, I'll start at that end and you start the other end. Just show and ask. Doesn't sound too bad. Let's begin," Tina said taking the lead.

What followed was the two of them spending a good part of the day asking people about Isabelle. It was repetitive work and even getting people to stop and talk to you was hard to accomplish and stressful.

Most thought Luke and Tina were yet more sales agents or surveyists promising to only take a few moments of their time. Hours and hours they were hard at it without any fruitful results to show for the effort. Eventually, they both sat down on a bench exhausted and disillusioned.

"Not an easy lark as we first thought, eh?" bemoaned Tina. "Like finding a needle in a haystack. We're gonna need a lottery winners' luck if we even get one person to say anything other than, "sorry I haven't" or "no thank you, I'm not interested" or "sorry, I haven't got time, I'm in a rush". Life is definitely faster down here mush."

"Snap! Or ditto, I think. Hours and hours we've been at it and we're as clueless as a village idiot taking a Mensa test. Everyone in London is in such a rush. (He looks at Tina's lucky charm necklace that is not in the right position on her neck). Your unlucky lucky charm thing is lopsided. I'll do it right for you." Luke grabs hold of the charm and proceeds to right it.

"Thanks," replied Tina.

"No probs. Probably, the most useful thing I'll end up doing today. (He is still holding the charm). I wish we had some luck come our way. I wish somebody would just come up to us right here and now and tell us something useful that we could go on, some sort of a lead or summat."

Just then there is a sparkly glint from the lucky charm. It only lasts a second and is missed by both Luke and Tina. Luke lets go of the charm.

"There, it's dead straight now."

"You know, with all this waiting around, sitting around, I should have brought my book down that I'm reading from Bolton," said Tina.

"Then you wouldn't have total eyes on the job at hand, miss important details," replied back Luke.

"Of course I would. It only takes a moment to scan the place, to look around. I'm on a really interesting chapter where this large group of uni students decide to swim naked in the river, that's butt naked."

Luke's interest suddenly perks up. "Really, have they got a film version of this book?"

"Typical bloke aren't ya! Dispense with the written word, bring on the porno film," lambasted Tina.

"No! If it's tastefully done, especially by the geek squad, then they're known as art house films." They both giggle at that.

They both just sit on the bench people watching, both silent for a while. Suddenly, this quiet moment is broken by a dishevelled looking bloke standing right next to them. "Excuse me nice people. Have you got a light for me ciggy?"

Luke looks at the figure in front of him. He must be one of those homeless types, about fifty years old and unkept. "Funny enough mate, even though I don't smoke I do have a lighter, belongs to a mate of mine. (He gets the lighter out and sparks up a flame and puts it close to the stranger's face). There you go squire."

The dishevelled stranger brings his cigarette (in mouth) close to the lighter and lights it. As he is doing this, he casts his eyes on the picture of Isabelle, plainly visible on Luke's lap.

"'Ere, I know that girl, why have you got a picture of her? Are you related to her?"

"Yes!" exclaimed both Tina and Luke.

"She's—my sister. She ran away and our mum is hysterical, crying and making herself poorly. We came down here from up north, Bolton, to find her as quickly as we can before she gets into any danger."

Luke hands him the picture to get a better look.

"Yes, that's her alright. Saw her a couple of days ago, hanging around here. It's where all the runaways gather you know. King's Cross is famous for it. This mare was all posh and that, right little hooray Henrietta sort."

He looks at Luke, obviously the opposite of posh as you can get, Luke realises this.

"I don't buy into all that wealth stuff. I moved out of the family mansion ages ago. The black sheep of the family sort of thing, I live off my own money, money I've earned by working hard," informed Luke. He gives a quick look to Tina, who gives him a snarky look back.

"Is she still here, comes here? Have you seen her recently?" asked Tina.

"Can't say I have. Not since she hooked up with that rat boy Pops character, this here station is his hunting ground you see," the man replied.

"Pops? Who's this Pops guy? Where can we find him?" asked Luke.

"You know what, I get hungry and when I get hungry my memory goes funny," said the man.

Now Luke is no fool, he has seen this shake down ploy plenty of times on the telly. He gets out ten pounds and waves it across the man's face.

"Will this help keep your hunger at bay and your memory seriously unfunny?"

The man grabs the note with relish.

"Now let's see. Pops is the head honcho around here. He usually gets first dibs on the newest fish—that's the runaways. There's nothing that he doesn't know about around here."

"How can we contact him or see him, this head honcho Pops?" asked Tina.

The man laughs. "You don't. He sees you, you don't see him. That how it works. Undercover cops do the occasional sweep across all the stations now and again. You can't go drawing attention to yourselves."

"How do we get him to see us?" asked Luke.

"Use your loaf man. He comes here, searching for new fish, fresh young skirt off the trains and coaches. You know, sweet sexy pretty things. I know, you could use your woman. (He looks at Tina, then so does Luke. Tina looks at them both sternly, in a way that is warning them to be careful what the two of them say next). Maybe not."

"What does he look like, we could just wait for him to turn up?" Luke asked.

"Oh that's easy, he's kind of a bulky build, tallish, about twenty-eight years old. He's got this dread lock blonde beady hair like those Jamaican Yardies but he's no blackie, he's a white dude. He has some piercings and tattoos around his body and he wears these big circle ring type earrings in his ears, like women wear."

"I think I'm getting the picture. There can't be that many about with that description in the world, not even here in London," assumed Tina.

"Take this my man, this is my card, call me if you see this Pops fella anywhere else or you see Isabelle. You do have a mobile phone, don't you?" asked Luke.

The man takes the card. "Mobile phones! I normally do, but sometimes I have to sell 'em to buy my medicines if you know what I mean? I haven't got a phone right now on me but I'll nick one today and give you a bell if anything comes up. (He looks at the card). Ooh, your name's Luke—Woam. That's a funny name, young man, that's how they give us our soup down at the night time soup kitchens."

"If you provide us with anymore good information, there's another tenner in it for ya', pal. Lots of 'medicine' money," said Luke

"Cushty, real Cushty. If that's all then, I'll be getting off now. Those night time tourists give you even more money than the day time ones. TTFN young searchers. Good luck and have yourselves a very happy Christmas."

The man goes off.

The intrepid two now have something to go on. They relocate and sit down on another bench that will roughly allow them to see all the key areas and doorways and more importantly, who comes in or out of them. Now it becomes a stake out, just sitting and observing—a doddle.

About two and half hours pass and still no results.

"Aw, this could take hours and hours," moaned Tina, as she closes her eyes for a second or two.

"Took!" replied Luke.

"Pardon?" said Tina back on alert again.

"Not take but took! I think our Pops fella has just popped up, surfaced, look over there."

Tina looks in the direction Luke is pointing. They both stare hard and indeed a very likely match has walked in.

"He matches in all the right areas, I think we have our man," enthused Luke.

"I totally agree. I think it's him, has to be," concurred Tina.

The helpful homeless man from earlier was spot on with the description and now the case of the missing teenager is stepping up a gear.

"He's kind of looking around like he's suspicious of things—people," said Luke.

"He would, remember what that hobo guy said, the police sometimes lurk around and this geezer, if he is Pops, would definitely behave like he's doing—scouting for the Police."

"Well, the hobo was wrong about one thing, we're seeing Pops, he's not seeing us!"

"I know I keep saying this Luke, but what now? We can't just roll up to him and demand the whereabouts of Isabelle. He'll deny everything, tell us nothing then probably get some of his druggy goons to beat us up," warned Tina.

"Yeah, he could and probably will do all of those things. We need a plan. Luckily, my sugar puff, I have a kind of a plan in my head. I knew we might across this type of situation at some point so thought about it all the while we were sitting down."

"Oh yeah, what?"

"Hear me out, see what you think. I thought, with these kind of scumbags, you have to tap into their kind of world, on their level, you have to give them what they seek. It's not take but give."

"What? Give them—him what?"

"Business—business and money! It's the reason good and evil exist and the only time they see eye to eye and co-exist. Every empire that ever existed has all been about business and of course, the immense wealth and power it brings."

"OK—what are we giving him and you'd better not say the wrong thing, matey?" warned Tina. "We know what his business is and how he makes money from it. It better not involve me in any way, shape or form."

"A different kind of business, Tina. In fact, it's the world's oldest profession and trade. Is your lucky charm wearing off already, left your brain back at the hotel?"

"No I haven't, what kind of business?"

"I'll tell you in a bit, just follow me."

Luke gets up from the bench and walks slowly off without explaining further and Tina follows, a little annoyed that her 'partner' is not forthcoming with any clear details of 'his' plan. Tina is thinking this partnership is more like 'a boss and employee' set up, something she is not prepared to accept. But she decides to keep her thoughts and feelings to herself for now, it is too early in the newly formed company to start kicking up a fuss. The teething problems can wait for another day.

Chapter 14
Pops

Luke and Tina walk towards the direction of where Pops is. They slowly get closer.

"Tina, when I say so in a minute, just stop and stand still and look like a right peed off she-devil, like a woman scorned."

"Way ahead of you, pal; I might already be," whispered Tina to herself. Then says a bit more loudly, "Is this part of your plan?"

"Yep! Right, stop here and look real angry, love. I'm going over to talk to him. Wish me luck."

Luke walks over to where Pops is standing, who is still casing the joint for anyone resembling the law.

"Excuse me, are you Puppy, Poppy—Pops?"

"Who the frick are you? Do I know you, mate?"

"No! But I've been told to ask for a guy called Pops, is that you, for some business I can bring your way?"

"Have you now, who've you been talking to? I ain't exactly in the business phone-directory."

"I've just been asking certain characters, not here, downtown in some right unsavoury hell-holes, it was scary, I can tell you that. But they did say I should try a guy called Pops in King's Cross and described you."

Pops gives a long hard look at Luke to see if he is anything other than a young, average lad about town. He decides Luke is too pathetic and too young looking to be an undercover agent or indeed anything of threat.

"I might know someone of a similar name, who's asking and why?"

"I and my girlfriend are going back home tomorrow, but I really want to leave London on a high. I want to hook up with some—babelicious booty, a lady of pleasure, as a goodbye present to myself. You get my drift?"

Pops looks hard at Luke again. "You say you're here with your girlfriend, home boy, is she like giving you permission for all this? Is she OK with this cheating on your gal business? She ain't retarded, is she? Is she fronting the dosh as well for this present to yourself?" Pops had managed to cluster together a lot of quizzing questions.

"Oh no, far from it. She thinks I'm over here talking to you about buying some—dope, gear!"

"What do you mean she thinks? Where is she?"

"She's just over there, waiting and shit." Luke points behind him.

Pops frantically looks where Luke is pointing. He sees Tina a little way off looking all angry.

"Jesus, fricking hell! You bring your—gal to discuss pussy? You must be nuts! I sussed you weren't no undercover but you're a total bloody lunatic man." Pops gives another look at Tina, he becomes a little calmer, almost frowning. "Urgh! F me sideways, mate! I can see your problem dude. No wonder you're looking for pussy. Man, that's your gal, that puke inducing tub of ugly lard? I'm almost inclined to let you have a freebie. Even I'd look for gals or turn gay if that's all I could get."

Luke makes an angry face for a split second then gets back into role play. "Yeah—can you help me? My girlfriend is staying at the hotel tonight so I got tonight to do the business. I want pussy, please say you can hook me up. Maybe throw in a bit of the old ganja as well."

"I might be able to cater to your needs but strictly at the right price, what are your preferences, what kind of goods are you after, Mandingo? What kind of skirt do you want to flirt with?"

"Young! I mean not really young, I'm no pervert."

"Don't matter to me if you are, it'll just cost ya' more—harder to get ain't it. How young you looking at? I mean, you're barely out of school looking age yourself so how young ya' wanting 'em, a baby, four, five-year old or are you going for the oldies—the nine, ten eleven plus range?"

"Oh God no! No! No! Never, nothing like that. (It is a genuine reaction of disgust from Luke, this needs no acting, then he composes himself quickly so as not to arouse suspicion). Around fifteen or sixteen max. No younger or older."

"Boy! You've really nailed it down to one size fits all, haven't ya'?"

"Yes, it has to be that age. Also I want her to be like—posh and sweet and white. I'm from the north so my preference would be with a northern sort. Also, no trashy druggy types or tattoos or looking like Goths or trans-genders and shit. She needs to be clean like freshly laid snow and white. Have I already mentioned white?"

Pops looks at Luke with a bit of concern and thought when Luke said that. Luke is a little annoyed with himself too, has he said too much or something to give the game away?

"Your requirements are—pretty specific, matey. I'll look up in my list of royals for hire to see who's available, shall I, my Buck house list?" Pops laughs a little.

"I—just want a clean pussy, nothing that will give me the craps or like an STD, 'cause that will mean my girlfriend will find out about it."

"It will cost ya', you want the goods straight from the premium shelf, top draw stuff don't ya'? You're one of them who wants to raid the orchard instead of buying from the market. We're not talking pocket money for your fantasy wet dream."

"It's OK, I ain't rich but money—will be no problem, worked hard for it, so spend hard, I always say."

Pops looks about the vicinity.

"Shit! The feds, let's move. No, we're better splitting up. Listen, meet me in the freight bays, it's over that way, be there in five minutes and bring the readies, a whole bagful or no dice."

"How much, exactly?"

"For what you want, no less than five-hundred! Five-hundred or no deal!"

"That's—a lot—but OK," replied Luke as Pops flitters away.

Luke goes back to Tina.

"How'd it go, seems it went alright, he did not beat you up and you were talking a fair bit before he hot-footed away?" asked Tina.

"Good. Better than expected really. He totally bought it that I was looking for some totty—posh young totty."

"Totty? Charming, that is! So, why did he suddenly leave just now?"

"Oh—he spotted the police, I think. People like him see police everywhere, don't they? He told me to meet him in the back of the station, where the loaders work. (Luke looks at the lucky charm on Tina, it is lopsided again). Your charm thing is out of place again, can't stay in the right position. Let me fix it again."

"No! You know what, I want you to wear it. It's bringing us luck—or at least changing it for the better." She takes the charm necklace off and proceeds to put it on Luke.

"I wear it? You know how I feel about that tacky good luck trinket thing and you want me to wear it?"

"Yes! (Tina puts it on Luke and tucks it inside his clothing). There, The Lady Wizard of Bolton has given you luck. Oh! Just out of curiosity, he gave me a right creepy, weird look. Explain to me how you can negotiate with a pimp for a piece of underage, totally illegal crumpet when the pimp can clearly see the girlfriend of the client looking straight at both your pathetic asses?"

"Fair question—I told him that you thought I was looking to buy dope for both of us to shoot up on our last night in the big city, a farewell high. He believed me."

Luke finds his way to the non-passenger freight part of the station. He then sets about finding Pops, he sees him fairly quickly and goes to him. Some freight workers can be seen doing their job in the near distance but they seem oblivious to Luke's and Pops' presence in an area that clearly must be off limits to the general public.

"You got the money?" asked Pops straight away.

"Not all of it, but I will have it all in a jiffy, I didn't know it was going to cost that much. I need to get it," replied Luke.

Pops becomes a little angry at this point. "You're not jerking me off are ya', pal? No one walks away if they cross me! Are you feeling me?"

Luke almost laughs out loud but just manages to control it. What he finds funny is Pops' choice of words like 'jerking' and 'feeling me'—these sexual words when talking tough and being threatening, all whilst wearing girly earrings.

"I'll have the money, I've got a few hundred on me and the rest I can easily get from the till machines in the station. Now, what can you offer me—for my money—hundreds of pounds?"

Talk of money sedates Pops again. "Well, I have got this girl, maybe around seventeen, comes from a rich well-to-do household. Only been in the game like a week. Real sweet, real clean and—kind of posh. She says 'thank you' and 'please' and good polite shit like that when she talks."

"A week ago, have you got anyone newer, real fresh meat, like only couple of days old? I want the best, I was hoping to be her first client."

"Listen John, if you'd come along only yesterday or was it day before, I forget, I could of supplied you with the very best. True, I would have charged you a lot more than a measly five-hundred sovs but I think she would have fitted your demanding requirements perfectly."

Luke's ears prick up. "Oh yeah! What was she—some runaway royal that the monarchy is keeping secret from us and only you and the secret service guys, the MI5 know about?"

Pops laughs at this. "You're a funny guy, John. She was no royal but she sure was a rich posh tart and young too, from up Blackpool or was it Bury or was it Bolton? I made quite a killing with her. I had no problems shifting her, in fact, I had a bidding war on me hands once I let my—more discerning clients know of her.

Good pedigree birds like her don't fall into my lap very often, oooohh, you should see the ones I normally have to deal with. I think they get spaced out on drugs just so they don't have to look at themselves in the mirror in the mornings. (Pops laughs at his own joke, then gets out a cigarette. He looks for a lighter but cannot find one about himself). Have you got a lighter, matey, I've seem to have mislaid mine?"

"Who's the lucky guy—the winning punter, for this angel, who's becomes her guardian sugar daddy, shall we say?"

"I can't tell you that, Sonny Jim. Information like that—is confidential between me and my clients. I keep that info in my little black book right here (he taps his top right breast part of his coat). All I can say is he is very rich, very rich indeed, needs to be—and has a title or something. He lives in the city in a big multi storey house, so this posh bird has hit the jackpot. Not bad for a runaway, beats the back alleys and drug dens. Have you got that light or what?"

"Sure, has no one in London got a lighter?" Luke said mostly to himself as he gets his lighter out of his pocket. As he takes out the lighter, one of his business cards falls out onto the floor and Pops sees it.

"You've dropped something pal, I'll get it for ya', look after yer' clients and they'll look after you, that's my motto. (He picks up the card before Luke can react and reads it). What's this? 'Luke Woam. Missing Person Finder'. What the frick! Who are you, dick face, speak before I bash your head in?"

"I don't think so, you pimp scum," shouted Tina as she races over to the two, both of whom are surprised at seeing her. She must have been nearby but out of sight but not out of earshot.

Luke then grabs the business card from Pops' hand and puts it away.

"You need the help of yer' woman to fight me?"

Pops swings his fist towards Luke, who ducks out of the way just in time. Just then Tina and the momentum she has on her side, smacks right into Pops, they both fall down to the floor, Pops comes off the worse as he bangs his head on the floor and is a somewhat dazed. Luke helps Tina get up, then he half unzips Pops' coat and pulls it half down so that his arms are rendered inactive. They get him up to his feet. Luke gets the little black book from Pops' coat's inside pocket, which is now on the outside due to his top half of his coat being inside out.

"You're a marked man, you're finished—dead man! Both of you," shouted Pops, a little blurrily, still feeling the effects of the knock, but recovering fact.

"Is the MI5 going to come after us? Are they into protecting metropolitan sewer garbage like yourself?" asked Luke.

"Call the police, why don't you? Make use of the taxes you don't pay to the government," joked Tina.

"When my boys dump you in the woods, I'll tell them to call the RSPCA for you, love," replied a cocky Pops despite his predicament.

The lucky charm is out of position again, on the outside instead of tucked inside. Luke grabs it to put it back inside whilst looking at Pops' extra-large circle earrings.

"I wish a loader with a chain hook would swing by right now!" Luke murmured to himself. A sparkly glint appears for a second on the charm.

Just then, a small loader driven by a worker wearing head phones complete with tinny music blaring out, comes out of nowhere and heads their way. Luke seizes the opportunity to hook Pops' right earring onto a conveniently place metal hook on the loader as it whizzes by them. Pops has no choice but to run alongside of the loader as otherwise his right earlobe would be ripped apart. He is cursing but the driver cannot hear him. Luke and Tina laugh as they see this funny sight.

Chapter 15
A Solid Lead

Luke and Tina rest on a bench inside the station but at the opposite end of the freight area. They look at the little black book. Luke is turning the pages one by one when something grabs his attention.

"Hey up! This looks promising. It says, "Premium goods delivered, 16th December. £3,500. Sir M. Bainbridge, 135 Belgravia Drive, SW17". That's only a couple of days ago, fits the timeline perfectly to what Pops was saying about the posh girl he flogged," said Luke with glee.

"Flogged! What kind of way is that to talk about a young girl? She was kidnapped and sold—trafficked even. This Pops guy didn't flog the buyer a second hand car you know!" Tina remarked, rebuking Luke on his choice of words.

"Sorry—I didn't t think. You're absolutely right, as always."

"Alright—no need to apologise, you were just saying it like most blokes would, that's all."

"This book, it's useful evidence for a case against this Pops and his clients."

"You're not thinking again, Luke, my little toy box detective. Pops doesn't say what he sold to this toff. It says 'goods' in the book, it could be anything—it could well be a second hand car. Not that a rich toff like this Sir M. Bainbridge would buy anything like that off lowlifes such as Pops, but my point is still valid, so this book and its entries are not kosher as evidence. All coded stuff ain't it."

"Listen to you baby cakes—you're on fire!"

"And you're not! This is pretty serious stuff we're getting into, suddenly the money side of it seems far away. There are more people involved now, a mix of thugs and the rich and powerful," warned Tina.

"I agree. We're getting deeper into the murky dark underbelly world of a seedy London that tourists like us, don't ever see. And we're not even in the real gangland areas of London where wearing the wrong colours or wrong brand designer trainers could potentially get you killed."

"With the trainers we're wearing, the gang members will kill themselves laughing if anything. Anyway, let's call it quits today. We can hunt down that address tomorrow," Tina suggested.

"Are you sure? Timing could be everything, especially now Pops knows we've got his book. But I do agree it would be beneficial to our health and wellbeing if we made ourselves scarce from this place. He could return with backup any moment now."

"In contrast, time is on our side, if you mess up by losing a very important book containing highly classified intel, you're not going to inform your clients are ya'? That wouldn't look good on him. But you're right about us going from here. Come on let's head back to the safety of the hotel."

"Wow! Move over Sherlock! There's a new master detective in town. Good to go, your mightiness!" Luke joked, impressed with his girlfriend.

"Oh be quiet, you big buffoon!" said Tina.

It is night time and both of them are in bed. Tina is fast asleep, maybe the brilliance of earlier on has made her happy and able to sleep better. Luke, however, is awake. He is toiling over the day's events and other days. He is particularly thinking about the lucky charm and how in the past few days they did indeed get some amazing luck in the nick of time.

Now, he also knew he had wished for those things to happen and they did. He does not make the connection that he was holding the charm in his hand at the time of wanting the good luck. He thinks a little bit more then he shakes his head.

"Nah! We live in the real world, this sort of nonsense simply does not happen." He speaks out loud then he realises Tina is asleep next to him. He looks at her and is relieved to see she is still asleep.

The next morning, the two searchers are up bright and early and are fairly near the address of a certain Sir M. Bainbridge, maybe a few streets away.

"It's another world, from where we're from, don't ya' think?" remarked Tina as they gaze upon the white marble majestic buildings around them.

"Yeah, but I think London is good for a holiday but not to live in. There's way too much traffic, pollution, arrogance, high prices, there's no let-up, even if you go miles outside the centre. Living expense is just too high. Even if I was rich, I would still not live here. I'd come down here a lot, but not live," replied Luke.

"Me too. A good party and holiday destination but not to live and bring up a family."

As they walk and talk, unbeknown to them, they are being watched. It is none other than Pops and his gang of three. He figured the two would wind up around this particular client's pad sooner or later judging from Luke's special interest in a particular sort.

"It's them! It's those two, I'm a genius, a fricking genius. I'd knew they'd come here," raved Pops at his own reasoning prowess. His cohort of three look at their targets.

"Two! The way you got beat so easily and you described it, I'd thought there were more of them. One's of them two is a girl too—I think?" said Mozzy, a gang member.

"There were more of them, many more. People like them only fight in mobs. I fought like a tiger, man. I took them all on but even I can't defeat an army. Besides, it's these two that I really want the most, the leaders. And guess what, I know this dude's name—it's kinda funny sounding."

"Funny, what is it? Dick Long, Ivor Biggun, Ben Dover, Justin Sider, I've seen some right funny names on the internet," suggested Chayse, another member.

"I've seen them too. Can't believe people have names like that, man!" said Tommo, the last of the three.

"It's Luke Woam, like in hot and cold. But he spells it like W-O-A-M, Not W-A-R-M." announced Pops.

"Luke Woam! Hey! That's how you like your beer, isn't it, Chayse?" said Mozzy and laughs.

"No! That's how you drink it," replied Chayse.

"Cut it out you two. I need to get my book back and those two have it. Come on, let's get them," instructed Pops and walks off followed by the three.

Luke and Tina steadily walk in the direction of the address. Suddenly, out of the blue appear Pops and his three goons, in front of them.

"Well, well, well, lookeee here, if it ain't the small time outfit of the missing person dicks. You've beamed down to the wrong city pal. I got you right where I want you, on my planet, my turf and without—the rest of your gang this time," said Pops, very happily.

"Gang?" said Tina.

"There's no point calling for them, I know they're not around. It's just you two red shirts here and guess what, you're not going to be beaming back to the mother ship like permanently? (He produces a knife). Who's gonna be finding you two when you go missing, tell me that dipshits? Grab them boys!"

Just as the goons are about to pounce, a policeman appears out of nowhere from the heaving crowds. The four goons stop, Pops hides his knife quick time. The policeman is very close now.

"Good day to you, sir," said a very relieved Luke to the Policeman to make sure they get his undivided attention.

"Good day to you too sir, everyone," replied the policeman.

"Excuse me sir, can you direct us the way to Hyde Park please, we're kinda lost?" asked Luke. "These four gentlemen don't know their arse from their elbow even though they are locals." Pops and his mates just put on a forced smile and reluctantly self-gag.

"Hyde Park! From here, well, all I can do is point you to the nearest tube station, Hyde Park is easy to get to, using the underground. You're lucky a tube station is right round the corner," replied the policeman.

"Oh good! You've saved the day officer, a real public servant, thank you indeed!" said Luke. "Come Tina, let's us go." He gives a really smug look to Pops, who is trying to act all cool and calm. "As for you four wallies, we would have got better directions asking Nelson on his column. Come Tina my love, I think we've outstayed our welcome here."

"Certainly," replied Tina. She looks at the policeman. "Thank you also, Mr policeman officer, you have a good day now."

The policeman laughs. "Oh—I think I need to explain, I'm not a policeman, not a real one—this is just fancy dress. Well, not fancy dress, more like work clothes really—I'm a stripper-gram! I'm booked to a hen party that I'm on my way to now. I must agree, it does look pretty convincing though, so real I fear getting arrested," replied the 'fake' policeman.

To that confession, everyone reacts swiftly. Luke and Tina bomb it away, followed by Pops and his goons. The fake policeman looks at all six of them running away like the clappers.

"Why they running away, I just told them I'm not for real? It's not like I can arrest them." He shakes his head and walks off.

The chase is on. Running in the busy streets of London in difficult. There are people everywhere getting in your way. The funny thing is, not many Londoners or tourists are batting an eyelid at the frantic running of either party. Is it a normal thing down this way?

Pops and his three mates run fast after the two. The streets being busy and Pops being bulky, coupled with being in the lead, it was only a matter of time before he collides with some innocent member of the public, just minding their business. He heavily shoulder-barges a young twenty-something mum who has her six-year old daughter with her, the mum feels it good and proper. The other three run a little ahead and then stop and look back.

"Bloody hell fire, you clumsy idiot! (She looks at Pops very angrily). You dickhead! That really hurt me!"

Pops takes offence at being called some tasty offensive names but he was at fault so tempers his anger and response. "Sorry, our lass, my humble apologies."

"Your humble apology isn't gonna fix my broken shoulder, is it, you bleeding blind crackhead?"

This second insult was one too many for Pops and his anger begins to show. He looks at the daughter, who is mix-race black, the mum is white and native British. "I said I was sorry woman. Aaah, is that your daughter, how sweet?" said Pops with a quick change of mood and a smile.

The woman is not swayed or mellowed by Pops' change of tact. "Yeah! Don't change the bloody subject!"

"You know what, she—looks absolutely nothing like you! Maybe Shenequa looks more like one of her other ten half brothers or sisters on her father's side!" Pops continued saying and instantly darts off to the others waiting for him. All four run off together. The mum shouts at Pops but he cannot hear her, maybe just as well. This was Pops at his racist best.

Meanwhile, the two being chased are still trying to put distance between them and the four goons. "We need to get off the main busy streets, let's go down a side street!" suggested Luke.

Tina had already started to look around a while ago. "This one, quick, down here."

Both of them dart down this narrower side street, by far less busy.

Pops and co. soon reach the point where the main street joins this side street, they all stop. Pops laughs. "We've got them now, this is what happens when you mess around in someone else's back yard. Come on, this way boys!"

The four do not go down this particular side street but instead continue to run down the main road. Obviously, being from these parts, they know the layout and all the shortcuts.

Luke and Tina run but all this forced physical activity is taking its toll.

"I'm knackered, Luke!" gasped Tina as she stops for a breather, so does Luke.

"Me too. We haven't even been running long either. We need to continue though, can't rest for too long." After only a few precious seconds rest, they slowly build up speed again in their running. Luke looks back and says, "Can't see 'em, funny, they weren't that far behind us. Maybe coming down here has done the trick?"

However and most unfortunately, up ahead in the near distance, at the other end of this narrow street, they see Pops and his goons suddenly appear.

"Shit, shit, shit. They're ahead of us. We can't go that way!" said a despondent Luke. Tina looks and is also disappointed.

Tina looks down the way they came. "That side ginnel we passed back there, let's try it."

"That is almost certainly a dead-end, most likely."

"Could well be but we might find a doorway or something."

"Yeah! I bet it's a doorway to a Chinese takeaway or laundry like in the movies. We might have irate Chinese chefs with meat cleavers chasing after us as well," Luke joked.

"Come on, funny bones, let's see shall we?" said Tina and is off, followed by Luke. Pops and his crew, upon seeing their quarry running away from them and their planned ambush failing by not being timed right, run down the side street after them but with slightly more vigour now.

The running is the limiting factor here. For Luke and Tina, being modern urbanites, exercise is for other people—health freaks, salad eaters. Jaw and hand/finger muscles are the only muscles to be well exercise in the west and the wider developed world, plentiful food and electronic devices being the culprits. Evolution has got a formidable twenty-first century problem to overcome—another mass extinction needed?

Tina and Luke get to the ginnel and run into it for a short distance, it is a dead-end but there are a few doorways to be seen. Tina stops again. "Stop! I think I'm gonna puke."

"All this running, it's bad for your health!" joked Luke.

Tina laughs. "You've become a right comedian in the face of danger."

"Yeah, I must write to the top comedians and tell them what I've discovered. Might give a reward. Just pop down to South Central LA at night, wearing your most expensive Rolex and gold ring, talking on your latest i-phone. All that danger will give you inspiration no end." Tina chuckles at Luke's comment for a second.

"What we need now is some good luck, a shed load of it," sighed Tina.

"I agree. Your lucky charm needs to earn all its five pounds cost like right now." Luke has a very quick flash back at all the good luck they did have in the past few days. "We did have some good luck but that was just—fortunate good luck," he then added, for ever the unbeliever.

"That policeman came at the right moment, that was the lucky charm at work," replied Tina.

"Nonsense, that was coincidence. Besides even if either of us wished for a policeman to appear, one didn't. He was a bloody stripper-gram, about as opposite to a police man as you can get apart from being a crook," Luke replied.

"Same effect though, same result. Who cares he wasn't real."

"I suppose so, did the job of saving our hides, I guess," admitted Luke.

"I'm telling ya', have faith in the lucky charm. Where is it, are you still wearing it?"

"Yeah, I am, it's 'round my neck, where you put it, tucked nicely away. I don't know why I'm wearing it though? Along with 'Luke the Puke' kids at school used to call me 'Luckless Luke' on account of not having any—good luck that it, plenty of bad luck, bucket loads.

Jesus was born on earth to rid man of his sins, I was born to rid every person of their bad luck. In others words, I get it, so they don't have to. In a way, I'm doing God's work, maybe that's why I was named Luke, wait till I tell the Padre, I'll be a hero to him instead of a loser."

Tina goes and holds the lucky charm in her hand but it is still around Luke's neck.

"We got no time for you to feel sorry for yourself, some other time maybe. I'll show you. What we need is some wheels, a nice motor bike would do right now with its engine running and a full tank of petrol and the owner somewhere else. So come on lucky charm, do your thing."

There is that glimmering sparkle again, unseen by Tina and Luke. She lets go of the lucky charm, Luke puts it under his clothing again.

"With that optimistic tall order, you should have bought the more expensive deluxe model lucky charm with turbo boost, not the bargain basement model," joked Luke.

"Come on, let's go. I've skipped the puking stage, I think I'm moving straight onto the heart attack stage next," said Tina, hopefully joking too.

"I want to say, "who's the comedian now", you are joking I hope?"

"Relax, Mother Theresa, I'm joking! It's not quite stand-up comedy, more, fall-down sadness," replied Tina smiling, reassuring Luke.

"I'll just check if any of these doors are open," said Luke and he very quickly checks and finds they are all locked. "Nope! Better head off."

The two run on from the ginnel until they come to a side yard surrounded by back doors to their left. The look with utter disbelief at what they see parked there. It is a medium powered motorbike, still running, with no one around. Luke and Tina just freeze with shock.

"That's a motorbike right there!" said Luke, eventually.

"With the engine running," added Tina.

"With the owner—somewhere else!" said Luke.

"That's lucky! That's a shed load of luck!"

"That's—freaky, unreal kind of lucky."

"Let's get freaked out later, get on the damn thing," shouted Tina.

They both get on with Luke in control of the driving. They manoeuvre the bike into position and accelerate off back the way they had come.

Pops and his mates, just then, turn right into this yard space but are greeted by a fast moving motorbike coming towards them. The collision flings the four goons heavily against some bins and things and then they fall flat on the floor. Luke and Tina zoom off to safety.

Out of a doorway in this yard comes a courier with his helmet still on. He sees his bike gone and four hapless goons on the floor. He rips his helmet off and looks very angrily at Pops and his buddies laid out on the floor.

"Oh not again. Bloody hell! I just went in for a second! I hate London!"

A bit later, Luke and Tina have left the motorbike parked up in a busy area with the key put into the storage space compartment of the bike.

"That should be fine and we should be fine as well if the three dozen CCTV cameras we've featured on all happen to be on the blink!" hoped Luke.

"Yeah! Oh, thinking back to what you said about South Central LA. Who needs Rolex watches and expensive stuff to be a target? It's like what you said, just wearing the wrong colours on gang turf is all ya' need to be in real danger. Now that, should get the comedy juices flowing," laughed Tina.

Chapter 16
The Party

It is early evening, getting quite dark and Luke and Tina are scoping Sir M. Bainbridge's residence from behind a bush, a safe distance away. They see that their target is holding a party that is by invitation only with a doorman checking guests for the all-important pass at the bottom of the entrance stairs.

"Damn! You need an invitation to get in," said Luke disappointedly.

"At least we're dressed suitably—well suited and booted, if we by some miracle end up getting in. Dressing up was my idea, of course," said a smug Tina but she too is disappointed about not looking likely to get in.

"We need a pass!" said Luke.

"Way to go, Einstein. You've sussed out our problem."

"Sorry, I was just thinking out loud. We need some extreme good luck like we had this morning."

"Oh, you mean when my lucky charm saved our arses in the nick of time."

"It was luck, just abnormally good, kind of good luck, I must admit. That was the kind of luck that lottery winners have when they buy on a whim last second or with their last pound, you've heard the tales, 'shall I feed the baby or spend the pound on the lotto?'

The bike probably belonged to some courier delivering packages and left it running because who is going to nick a bike there? Couriers are ten a penny in London and they all work piece rate, so none even bother turning their engines off to save time. Besides, his luck was good too—it was stolen by us and we made sure it was left where it could be found quickly and hopefully returned to him within the hour or two. He, I'm sure, had no lucky charm, he had us!"

"Still the unbeliever, I see. And, it could have been a woman courier, so stop being so—back in time with your attitude. Girl power, remember! We have escaped the confines of the kitchen."

"OK, let's test the charm. I wish our luck is so good that a pass in both our names on it is behind that bush over there. Let's see if one is there shall we, Madam Rose Lee Tina." Luke wished for this but he was not touching the charm necklace when he said it.

They both go over to the bush in question and Luke rummages around the undergrowth to find nothing. "No, there's nothing here apart from creepy crawlies. That's one to me and zero to the lucky charm."

"Alright, Mr Doubter. There are about a hundred party-goers hustling around inside. How we getting in, break in around the back or something without somehow being spotted? Have you ever broken into a house?"

"Of course not! But I do have an idea about getting in—like them (points to the guests), through the front door."

"How?" Tina asked rather curious as to how her boyfriend is going to pull this off.

"With cunning and brains—and dare I say it—with a bit of normal everyday luck thrown in as well. You wait here, whilst I pop down to the shops to buy something integral to my plan. See ya' in a bit, darling."

Luke goes off without waiting around for Tina's questions about his plan. Like at the rail station, he has failed to communicate his plan with his so-called partner.

Tina watches Luke go off. "Cunning, brains and luck? Well, at least he can wish for luck in the absence of the other two. Both of us need luck in fact, dare I say it, some pretty hefty amount of good decent luck, again."

A short time later Luke returns. He does not show Tina what he has got from the shops but instructs her to follow him towards the party house. Tina pleads with him to tell her of his plan or what he went to the shops for but he remains tight-lipped. They get to the bouncer checking on the passes.

"May I see your invitation, please?" asked the bouncer.

"Certainly, sir. One moment, I'll just get it for you, my good man. (Luke said this in a rather posh voice and searchers his pockets for the elusive pass). Now, where did I put that dastardly thing? I know I've got it somewhere."

"Oh come on darling, I do want to get in and meet your family that I haven't seen since we all had that jamboree in Monaco. Your uncle Bainbridge is so kind inviting us tonight. I saw you put it in your pocket when I was generously spraying on the Chanel No 5," said Tina, adding to the pretence even though Luke had not even briefed her, she was improvising.

111

"I wonder if I left it in the Bentley—being a convertible I do hope it hasn't blown away. I know it is awfully nippy these days but I do love a bit of cold air rushing through my hair when I'm driving. (Luke turns his back to the bouncer but by now even Tina is getting worried as to what Luke is going to do to get past the bouncer). Aah! Found the blasted thing!"

"Oh! Jolly good show!" said Tina, it is the only thing she could think of saying, still nervous and dubious about their chances of getting in.

Still facing away from the bouncer, Luke opens a tub of green slime and puts a small scoop in his mouth. He then gets out a card with similar dimensions and colour as the invitation. He turns back towards the bouncer.

"There you go sir, one invitation from my dear old uncle to his esteemed party. (Suddenly, Luke sneezes and green stuff is deposited all over the card. It looks just like snot but really it is the slime, of course). Oh, sorry about that, dear chap. I am allergic to cheap food and my girlfriend insisted we eat from a decidedly dodgy takeaway. Bad mistake—bad mistake. I'm having an awful reaction to it, must be all the chemicals and pesticides they put in the food nowadays. Here's my pass anyway."

The bouncer looks awkwardly and disgustingly at the pass all covered in what he thinks is snot. Lucky for Luke, the lighting is not brilliant both naturally (night time) and from any nearby light source from the house "You are good to go in sir, madam. Enjoy your—uncle's party."

"Jolly good of you, Jeeves. I'll mention it to my uncle, might hire you for his impending—House of Lords party. Come on my dearest, it's time to flowcha! Let's meet the old codger of a soldier shall we, can't wait."

Luke and Tina walk past the bouncer and up the stairs. As Luke is walking up, he tosses the slimy pass down into some big bushes. Within the bushes are two teenagers, boy and girl all feeling romantic, they close their eyes and are about to kiss, their mouths are really close and about to touch. Just then, the slime covered pass falls in between their mouths and is held in place there. The two kiss the pass from either side. They open their eyes when they realise something is not right here. They see the pass fall down all covered in green stuff. They both yell in disgust.

"You got us in, I'm impressed with you, Luke Woam," admitted Tina.

"Well, they don't call me Mr Smart for nowt, you know!"

"Mr Smart! Who calls you that? I've been around you or with you most of your life, I never heard anyone call you that."

"OK, no one calls me that. Although no one has actually said that but it still stands!" insisted Luke.

"Yeah, OK. Stands as solid as a very drunk one-hundred year-old codger who's lost his Zimmer frame and waking across polished, soapy wet marble floor!"

Luke says nothing, he just looks hard at Tina, maybe trying to convince her with a hypnotise-style stare.

Once inside, the intense pressure is reduced somewhat since there are dozens and dozens of people here and there. The two make their way to the large reception hall like room where most guests have collected.

"I know I keep saying this, but now what? She could be anywhere and I don't think the host will take kindly to us searching around the house," Tina asked.

"It's a party! Let's party so we don't look out of place. Let's split up too, you know, just mingle and eat and see what we're dealing with, sound OK to you?" suggested Luke.

"Oh yeah! Eat, drink and be merry, all in the name of work, just try stopping me, slave-driver. See ya' in a bit, work slow, won't ya'?" Tina goes in a flash.

Luke looks at her disappearing. "I'm glad you liked my idea."

He too goes over to one end of a long buffet table, well away from Tina. He stands next to an old timer gentleman with a white beard and white hair. Luke picks up a sausage roll and bites into it and makes a satisfying sound.

"Great party, squire—your Lordship! Such great food too," said Luke to the old timer.

"Er—I suppose so—yes!" replied the old timer, trying to figure out if he knows this young man.

Luke decides to have a little fun, purely in jest mode. "Say, Mortimer, what price are pork bellies lately? Give Randolph my regards."

"I—haven't a clue, young man."

"Neither do I for that matter. (Luke takes another huge bite out of the roll). Tell Randolph that you two should invest in these sausage rolls, they're bloody delicious! Someone out there is going to make a killing with these, not just pork bellies."

"I must be off now, young man—nice talking to you," said the old timer as he hurriedly goes off, with a plate of food in tow. Luke says nothing but just looks at him walking away and smiles.

The old timer goes and sits down next to another old timer. "I say, Randolph,"

"What is it, Mortimer?"

"Do we know that young fellow over there by the sausage rolls, he seems to know us?"

Meanwhile, Tina is stacking up her plate with party food and has built a small food mountain. Be honest, who doesn't do that at buffets? Two well-dressed, slim, leg-tall, posh ladies on the other side of the table are picking at food. They look at Tina in a condescending way.

"How about a trifle more vol-ou-vents, Amelia?"

"Oh, you are kidding me, Frances? I'm watching my weight constantly. A lady should always look after her figure."

"Quite right, darling. I totally agree. One should have pride in one's appearance, especially us gentry women," replied Frances. Both speak with volume so that Tina can clearly hear all their conversation. "You know, when I'm driving my Porsche in the ghastly suburbs, ordinary people stare at me, I mean, haven't they ever seen a posh lady in a Porsche before?" wondered Frances.

Amelia laughs. "My dear, they probably think you're royalty—either that or they probably want to car-jack you, steal your car."

They both laugh as they purposefully keep looking at Tina and her less classy attire and her plumpy appearance. Tina stares back but says nothing for a few seconds. Then, she picks up two cheese and pickle sarnies from one of those upright triangular sandwich lines they always have at parties and slaps them down on her already burgeoning plate. Next, her eyes fall on a tray of Tandoori chicken legs, she picks one leg up.

"Oh how appropriate, all legs and no breasts! Now, who does that remind me of?" said Tina loudly.

She then looks at the two ladies and makes an intense expression. The two ladies walk off, after being unable to get a response from Tina in a way they had hoped—they were out to insult her, not the other way round.

Just then Luke appears alongside her. "Blimey babe, sure you got enough?"

"Oh—don't you start," replied Tina.

"Enjoying the posh do? How's it going so far?"

"Well, on the party front, good. The food's nice—really top notch. On the job at hand front, zippo! Also, shame about the people, what a lot of front they have. What can I say about them? They're unreal—not like us—they're not normal at all."

"Listen, I'm planning on slipping out of here and starting the search of the house. Give me a bell if anything happens. I don't yet know what the host—Sir M. Bainbridge even looks like yet. Hope the detective work will answer that one."

"I don't either, it could be anyone of these posh toffy-nosed twats! Eh up! Someone is about to give a speech and he looks like he could be our man."

Luke turns and looks to the front and sees a fifty-something aged guy, all expensively dressed, who certainly does fit the bill of possibly being Sir M. Bainbridge.

Chapter 17
Sir Marcus Bainbridge

A man stands on a footstool to get an elevated position and faces the guests, as they him.

"Good evening, ladies and gentlemen, thank you all immensely for attending my not so humble party, I sincerely hope you are all very well and happy. Might I just clarify that although we are in the Christmas season, this is, like the first Die Hard film, definitely not a Christmas bash, that party is scheduled for next week. For the odd one or two of you who might be here for the first time, I am Marcus—Sir Marcus Bainbridge, your gracious host this evening, although if those nice rumours doing the rounds are true, I could very well be Lord Bainbridge shortly—so watch this space on that one, because I will be.

Anyway, let me start by saying this secular party has two functions. One is that my yearly results for all of my companies are in and fair to say, the Champagne will flow like Niagara Falls for another year at the very least— another super successful year! Hurrah! (Everyone says, "Hurrah!"). I seem to be making so much money, I'm drowning in it; I sneeze one-pound coins, no kidding. My sponsored charities are praying I get a raging flu this winter. If you get a Christmas present from me next week and you're not pleased with it, don't worry, the wrapping paper will be made of fifty-pound notes, let's see who gets the biggest one?

Lastly, on the financial side, I've got this sweet business deal in progress as I speak, literally all tied up (he laughs). Should come out smelling of roses on completion of that one, fitting really as I have got a special penchant for freshly plucked young roses. (Luke and Tina look on and listen with scorn since they know what he was meaning by all this disguised talk of young roses).

Secondly and one I would say is much, much more important, it is a charity fundraising event, a benevolent fund, being for the benefit of numerous local charities. For that reason, I will be holding a raffle later on to which I will be most generously contributing towards. As you already know, I am a fervent disciple and campaigner for family values, so much so that I've simply lost count on how many groups I am patron to. Anyway, that's enough about my good causes, it's party time so enjoy the food offering, this time around, just like the supermarkets nowadays, we have a world buffet aisle on offer.

For those of you who have fallen on hard times we do have doggy bags available when you stagger home. (As Sir Marcus and others giggle, Luke takes a couple of small side steps away from Tina. Ordinarily, this is neither here or there but Sir Marcus does not recognise Luke or the woman he is standing next to as his gaze falls on them).

Oh, I'd just like to add, I know what some of you might have thought or be thinking, that I was going to imminently announce my engagement to the lovely Lady Somerton tonight or Vanessa as I get to call her. She unfortunately can't be here with us tonight as she is away doing vital work abroad. (He glances at Luke and Tina again before back to his guests). Now, where was I? Oh yes, but it's not to be I'm afraid, although watch this space on that one as well, any old excuse for a party, eh? (He laughs as do most guests).

Our aristocratic pedigree and social standing are such a perfect match it's simply unbelievable, nay terrifying, my heart has been smitten in a way that not even the single most excellent business deal I've ever completed can even come close to the business of when we get married. (The crowd cheer. Luke takes some more side steps away and seems to be heading towards a door to his right. Marcus picks up on this like a hawk as no one else is moving). Excuse me young man, the door to the bathroom is that way, the other door."

"Thank you, Sir—Bainbridge," replied Luke.

"Do I know you, sir?" asked Sir Marcus.

"If fate had dealt a different hand, you might have known my mate, laughing Liam!" replied a daring Luke.

"I'm sorry, I don't know what you mean, can you explain yourself, you're rather ambiguous? What's fate got to do with anything? I don't believe in fate, if you want something, you have to go out and take it—get it yourselves. The business world deals with facts and figures and even better, certainties, not hocus pocus remedies and fate."

"If my mate's father hadn't come home early from his night shift, you could well have been his father!" said Luke but is unsure whether he had said the right thing. There were a few smiles from some of the guests, who were unsure if this banter was scripted and meant to happen, sort of part of the night's entertainment. After all, they have had quite a 'stand-up' routine from their host already.

"Impossible, I've never been to any slummy, deprived council estate, especially up north judging from your crass accent. I leave that to the brave missionaries. I do not know why they bother up there, many a missionary have been mugged or beaten and a good few of them were lucky to come back to civilisation with their lives intact. Now, I know I didn't hire a comedian tonight, so you must be here for the charity—receiving not giving obviously, from the look of you.

The raffle won't be for a while my terrible comedian friend, good people like us give, people like you take. You and your partner have certainly taken to the food, please tell your lady friend to leave some food for the rest of us. (He laughs as do many others). I see the two of you have tried to dress in your fineries, your most expensive and desired clothes—or are they from up north? (He and some guests chuckle again). Where, if someone wears colour co-ordinated clean clothes, they are thought of as a snappy dresser, talk of the town stuff.

Anyway, I'll be the bigger and better person since it is a party, so why don't we break out the peace pipe? I put Old Holborn in mine, we all know what you and your brethren stuff into your pipes or should I call them bongs. You are excused, young vagabond, you can go the little boys' room now. Don't steal the toilet roll, it is expensive, it is from Harrods, now there's a good chap. (Again this produces giggles from the crowd). We will inform you when the raffle is so rest assured, you will end up with some handout cash in your pocket on top of the food in your stomach."

Marcus jesters to the butler to follow him when the crowd are mostly looking at Luke.

Luke knows when he is soundly beaten at the Mickey take stakes. He never would have guessed it when he made his joke at the start, that a rich pompous, super pretentious aging blue-blood would out-gun him in a slanging shoot-out match. A southern pounce out-shooting a gritty northerner—what is the world coming to?

So, instead of trying to win a losing battle, he just says, "Thank you, Sir Bainbridge. However, there is just one more thing I'd like to mention before I go the little boys' room. Your kind, the ruling elite, once occupied foreign countries through force and called it a glorious empire. Well, I am speaking up for the people of those countries by stating that when the British finally left, those countries regained their freedom back, their God-given right of sovereignty over their own land. It definitely, most absolutely was not independence, it was freedom.

It was just that saying the word freedom made the British rulers look bad, making them look like an illegal foreign occupying force, which in essence they were, so they simply changed the wording. Your lot—incredulously wrote down history the way they wanted to, not the way it should have been. You and your friends' ancestor's legacy is a lie and your wealth is based on oppression and plunder. It's a nice house you got yourself here, how did your ancestors ever afford it? Wealth from the colonies, I dare say, by way of the business end of a Mark II Lee Enfield rifle no doubt!

Oh, by the way, who are the beneficiaries of the charity funds raised here tonight by you and your rich friends? All your poor friends who have fallen on hard times and are down to their last million pounds in their private off-shore bank accounts, poor things." After that rant, Luke hurries out of the other door previously indicated by Sir Marcus. The butler, Benson, sets out to follow him but is hampered and slowed by guests who keep wanting his services.

Everyone in the room (many belonging to this empire-profiteering elite class) and Tina too, are silent. Sir Marcus does not react in any way angrily after Luke's outburst. He does not even do anything to throw the two out, that would make him look bad in front of his quests. As ever though, he uses it to seize the moment to his own advantage.

"Does he not look in the mirror now and again? Has no one told him he is British, well barely and white himself? He's batting for the wrong cricket team, the poor deluded chap. Besides, the empire isn't lost, it's all in bloody London. A minority British ruling over the majority ethnic inhabitants, ring a bell anyone? (The guests all giggle at this potentially explosive and racially infused comments bar Tina, she is not amused!). We in London are used to invasions year round. All sorts of people come here. To be fair, they have enabled us to win at sports at least, our medals cabinet would be empty without them. These foreign mercenaries have made the UK victorious in boxing, tennis, running, athletics, skateboarding and of course football. There's hardly any native white English stars out there. Mr Jones, Mr Smith and Mr Brown have been replaced by Mr Adewale, Mr Kowalski and Mr Nicolescu! But it's the dreaded northerners I detest the most, at least the foreign contingent bring their money with them also, allowing us to rob them twice in history. (He and the guests giggle again).

The northerners bring their crow bars, pliers and latex gloves, their drugs and foul language and spitting. I mean, up there in the badlands, the people and the police are shocked if there isn't a daily stabbing or shooting. I bet the safest place to be is in any adult education centre or a school or college—nobody bloody there! I hear a person, once did graduate up there and promptly moved south, the local newspaper reported that the whole region suffered a brain drain crisis thereafter.

I once heard that when the police searched one particular prolific burglar, they found about his persons: a pocket locking knife, another eight-inch knife, couple of screw drivers, some counterfeit cigs, a splif joint, cannabis, gloves and two cheap mobile phones. But the most truly shocking item recovered was an actual receipt, for a genuinely purchased item. (Members of the audience mockingly respond by muttering things like, "Oh my God!" or "I don't believe it!" or just simply "How shocking indeed!").

Oh, he had a Parker pen on him too. Probably could find no buyers for the pen! There's more ladies and gents, a certain unnamed council up there had plans to set up an anti-fraud department but a bent council employee fraudulently embezzled all the funds, he took the lot and then took himself off to the Bahamas. Another case I read about, one council's housing department was left homeless itself after an aggrieved tenant burnt down their offices after they refused him a six-bedroom house. That's one room to sleep him, his wife and all the little runts and five bedrooms to grow the cannabis in. He was on permanent sanction so growing drugs was the only income he had apart from the pocket-money his drug-dealing kids gave him.

So, you'll understand my dear people, that after 'Brexit', we should have something to sort out the north south problem. I thought we could call it 'Southxit', but it's a tongue-twister and sounds like sax-it or even sex-it when said real fast, can't have that spoken out loud in Parliament, can we? The northern MPs will love the name if not its purpose! Since 'Northxit' is just as bad and it's all about the south not north, I came up with, 'Shove-it—We don't need the North'. Straight to the point, marvellous! You've got to admire the Romans ladies and gentlemen, they had the right idea way back then, only thing is they built the damn wall two-hundred miles too north!"

The guests again laugh out loud with great satisfaction, Sir Bainbridge had suddenly become an impromptu and fully-fledged comedian and he knew it and revelled in it. He bows to their applauds.

"More! More! More! We want more, Sir Bainbridge," rang out from the pleased and entertained crowd.

Sir Bainbridge, loving the attention more than ever, obliges. "Go on then, I should hire myself out, make even more money, better than a boring business speech this. OK, I'm all for feeding the wanting masses, give then what they want. Let's try a traditional 'when God made you' joke. When God made the northerners, he ran out of stuff so he gave them an I.O.U., a bit like the pharmacy give you when they are out of stock of your particular medicine. For the northerners, their I.O.U. was for brains, looks, manners, honesty, integrity, clean language, etc. They are still waiting to receive them. That truly is all folks! Enjoy the party of parties!"

The audience give Sir Bainbridge the loudest clap, he has them eating out of his hand. What started out as a dig from Luke, finished as a triumphant ego buzz-trip for his opponent. Not ideal, not ideal at all.

As for Tina, who is still a little angry at being made fun of by Bainbridge, is wise enough to keep her temper under control. Their mission is more important than causing a major ruckus over weight and world of (past) empire. Besides, all she has to do is just go on eating.

Luke finds himself in a hallway and looks ahead. "Ah stairs! Stairs to some bedrooms. A good place to start." He makes his way up the stairs as quietly as he can. Just as he disappears from the upstairs landing and out of view, the butler comes out of the party room door and heads towards the downstairs toilet and opens the door to find it empty.

"I thought so, just another pilfering thief!" concluded the butler.

Luke enters what he susses to be the master bedroom. He enters and closes the door, again quietly. "Wow! Call me a bread and water peasant but this is one hell of a classy bedroom. (He goes over to the extra lavish four-poster bed and dives into the middle and wriggles around). I could live here, just in this bed alone. (He gets up and goes over to the main chest draw, not to the make-up desk as it is obviously Lady Somerton's domain and unlikely to harbour any incriminating evidence. On the chest draw, he rummages through the CD collection box).

Time to check out the music, what do toffs listen to nowadays I wonder? (He flips the CDs). 'Spice girls'! 'Eternal', 'Britney Spears', oh my God, 'Shampoo' (He sings), #Uh oh, we're in trouble, someone's come along and it's burst our bubble, yeah yeah#. (He stops singing). Man! This guy is not only a pervert paedo, he has such bad taste in music! Should be locked up on both accounts. (Luke then looks around until his eyes fall on the wardrobe. He goes over and opens it to see many quality suits hung up).

Well, lookee here, now this is more me and my taste. (He looks about and sees a black bin liner in the corner. He opens it and sees a coat inside—a coat that could well belong to a rich trendy teenage girl). A Moncler coat, that is expensive. (He picks it up and puts his hand in one of the pockets where he finds a scrunched up post-it note, which he unravels and reads out loud).

'Hi, Isabelle, can't meet you at dinner time, luv Emily'. (Stops reading). Ah ha! I think that's called irre—irrefootable—irrefu—table evidence. So she is here or has been! A note from a school friend of Isabelle no doubt." Suddenly, Luke hears the floorboards outside creak. He looks at the slightly messy bed and the CD box with its lid open in quick succession. He hears the door handle slowly being turned.

The butler enters the master bedroom door and goes in. He stands in the middle and observes the room. There is nothing amiss, nothing out of order. The bed is made just like he had left it in the morning, the CD box is closed, the wardrobe is closed. Having been satisfied that all is OK, he walks to the door. He begins to close it from the other side when he stops short of clicking the door shut.

He has a think, then he goes back into the bedroom. He walks right over to the four-poster bed and stands by it, after a second or two he crouches down and looks under the bed. Nothing! He sighs a bit out of disappointment and gets up. He checks out the wardrobe by opening it and again nothing. "Maybe he is here to nick the toilet paper after all and the Mount Fuji lava crystal body wash perfumed with an elixir fusion of passion fruit and water Lilly." The butler leaves to continue his search elsewhere.

Under the majestic bed, Luke drops down onto the floor with a thump from where he was—clinging to the wooden framework of the underside. A right clever trick! He gets up and rubs his arms a bit due to the intense holding action he has had to do. He looks at the bed then says in a French accent, "I most definitely prefer the top side of the bed, Josephine!"

Luke stealthily makes his way down to the party room and hooks up with Tina again, the butler is not in the room so must still be searching.

"Find anything?" asked Tina.

"Luke Woam—Missing Person Finder has landed! We are officially on the score board," exulted Luke.

"What? You've found something?"

"Indeed I have—irre—irreee—oh—hard evidence. A coat belonging to Isabelle."

"Where is it, did you get it? Obviously not, have you hidden it somewhere?"

"No, I searched the pockets and there wasn't anything in it apart from a post-it note and I couldn't hide a coat about my persons, not exactly pocket-sized. I was very nearly rumbled so I just left it where I found it."

"You certain it was hers? Could it be a daughter of his, soon to be Lord Snotballs!"

"Certain, the post-it note had her name on it, the friend who wrote it is called Emily, remember her brother Archie mentioned an Emily to us."

"Yeah—it all makes sense, I'm certain of it too now. She's either here or been here. My guess, if she is here somewhere, she'll be all tied up or drugged and that or both, just like the creep joked to the guests."

"Honey, we'd better flowcha out of here now as we might be in danger ourselves. Bertie the Butler is snooping around looking for me right now as I speak. And Bainbridge is giving me the evil eye."

"Agreed, the other danger is I might end up eating all the food off the table if we don't make a move soon. Beats beans on toast, I can tell you that!"

The sleuthing duo make a quiet exit from the room and building. They are mighty glad to be outside in 'safe' night time London. They make their way home.

Inside the party house, the Butler is standing next to his master, Sir Marcus Bainbridge. The party is still in full swing.

"It's pretty obvious he was snooping around," figured Sir Marcus.

"There is nothing missing, sir. All the household items are still there from what I can gather," replied the butler.

"I wonder what it was they were here for, looking for, besides the expensive free food? It is a bit worrying coming so quickly after I received my package? Too much of a coincidence, the girl and these two being from the lawless lands up north, I'd say more suspect than chance. Oh—the girl's coat, did you get rid of it like I said, the one that got left behind when we moved her? Destroyed it, not just put it in the bin outside? The police probe every nook and crevice these days."

"Oh blast! I forgot to do it sir. Sorry about that, sir, I put it in the wardrobe, force of habit I'm afraid. I will destroy it immediately; it will not happen again I assure you master. As for the problem at hand, shall I put the boys onto the two uninvited guests, sir?"

"No! I have a better idea, sometimes brains are better than brawn to sort out troublemakers. Tell that waste of space Pops to get in touch with me ASAP. He's got some explaining to do, I think he might be withholding some vital, need to know, information from me. Now, go and get rid of that bloody coat"

"Very well, sir. I shall carry out my duties." He starts to go off.

"Oh, Benson, you did check the toilet paper, didn't you and the body wash?"

Chapter 18
Sophia

Sir Marcus, Pops and a very eloquently and seductively dressed high class lady are all in a Range Rover, being driving around the working parts of the back streets of London by the very loyal butler, Benson. It is where all the workers of all description come to local cafes and sandwich shops, in other words, the real beating heart of ordinary Joe London, away from the rip-off tourist areas and prices.

The car drives around without haste, since the occupants are on a mission and are busy looking out of the windows at the numerous affordable eateries.

"What a dreadful part of the city this is, I hope I don't catch something, something airborne?" complained Sir Marcus. Sophia mutters in agreement.

"Nah sir, I been living here all my life, look at me, prime example of a healthy male human being, like a choice cut of lean tender beef, don't ya' agree, Miss Penelope?" boasted Pops as he gazes at her, in fact, he had been eyeing her up more than looking out of the window so far.

"It's Sophia! Sir Marcus has told you many times already, do remember it," replied Sophia.

"A beautiful name for a beautiful lady, I must say. Sophia—sounds like—Sobhia—a Paki bird I knew once. Then, there's Susan—I," Pops said but is cut up by Sophia.

"Susan! What a ghastly name! I can imagine you would know a 'Susan'."

"Can you stick to what it is you're here to do, we've been looking for well over an hour now. You said this is where—people like you and them—commoners, come to breakfast. So keep your eyes peeled and stop talking. God knows, this mess is all your creation, that I have to, now, personally sort out," Sir Marcus said in a raised and annoyed voice.

"Will do, your Lordship, will do. If you let me, I and the boys can deal with it our way, you won't have to worry about it no more, we make problems go away, forever. If they're here, I will eyeball 'em out, no probs," said Pops and began to look in earnest again but this time out of the window for a change.

Sophia looks profoundly at Pops. "Yes, do! I too detest this part of London. Once I was unfortunate enough to be driving at night through these parts and I can swear I saw some women group urinating together just off the main road, like it was normal behaviour. Can't imagine what their men were doing at that time, probably urinating on each other, then having a mass brawl in the middle of the road, followed closely by the women."

"The mass brawl happened probably because when the two groups got back together, they all found out everybody was sleeping with each other behind each partner's back. It's common occurrence in the lower classes; one could say even, a rites of passage," added Sir Marcus with more than a touch of a deprecating viewpoint.

"I am tiring fast, Marcus darling, must we continue this wild goose chase much longer?" complained Sophia.

"I understand, my sweet heart, but it's a job we need to sort out, just persevere a bit longer, I beg you," replied Marcus.

"I know! Do you lot want to hear some badass jokes, I know some, about Gypos?" asked Pops, thinking he can entertain.

"No!" came the joint reply from Sophia and Marcus.

Pops, eager to tell his jokes, ignores their wishes. "What's a Gypos' favourite book? None, 'cause they can't read! (Smirks). If they could, it'd be A to Z of Ireland or England. Why do Gypos hate prison more than normal people? Because they have to stay put in one place in their cells! Geddit? (There was no reaction from the other three occupants). OK, why are Gypos banned from airports? 'Cause they keep nicking the travellators! Funny, eh? (Still no reaction but Pops is oblivious).

What word do Gypos hate the most? Stationary! That's a real belter! There's more. Why did the Gypo kids run out of school? Because the teacher told them they were going to be put into school house groups! Now, that's a scorcher, that one. What about, why is a heart like a Gypo? Because a heart never stops moving, it keeps going and whenever it does stop, it causes massive problems! That one is a killer, my personal favourite! (Pops laughs out loud, he is the only one laughing. Benson had smirk after the last one but quickly ended it). I've got another kind of similar one, why do Gypo kids do bad at school? Because they hate using stationery. Now that's a different word to the first one you see, the first one is all about not moving—"

Pops' jokes did get a frustrated reaction at last. "Stop! No more, that's enough! Just keep an eye out for what I have asked you to do!" bellowed Sir Marcus. Pops resumes his look-out job to the immense relief of the other three.

After a short while, Pops sees the two targets sitting inside a cafe. "Stop! Alfred, stop, stop the bat-mobile! It's them, sitting right there, inside that cafe. I was right, I told you they'd be somewhere here." Benson gives a look of annoyance at Pops for getting his name wrong too but stays quiet.

The Range Rover comes to a halt on the kerbside very near the cafe so that the vehicle occupants can easily see inside of it. The cafe is a typical sized corner type.

"My dear Sophia, take a look at your quarry, it's the young couple sitting under the picture by the wall."

"Yeah! The fat bird sitting with the skinny toss pot, they're from Bolton you know," added Pops.

"I thought bread was the only white thing that comes out of Bolton!" remarked Sir Marcus in a serious expression.

By now, Sophia had lit a cigarette that was tucked into one of those old fashioned long holders that you only really see women in movies using. She looks in the direction of the cafe.

"At last, all this hunting has made me hungry for another love fool. (She looks hard at the two targets, especially Tina, she frowns). Really? Sir Marcus, you're willing to spend a fortune hiring me when even a ten-pound slut could do the job all too easily."

"Err—what do you mean darl—lady—Sophie—I mean Sophia?" asked Pops, but Sophia does not even look at him.

"Quality work demands high prices, I am a successful business man, I should know how much to spend or not to spend. You are worth every penny, my dear," replied Sir Marcus.

"Why thank you sweetheart, but with that—troll in there, it won't even be a challenge. I was hoping for a bit of a contest, just to make it more interesting for me, I do like to be stretched now and again. But with this bag of beans—let's just say, I probably do more stretching when I get up in the mornings," remarked Sophia.

"I can be a challenge for you, your ladyship, I'm sure I can stretch you out like a rubber band," added Pops.

Sophia blows smoke into Pops' face. "Are you still here, your usefulness ended the moment you spotted them? You can go back to the gutter now." Pops does not react to the insult; he is punch-drunk in love and in awe of the beauty he sees before him.

"I can be very useful, your ladyship. If you ever need someone to unpick a wedgie for those times when you wear a super sexy dress, then I'm your man. I'm good with me hands you see, delicate they are, could have been a brain surgeon me," continued Pops. Sophia is lost for words at the vulgar thought of him unpicking a 'wedgie'.

"But instead you ended up as a third rate pimp, a flesh merchant. And talking about brains, pity you bashed the head teacher's brains out at school and got expelled, otherwise you could have been a contender, right?" commented Sir Marcus, obviously in irony mode.

"That's right, boss, spot on, I could have been a contender," said Pops little realising Sir Marcus' comments weren't meant to be complimenting.

"Brain surgeon? It is a pity as your first patient could have been your poor old head teacher, better still, you could have operated on yourself," joked Sophia. "No danger of damaging something that has never worked!"

Pops laughs. "Oh that's funny, Miss Sophia. You are a very funny lady. And a very beautiful lady. Add in cooking and you'll make a perfect wife, just need the right sort of geezer to marry. But right now you make me wish I was a fairy tale Prince Charming so I could charm the pants off you."

"Oh my God!" gasped Sophia.

"And back to reality people, I just want the job done quickly, without much fuss and right," said Sir Marcus looking at Sophia.

"OK, Marcus, it's your money. Time to work off the diamond you are going to give me on my next birthday," said Sophia as she made moves to exit the vehicle.

"Consider it done peaches, the pleasure will all be mine, my princess," replied Sir Marcus.

Sophia leaves and closes the car door. "I Know, I'm expensive but damn I'm worth it!" whispered Sophia to herself as she walks off towards the cafe.

Inside the car, Pops is still smitten by Sophia, he is right up against the window watching her walk away. He starts to make moaning/groaning type noises. He realises and looks at Sir Marcus, who in turn is looking right at him in a confused and disgusting way, so is Benson.

Sophia enters the cafe and immediately locks eyes on Luke, who is sat facing the door, with Tina's back to her. Luke, just like Tina, is looking down at his breakfast. When Luke does look up, his gaze falls straight away on this beauty of a woman standing near the door area, looking well out of place in this cafe and the whole area.

He just stares, Tina is still looking down, busy hacking away at the full English. Sophia blows a seductive kiss to Luke, he reacts like he has been physically kissed for real, after that, he just has a stunned like appearance, stunned with admiring love.

Sophia walks slowly to the empty table in front of Luke (and behind Tina) and picks up a serviette and proceeds to writes down her first name and mobile number, shows it to Luke and puts it upside down on the table. She then looks at Luke again, blows another seductive kiss and leaves the cafe. Not bad five-minute work for the money and diamond she will earn from it.

Tina finally looks up at the inanimate, love struck Luke. "What's the matter with you, you alright? You look like you had the winning lotto numbers and then found out your tickets' out of date."

"Yeah! You could say that. No! I mean—it's just this coffee, it's really tasty, I think I'll ask the owner which country it's from or rather which brand they use," replied Luke.

"Whatever Trevor, it's OK but nothing special I'd say," replied back Tina as she puts some headphones into her ear and starts to listen to her music.

Two Japanese tourist type couple walk into the cafe. They sit down on the empty table in front of Tina and Luke, one recently vacated by Sophia, the one with the marked serviette on. They put all their expensive electronic equipment on the table like smart phones and cameras.

"Don't show all this valuable stuff for all to see, I don't feel safe around here. Not good part of London," said the Japanese lady to her husband in Japanese.

"Don't worry, we are safe in cafe. Besides, all Westerners think us Orientals know martial arts, any sign of trouble, I'll just make kung-fu and karate noises and put my hands like this," replied the husband also in Japanese and makes out a kung-fu pose with his arms.

"You're no fighter, you fix photocopiers. You look like someone who fixes photocopiers."

"Like I said, we are very safe in cafe. Out there I will hide the equipment and my Rolex."

"Good! Now, I feel like a full English for each of us," said the wife.

Luke stands up and looks at the Japanese table. A few minutes ago the table was empty, now it has people on it. This is a bit of a problem as how do you go about obtaining the serviette? What if the tourists cause a commotion, then Tina will inevitably find out? In the end, blind lust wins the moment, caution loses out and Luke just goes for it. He goes straight up to the two tourists who were looking at the menu but now are looking up at this menacing rough looking bloke standing right next to them.

Luke raises his right hand, the Japanese tourists have an expression somewhere between confused and scared. The Japanese man uses his hands and arms to cover as much of his equipment as possible on the table. Luke suddenly, with the speed of a cobra's strike, grabs the serviette from the table. The Japanese man covers and grips his equipment even more, his wife just looks on in immobile shock.

"Sorry to bother you but this is mine, I left it here. Merry Christmas and have a good day. Oh, that is if you lot celebrate Christmas in China or Japan. My guess would be you're from Japan, right?" To that, Luke spins around and goes to the counter to ask the counter staff member about the coffee. The Japanese tourists just look at each other with disbelief and relief. They nervously start to look at the menu again. Tina is oblivious to everything.

Luke returns to his table.

"Did you find out, about the coffee?" said Tina but loudly, she had headphones in so did not realise her volume.

"Whoa! The headphones, take the phones out, Tina," replied Luke and pointed to his own ears as some other customers in the café look at Tina for a second or two.

"Oh shit! Was I too loud?" said Tina, again loudly but this time she removes the phones after saying it. She asks in normal volume, "Did you find out about the coffee?"

"Oh, they said they get it in bulk in large size packs, especially made for the cafe trade. So it's nothing special like."

"Thought so. Any back street cafe isn't gonna sell Chelsea and Knightsbridge quality coffee round here, are they?"

"Nope!"

"So, what's the plan, what are we going to do now, after this nice bit of real east end brekky?"

"Stick to buying cheap basic coffee and be happy about it. (Tina looks unamused at him). Just kidding, my love. I don't really know what our next move should be, what with being new to the business of finding people. Telling the police won't do any good. This is a very rich and very well connected aristocrat we're up against, who are we against him, this pretend charity king. Not forgetting, we know he's most likely moved her somewhere else by now and most probably got rid of evidence like the coat I'd seen, evidence we could have used, real proof."

"Yeah, things are not going our way on that front. What we need is concrete."

"Concrete?" asked a confused Luke.

"Yeah, beyond doubt kind of thing," replied Tina.

"Concrete proof you mean?"

"Yeah! What else?"

"Tina love, why don't we take the day off today, give us time to think about our next move on this Bainbridge guy, what do you say?"

"Sounds like a good idea to me, I won't say no, clear our heads."

"Good, I was thinking we check out some more tourist sites like the British Museum of Natural History again. I could spend a whole day in there. At night we could check out the famous nightclubs up West End."

"Whoa, slow down Speedy Gonzales! One small but significant breakthrough in our first case, a name and residence and you're in a jubilant mood already."

"Well, you know, if we crack this one, the money is kinda alright in this lark. Plus, we can always be together like, you know in work, the business."

"Like a dream team, but we're a long, long way from cracking anything, except maybe our heads right now, but things are shaping up, albeit very slowly, I'll give you that, darling?"

Luke takes a quick look at the serviette in his hand under the table. "Shaping up nicely, honey bun, like a dream just as you said."

Chapter 19
A Day Out

So, as it was decided the day before, today will be an off-the-case day but crucially, it will still officially be an expense day, so poor old Mr Haversham will be paying the for the good time and maybe some of the venues without even knowing about it. Cheeky, so very cheeky from the crafty duo.

"Here we are again, armed with the wonder that is the all-day pass, let's paint the town red," bellowed Luke as they are standing in a tube station.

"Why not? Let's make the most if it, back on the case tomorrow, right? After all, we are our own bosses and we certainly can't sack ourselves!" said Tina.

"Too right! Let's flowcha."

So they were off. They had many things on their list and the sooner they started, the more they could cross off the list.

They went to Camden market, up the Shard, they even went to Green street, Ilford, east London and had a curry in the Asian sector. They were all whistle-stop tours apart from the curry house stop. At present they find themselves in the Bluewater Mall, the Museum of Natural History did not get a look in today. They are idly strolling around in the walkways when they come across a salesman demonstrating washing power, so both decide to stop and listen in in the hope of maybe getting a free sample—they are Northerners after all. One can take them out of the north, but everywhere they go, they always take their northern habits with them!

The salesman reels off his banter whilst holding two pieces of cloth, one in each hand. "Right, ladies and gentlemen, if you look at these two cloths, the cleaner one, on your left, my right, has been washed in the totally brand new formula Spark powder. You will notice it is way brighter, whiter, cleaner, simply dazzling. It's a win-win result for all your clothes, coloured or not. It also leaves them smelling fresher like if they were new, just bought from the shop." People are nodding in agreement.

Luke makes his way to the front with Tina next to him. "So, what you're saying to us, mister, is that the old Spark, that we are all currently using at the moment, is a load of crap?" some people laughs as the salesman looks at Luke in slight annoyance.

"No sir, I'm not. The old Spark powder is still wonderful stuff," replied the salesman.

"But look at that cloth on your left, our right, the one washed in old formula Spark, I wouldn't call that a dazzling clean cloth, like you yourself just said. Yet, I remember when it came out new a good few years ago now, you lot at Spark said it was the best thing ever. Everyone saw it, it was on the telly about ten times a day.

The clothes back then certainly looked better than this cloth here. But now you're telling us it wasn't the best thing ever, just OK, because as you can see right there, it leaves your washing slightly dirty. We were sold a lie and I bet in a few years' time you'll be telling us this newest Spark is a load of tosh because the even newer new formula X Spark is the new king in town! I rest my case folks." Luke looks around to see everyone looking at him and being influenced by his musings.

The salesman picks up a couple of free mini sample boxes and puts them in bag. He goes over to Luke and Tina real close, his face is only an inch or two from theirs.

"Here, free gifts from the nice people at Spark. Now kindly sod off and have yourselves a merry Christmas somewhere else and let me get on with my job! I've got bills to pay like everyone else." The salesman said it very quietly for obvious reasons.

"I think we do need to move on, Luke, whadya' say? We got what we came for."

"I think you're right," replied Luke, much more quietly. Both then flitter away.

Luke and Tina casually stroll the walkways when Tina sees a kiddie's ride, the coin-operated seated rides that are the saviours of many a parent when on a shopping trip out. Tina walks up to it and Luke follows. This ride is tucked away from the main busy areas.

"You know what, sweetheart, I feel like going on this ride, there aren't many people about here, it'll be fun. Come on, there's just about enough room for two."

"Well, that leaves no room for me then!" replied a cheeky and daring Luke, maybe taking his life in his own hands.

Tina looks at Luke all serious and that. "You'll cop an unfortunate one in a minute, lover boy?"

A bit later, the two see an up-market art shop full of funky art stuff of all descriptions called, 'Out of this World'. The window display items attract their attention so much they go in to look at the internal displays close up, something they do not get much opportunity to do back in Bolton. The two casually stroll around in wonder and awe.

"Good expensive arty stuff in here," said Luke.

"Grand! I think some of it is called art nouveau or art deco, might even be abstract art. There are so many names for 'em, even I get confused," replied Tina.

"You're a work of art, my dear. I could sell you in here, they'll be queuing outside the door to buy you. My name for you will be 'art fantastic'. Add that to your list of arty farty posh names and think of a number with at least a hundred zeros. That's the amount of money they'll need to cart you off to their mansions."

"Oh thank you, my darling, so are now so forgiven for earlier on," said a well happy Tina. Who doesn't enjoy a compliment now and again?

A posh white couple in their thirties walk in and go straight over to an art display object and look at it. They then discuss together for a short time before both approach a black male shop staff member.

"Excuse me sir, can we see the person in charge, the manager," asked the man.

"Of course, sir, madam. Speaking, I am in charge here, how may I help you today?" replied the staff member.

"Oh! The boss has left YOU in charge of the shop. Good, good! Good for him I say, hello to the twenty-first century and all that," said the woman in a surprised kind of way.

"No, I am the manager, ergo the boss and owner too."

"That's—wonderful, so this is your shop, you've opened an—art shop? Oh how—different—quite—" muttered the man but was cut up by the manager.

"That's right, sir. I thought about opening a bakery shop and calling it, 'Cakes and Shit' or even contemplated starting a cycle shop and calling it, 'Stolen Bikes and Shit'. Of course, that was after I nearly opened a ganja joint with the suitably apt name of, 'Weed and shit'. Luckily, in the end, to keep my mother's white neighbours from both sides of her house over in Hampstead Heath happy, I opened this here quaint little artworks shop instead. Although I have as yet to encounter another person of similar ethnic persuasion as me in the world of high end nouveau art. Now, how may I be of assistance to you on this fine wonderful day?"

The white couple react like they had just been hit by a sledge hammer. The stunned silent stare. "I think, Trudy, we need to go home and discuss this a trifle more. Maybe that Georgian chest drawer your mum offered us would be a rather better fit in the corner of the room, what are your thoughts, my dear?" said the man, slightly red in face and embarrassed.

"I think you're right, Simon. Why don't we go now and discuss this at home?" replied Trudy. Both then say a very courteous but guilty goodbye to the manager and hurriedly leave the shop without looking back. The manager just chuckles and goes about his business, like he was used to it.

Luke and Tina witnessed all of this and laugh their heads off loudly that other customers begin looking at them. The two then also exit the shop, as realistically speaking, they are not going to buy anything, are they?

Soon, like everyone when in a mall, they inevitably end up in the food court; it is a highlight for all concerned. Tina and Luke have a huge choice on what to eat. A person walks by them holding a tray containing a really tasty looking juicy burger complete with golden fries and a drink. Food to die for, for the young generation.

Tina is especially wowed by it. "That looks scrumdid—lee—o—ce—ous, hard word to say. You go and find us a place to sit down and I'll order two go-large meals of that, my dearest?"

"Yeah, does look good? Order me two as well, feeling peckish," replied Luke, who seems to have a death wish today.

"You'll be eating a fist finger unhappy meal in a minute if you're not careful, or a good old fashioned knuckle sandwich. Second time today!"

It is night time now and the intrepid two are in a night club up the famous West End. They are sitting on a table drinking. Their glasses are empty.

"Oh no, time to refill again and break the bank at the same time. Same again, love?" asked Luke.

"Wh—wh—Why not? Haven't had this boozy a night in ages."

Luke comes back with a pint for Tina and a coke for himself. Tina notices.

"Hey! What's this, is—is—that a bloody coke, again?" asked a tipsy Tina.

"Yes, love. I don't feel too brill, thought I'd lay of the booze for a bit. Could have been that burger—too rich."

"Bit? You—you've—only had cokes and silly pop drinks, no alco—alcoholic drinks all night. Can't you handle the hard stuff anymore, going soft are we?" teased Tina.

"You watch, babe, I'll drink you under the table another time when I'm feeling up to it, when my stomach feels up to it."

"Good! I'll drink to that and you'd better too, a proper drink like right now, well, the next one you buy, not this children's party pop you are knocking back!"

It is the next morning, in their hotel room, both of the two party animals are not up at the usual early time due to the nocturnal activities of the night before. Tina is still out of it. Luke is way more alert than Tina because he is buzzing, the reason?—the only hangover of being on a cola binge is your sugar level, probably a level only an injection of insulin can cure.

He very quietly gets out of his side of the bed so as not to wake Tina. He tips toes and picks up Tina's phone from her bedside cabinet, turns it off and puts it on top of the wardrobe. Just then Tina stirs and shows signs of life, her eyes open. Luke is not bothered now as his phone hiding mission has been completed.

"Oh—what a day—I mean—night!" Luke moaned loudly, a bit indifferent to how he is actually feeling.

Tina stirs much more to life now. "Don't even say you've got a hangover—'cause you haven't. Not on flipping pop drinks!"

"I wasn't gonna say that. It was just a heavy night, something we've not had for a while. But now it's the morning after and time to get back on the job. So get up and greet the day fighting style."

"Oh—sod the day! I've really got a genuine hangover, a proper alcoholic one. I can't—don't feel up to it today. I'm sorry Luke but I don't think I can support you today."

"Yeah! You don't look right, don't sound too pukka either. Hey, I wonder if they are diluting the drink with water straight from the river Thames."

"Nah! Otherwise we'd be dead by now, our bodies slumped somewhere between the clubs and our hotel. They'll be using tap water, but tap water in London sucks to high heaven. Way better up north with our hills and clean reservoirs." They both laugh.

"So, I highly recommend staying in and resting all day today, sleeping it off, recuperating like, a good convalescence has marvellous rejuvenating powers you know," suggested a sly Luke.

"Yep! You're right, Dr Dictionary, but don't bother writing me a prescription, it's bloody cheaper to get it at the chemist." Tina then laughs little.

"OK, good, good. (Luke makes a happy contented facial expression not intended for Tina to see). I'll just search around and try and find out as much information about old Bainbridge as I can. Things like if he has other premises around the city and stuff like that."

"Good idea, wish you luck."

"Thanks, I'll miss ya', but sometimes you have to work solo. Sometimes you have no choice but to be the I in ITEAM. Or you could say, be the missing I in TEAM—"

"What ya' on about, you bozo, just go? Bloody I and team, just makes me wanna throw up!"

Sometime later Luke, is indeed on his own in the big city, something he cunningly engineered to be this way. This was the reason he was drinking exclusively only pop shots last night, but making sure Tina was knocking back the hard stuff. Pure deviousness on his part. Anyway, he has his phone in one hand and the serviette with the number on it in the other hand.

"What possible harm could one simple, innocent meeting do? Nothing! I'm just making contacts in the big city, might be useful for my business. Yeah! Go for it, Luke, my son," Luke said to himself and then he dials the number and it starts to ring.

The phone call is answered. "Oh hello, is this Sophia I have the pleasure of ringing? Good! I'm Luke, Luke Woam, from the cafe yesterday, ring a bell? Good—again. Well, I was thinking, maybe we could hook up and discuss—erm—well—I don't really know what to discuss, but we could meet anyway—to maybe—find things to discuss—and—sorry I'm rambling. What? You don't mind—that's comforting. What do you say to a meet? Excellent! Most excellent! How about let's say I meet you in—Trafalgar Square in an hours' time? Great stuff! See you then."

Luke ends the call.

"YES! Posh totty pulled just by looks alone, now to unleash my charm on her, knock her bandy. Time to get lucky in plucky London."

Luke is standing in and around the famous landmark of Trafalgar Square, with his eyes scanning the place in nervous hope, is it going to happen for real? A brass, rough and ready northern ex-bread factory worker with little or no education who can't even spell a word like, etiquette or know what it means.

One who usually has less pounds in his wallet than he has GCSEs, waiting to hook with a sophisticated member of the so-called elite society of London, the normal preserve of fat cats in big cars. Whatever you call this miss-match: chalk and cheese, fire and water, matter and anti-matter, Luke simply does not care. He knows this Sophia and him are definitely no two peas in a pod, no Ying and Yang, no strawberry and cream. To him, both parties are ready to taste and experiencing life on the other side of the street or in their case, other side of a fifteen lane America-style freeway, so, everyone's a winner baby!

Chapter 20
The Hot Date

Sophia sees Luke standing in the near distance with his back to her. She walks over and stands behind him and coughs once gently, very ladylike. Luke hears the cough but can also smell her expensive perfume. Before turning around, he makes a joyous expression on his face then he turns to face her, beaming in smiles.

"Hello, Sophia, I'm Luke, Luke Woam from the cafe. So pleased to meet you, so pleased you agreed to a—dare I say it—a date?"

"You may. I'm Sophia—Sophia Belmont. Luke Woam—that's how I like my men, I don't like hotheads but I warn you, I am a lady of exquisite tastes, I like my action hot, I am an extreme socialite well known in the highest circles of the London high rollers and amongst the millionaire rat packs!"

"Well, my princess, I am also well known in the northern circles of the country amongst all the bread-roll—ers and millions of buyers of multi-packs!" I too dabble in hot and expensive tastes—sometimes.

Sophia has no idea what Luke is on about but still smiles.

"So nice to meet you, I was really hoping you would ring, I hope you didn't think it was rather callous or forward of me, too sudden in a pushy kind of way, I simply didn't know what came over me when I saw you sitting there in that dreary little cafe looking like a bored house cat, nay lost cat, in need of some real attention and love from a sophisticated lady of honour and breeding."

"Absolutely not indeed! I love the way you acted, it was like something straight out of a movie or book or even a television program. Not that I have read many romantic books or any books for that matter, but I'm sure that's how some of them are bound to play it out somewhere in one of the early chapters—I think. Sorry, I'm in rambling mode again, forgot to switch it off."

"It's OK, I like what you say, makes me smile, you make me smile. I've only just met you and already I'm feeling good about myself and good about you. Such a change from the dreadful lot I usually hang around with. They wouldn't know what a genuine good time was unless it was on sale for a few thousand pounds in a shop up Chelsea way. Then they'd all want one and then throw it on the scrap heap in one of their many rooms once the trend is over." They both giggle.

"Anyway, this is what I thought we'd do today, see if you agree, it's a little different to what you're probably used to my fine lady. First, a lovely walk in Hyde Park, feed the ducks then luncheon by way of the best burgers in the whole of London, Harry's burger van next to the park. I'm not from London but since we've—I've been here I've discovered the best burgers outside of Bolton. Lastly, a movie in Leicester Square. I've always wanted to see a movie in Leicester Square. So, Sophie my fairy-tale princess, is that a yay or a nay for a magical day out and about with your humble servant, Luke?"

"It's Sophia, darling. And it's a resounding yay from me."

"Good show, as they say down this way I think! And sorry, of course it's Sophia. So, let the royal fun and frolics begin."

For the next few hours, the twosome worked through the list. As for now, they have just finished watching a movie and are coming out of the cinema in late evening.

"That was kicking man, I just love watching a Christmassy film at Christmas, don't you? It's magical, I just don't know how they do it?" exulted Luke.

"Yes, best time for it, so clever of them," replied Sophia with a dash of sarcasm and a sprinkle of downbeat thrown in. Maybe cheesy Christmas movies are not her bag.

"I'm not religious as such but I do love the seasonal atmosphere around Christmas."

Sophia does not reply to Luke's merry comment or share his jubilant mood. She is much more in a sober kind of mood, definitely not on cloud nine like Luke.

"Thank you, Luke, for giving me such a wonderful time tonight. It was simply divine, an experience I will never forget."

It was said without too much conviction but Luke does not notice at all due to being blinded by the occasion.

Luke looks at her a bit surprised, in a super pleasant kind of way. "Really, divine? I've never had that effect on a woman before."

140

"That's because most women don't know how to appreciate the finer qualities of their men. Men are sensitive creatures and so too deserve to be treated with love, affection, feeling and respect, just like us women. Most women purposefully hold back their men, stifling their dreams and ambitions, chaining them to a life of mundane domestic hell. But don't worry Luke, my prince, today you were nothing like the deflated, shackled person I saw in that café. Tonight, you got your mojo back. You got it back in abundance with change to spare and you used it well all day."

"Good, good, excellent. So, in that case, we must do it again, I want to use some more of my new found mojo, that I never realised I'd even had or lost until you told me."

"I agree, but this time let me entertain you. How would you like to come to my place, meet my parents, say tomorrow morning around 8:00 a.m., have breakfast with us?"

"Whoa! Parents. Things certainly move at pace down here, swinging London, eh? Definitely a city of action. Tomorrow? Could be a little tricky, my love—you know, I had to concoct an ingenious plan just to free up this one day."

"Oh I understand, dear Luke. I'm ever so sorry, my darling. I'm being pushy again; oh dear, I have made an utter fool of myself, blind love can make one awfully foolish."

"Don't be! I would love to come to your house and meet the parents. I will clear my schedule again tomorrow to free up the day. I accept your humble invitation with pleasure."

"Oh great stuff, that's just jolly. 8 o'clock then. Here, this is my address." Sophia pulls out a piece of paper with her address already written on it. Sophia said this much spritelier, she seems to have rid herself of the 'feeling foolish' mood instantly.

Luke gets the paper. "Is that one you prepared earlier?" quipped Luke, to which both laugh.

"Well, it's time to go home already, time flies when you're in blissful heaven. Mummy and daddy will be expecting me home any time now."

"Yes, both of us should really be heading home, well, hotel anyway for me."

"I'll hail a taxi. You should set off now, Luke. The underground is not the best place to be at night times, so I hear, packed like sardines in a can only—people."

"Yeah, I know only too well, like sardine cans exactly. But just like the can, if you could only ring pull a bit of the roof and sit on top that would be a solution and a laugh. Of course, they'd have to raise the tunnel roof a bit too. Anyway, thank you for today as well, it's been just mega great and—well—see you tomorrow Sophia, it's time to flowcha."

Sophia tries for a second to comprehend what 'flowcha' means but gives up. So just says, "See you tomorrow, Luke, my very own Duke." Luke hears this with pleasure, it makes a change from being called 'Luke the Puke' or 'Luckless Luke' all way through his school days.

They part their ways and make their way home separately.

Much later, Luke slowly opens his hotel room door and closes it even more carefully. He does not switch the light on. He makes a face as the room is a bit niffy, he wafts his hand across his face. As he creeps about Tina stirs half-heartedly.

"Where the 'eck have you been all day and night?" asked Tina.

"You know, on the case. Why didn't you phone me, I missed you?"

"My phone is lost in the room somewhere but I just wanted to sleep so didn't look for it. Anyway, even sleep got a bit boring after a long while so I snuck out for a bite to eat. And that's it, my day. What did you get up to all this time?"

"I just—wasted most of the day to tell you the truth, been about as busy as a hibernating bear who has overslept. I watched Bainbridge's house for a couple of hours, nothing doing, then just walked about, thinking what to do next but for the life of me, not a Dickie bird of an idea came to me. Looks like both of us have had an unproductive day."

"Come here, Happy Harry, it hasn't been wasted. I got some much needed rest and you got some fresh air and rest too. Cuddle time, both of have been apart for ages, well—physically at least—'cause I had a dream about you. We were young carefree lovers on an island living in harmony with mother nature, at one with the animals—that it, until we had to catch and gut a big fish we caught for dinner. One has got to eat—even in dreams. Point is, we were worry free and very much in love."

"Sounds good. I too was in a dream world out there today myself, reality had abandoned me. (He mutters quietly to himself, so Tina does not hear). A dream I would like to have again. (Loudly again). It was a time of intense deep, meaningful—"

Luke's sentence is cut off by a loud burp from Tina. "Sorry 'bout that. I suppose it's better than coming out the other end and trapped under the covers, eh?"

"What about the other ones, the ones that did come out the other end, they didn't have the decency to stay trapped under the covers. I needed a gas mask when I opened the door just now and came in."

"You're still breathing aren't ya'? Oh, before you turn in, can you find my phone for me, I felt like I was in the stone ages without it, just leave it next to me on the bedside cabinet, thanks lovely," said Tina as she pulls the cover over her head to try and get back to sleep. She immediately pulls back the covers again. "I did have another dream too, I just remembered. A rather pleasant one, as it happens."

"Oh yeah, what?" asked Luke with a smile and eager to know.

"About David Beckham of all people. Lucky, lucky me."

Luke's smile disappears quick time, replaced by a disapproving look and frown. "Oh! Did you now?"

"Yeah! We met in a fancy casino in America, where I'd won a lot of money and he was totally smitten by me. Before I could say, 'Jack Robinson', he wined and dined me and gave me a tour of his football club. Later he invited me back to his place in Miami. When we got there, his bloody wife Victoria shows up from another room holding a shit load of her own label handbags. Both of them just wanted me to buy one of his wife's expensive handbags, all along it was just a crafty sales pitch. What a let-down tosser!"

Luke's smile returns as quick as it had gone. "You should have bought one, it would have doubled her annual sales. Plus, it would have made old Golden Balls happy!"

"After that, why would I want him happy? I felt more like giving him a taste of one of my special left-footed free kicks, a world cup winning free kick right in the joy department! The end of my right boot would have gone where the sun don't shine!"

"You're a two-footed player then? Stick around, once he recovers, he might want you for his team," joked Luke.

They both laugh out loud.

Chapter 21
Hot Date 2

It is very early in the morning and Luke has got up before Tina, just like yesterday, who is still fast asleep; this is because he cannot rely on a hangover to subdue Tina as before. He dresses super quietly and puts his phone in his coat pocket. He stops and thinks for a second, then grabs Tina's phone just like yesterday again from her bedside cabinet. The one he had 'found' for her.

He then smiles a sly smile and switches off her mobile and puts it in his pocket too. He nods in satisfaction, this time Tina's phone will not even be in the room. After that, he writes a note to Tina which reads, 'Tina, I'm acting on a wildcard haunch that could get dangerous so I thought best I go it alone. See you soon pumpkin pie.' He leaves the note on top of Tina's bedside cabinet, where her phone had been. He then leaves.

Sometime later, Luke gets out of a taxi and looks at Sophia's house. It too is grand but not anywhere near like Sir Marcus'. "Well, here goes nothing! The Princess and the Pauper."

Luke, Sophia and who must be Sophia's parents are at the breakfast table, a lavish breakfast is set out on the table.

"So, Sophia tells me your name is Luke Woam. That's how I like my bath water and it's a great way to describe things, but I've never heard anyone being called it before, what kind of name is that to have?" asked dad.

"Blame my mum on that one, she chose it, I got it. I think she thought it might be rather catchy, especially if I had become famous like an actor or pop star," replied Luke.

"Catchy? Rather silly, odd even if you ask me," continued dad.

"Very silly I agree—Luke Woam!" added mum and laughs.

"I think it is a lovely name myself," said Sophia in defence of her new boyfriend.

"You would! I'm sorry dear, but you do always pick the bad apples, talk about picking them from the market, you pick yours from the market waste skip," said dad. Luke hears but restrains himself, so does nothing.

"No, I don't!" insisted Sophia.

"Talking about rejects and bad 'uns, what do you do for a living Masterless Luke, how do you earn a—crust—nay—crumb, that is, if you do work at all and not intending to live off our lovely daughter's wealth cum inheritance?" asked dad.

"I—erm—" Luke was replying, whilst still trying extremely hard to ignore the wave after wave of insults but is cut up by dad.

"Come on man, how you do earn a decent day's wage in your pocket?"

"Yes sir, I work. I'm a—bakery operative in a very large factory. You were right, hit the nail on the head about earning a 'crust—nay—crumb'. There's plenty of that in a bread factory," Luke replied with a bit of humour and forces a giggle from himself.

"Bakery operative—you're a baker, a labourer. You make bread, working graveyard shifts in grimy factory buildings no doubt? The only positive is I suppose, is that you are producing cheap bread to feeds the masses so we're safe from a peasant revolt at least," insinuated dad condescendingly and chuckles.

"We do make bread products for Waitrose, now they're posh and expensive," informed Luke.

"Aren't our Christmas presents enough for you Sophia, my sweet pea? We got you everything you wrote down on the long list," chipped in mum.

Luke is listening to all this but is still defiantly disguising his true feelings in a slight smile, after all, he is the guest here. It is hard though, especially being compared to Christmas presents. He moves his hand and makes a spoon drop to the floor. "Oh, I dropped the spoon, I'll just pick it up." Luke bends down so his head is out of sight under the table. He clenches his fist in anger. After this venting, he sits back up normal as before. It was a private and secret protest.

"Luke," said mum. "It is every mum's wish that their precious daughters find a suitable partner to wed. In our case, though not unique to us, we desire a well-educated, sophisticated, preferably heir to a title and wealth, blue blooded boy. One with proven aristocratic breeding and heritage, maybe going back centuries. To be brutally honest and don't take it as an offence, you don't even get to the starting line, let alone the score board, in any of these categories."

"Here, here, darling, well said," concurred dad as he taps the table in unequivocal agreement. "The likes of him are better off on their side of the north south border. We should build a wall too to keep out the diseased and degenerate genes, shoot 'em on sight, I say!"

"Mummy! Daddy! He's a guest in our house, I have invited him. Please remember that, show some decorum," pleaded Sophia at last in Luke's defence. It was a long time coming.

Luke again purposefully drops a fork on the floor. "Oops! How clumsy of me again. I'll just pick it up."

As Luke is under the table, Sophia looks at mum and dad and smiles to them, they smile back. All is well with the three of them it seems.

As Luke is under the table, all those lucky incidents flash through his head in super quick succession. He makes his fist clench again and then he grabs the lucky charm (which had fallen out from under clothes) in his other hand.

"I wish Sophia's dear mummy and daddy would throw up right here and now!" He gets back up with a straight face. The three are looking at him. "Got it! Now, where were we? Oh yes, the north south divide. Well, I don't care about the north south divide as I'm from the west, Lancashire."

Before anyone could say anything, mum and dad begin retching violently, then both throw up on the table to the utter disgust of Sophia, but not Luke, he is smiling. After a couple of jet propelled expulsions, the two elders are feeling OK again, like you always do almost immediately after throwing up. The vomit, made up of mostly pureed breakfast ingredients, is all over the table near them and on them. The two are speechless with plain old shock of the very sudden vomiting action.

"Oh! Oh my Goodness! Are you two OK?" asked a shocked Sophia.

"Yes," came the dejected reply from the two shell-shocked duo.

"Luke, it's time we left. (She looks at mummy and daddy, both of whom are now beginning to get up). I'm glad you two are OK but I want you to know that both of you have shamed me today!"

"What have we done?" came the unison reply from mummy and daddy.

Luke is quick to get up followed by Sophia. They say their goodbyes and leave the room into the hallway. Luke even managed a respectful and courteous goodbye to the parents.

"I'm sorry about my parents. All they want is the best for me," said Sophia.

"Forget it, I'm over it. That's a wish for all parents the world over," replied a diplomatic Luke.

"Listen, on second thoughts, maybe it's better if I stay here, with them."

"Yeah, you should."

"Oh Luke, I feel gutted, let me make it up to you by taking you out to dinner to my favourite restaurant, just the two of us. I would really like that. What do you say?"

"Another day? I'll need a miracle to get another day to myself. But hey, why not? Just tell me the time and place."

"Seven o'clock at 'The Mayfair Grill', any cab will get you there."

"Can't wait, see you then, bye, I'm going to flowcha now," said Luke as he let himself out of the front door.

Sophia closes the door and turns around, she has a wicked sly smile on her face like she is pleased with her achievements, despite the surprise vomit setback. The seduction plan is still alive and kicking; her prey is still blissfully unaware.

As Luke is walking outside, he gets out Tina's phone and switches it on. When on, he sets it to play music on replay. This is a devious attempt at trying to run down the battery charge on the phone.

Chapter 22
Hot Date 3

Luke gets back to his hotel room in good time (he did not plan to, of course), well before noon. Tina is watching the normal boring daytime stuff on the telly, no choice as she does not have the use of her phone courtesy of Luke's dastardly deed.

"Well, you've certainly and suddenly taken all this finding people malarkey to another level. I don't like waking up all alone in bed in unfamiliar places like big city hotel rooms. We're partners remember, which means we work together as a team, two heads are better than one kind of thing. Just remember partner, my name does appear on the business card," barked Tina.

"I know love, but sometimes the work can be a bit dangerous or you need to be on your own, especially when doing risky covert operations," replied Luke.

"Covert operations! (Tina laughs). Have you bought yourself a Ladybird book on do it yourself black ops private investigations? What was it then, this super sleuthing you've been doing completely alone—solo stuff?"

Luke has to think before he answers, "I just tried to case this Pops geezer again, in King' Cross. Just in case he moved another one of his victims to a location belonging to Bainbridge or if he'd go to wherever they're holding Isabelle. Even did Bainbridge as well, to see if he himself might go to Isabelle's location. If Pops had spotted me, I would have had to run—fast." Luke was obviously saying things adlib, on the hoof!

Tina is looking at Luke looking at her. "Are you saying I'm—"

Luke cut her up. "No! I'm just saying I didn't want you to get hurt if the situation got violent. Anyway, that's all academic now, as I never got to see Pops or Bainbridge all time I was out there, they must be keeping a low profile."

Tina accepts his explanation even though she only half believes it—just. Her physique is not conducive to running and she knows it.

"Hey! I thought you found my phone last night, I'm sure of it, I saw it next to me before I fell asleep. I can remember you whispering it to me or was that me dreaming it? I've been all morning without it again, I'm past the stone-age now, I'm fast approaching losing my will to live stage."

"Oh yes, I did. But this morning I was checking the battery life on it and I put it in my coat pocket without thinking, along with mine. (Luke gets out Tina's phone from his pocket and looks at it). Here. (Luke hands over Tina's phone). Needs charging, though."

"What are we gonna do the rest of today, super cop?"

"First, stay here until your phone is somewhat charged. Then I thought we'd just be a pair of eyes near Sir Marcus' house, see if we can pick up on anything, he's got to surface sooner or later, can't see him jetting off on a foreign business trip at this moment in time. At night, I want to go on my own again to try and find Pops and his crew in order to follow them for a couple of hours."

"Another mysterious solo mission, coming thick and fast now. You're making a lot of important business decisions on your own lately and it's our very first case an' all. Which lollipop man or tea boy got promoted and left you in charge—of their old job? Answer me that one!"

"Funny! I'm laughing my head off. But seriously, Tina darling, we've just been through this, our business will require a lot of solo work both from you and me. For instance, if we need to follow a woman then it'll have to be you for obvious reasons. We need another breakthrough fast. I promise to make this the last one."

"Yeah OK, but like I said before, two heads are better than one, just remember. Oh bugger! I really want to tell you to shove it, all this solo stuff you're doing because I am somewhat angry at you! But, I'm not gonna."

"Tina! Sweetheart that would really have hurt me if you did say that."

"That's why I didn't. I'm all understanding, thinking of the business, aren't I?"

"Good! Now, get up and plug your phone in preparation to leave shortly," ordered Luke.

The bulk of the daylight hours were spent just casing the residence of Sir Marcus' place and just behaving like tourists as well. To Luke, it was killing time until night time, to Tina, it was doing vital case work. Wicked Luke! Nothing of value was gained from this new 'joint' line of attack all the time they were there. No sight of the elusive Sir Marcus.

Back in the room, Luke is ready to hit night time London again. Tina is still all understanding for now and just watching telly again, only the much more interesting night time telly. Her phone, needless to say, never gets any down time as usual as she is on that as well. It is the modern way for young people—phone and telly multi-tasking.

"Well, I'm off on my mission now. Wish me luck, darling," said a buzzing Luke.

"Good Luck, Luke. See you later, if I don't, I might be asleep, been doing a lot of that lately and it's brill to have the use of my phone again," replied Tina, rather happily too. Luke leaves as Tina's eyes flip constantly from watching the big screen to the small screen. When Luke disappears, Tina quickly puts on her shoes and coat and quietly opens the door and goes out. Obviously, she intends to follow Luke on his solo nocturnal mission. She has her own secret covert 'black ops' mission going on, clever lass.

Luke gets into a cab and goes off. Tina gets into another cab close by.

"Where to miss?" asked the cabbie.

"Just follow that cab, the one that just left."

"Oh brother, I've been waiting for a customer to say that to me for over twenty years, just like in the fillums. Yes miss, I can follow that taxi. No problem," replied a rather jubilant cabbie and he is off too, rather briskly.

Eventually, Luke's cab stops outside the Mayfair Grill and he gets out and just stares at the outside of the restaurant for a moment or two. Then Tina's cab pulls up less than a minute afterwards, they see Luke go in. Both the cabbie and her can see inside the restaurant since it has large uncluttered frontal windows. What Tina and of course, the cabbie see is Luke sat down with Sophia at a table for two, facing each other and in good spirits. The taxi two both stare for a few seconds. Tina has a tear or two rolling down her cheek as she sits and stares in total silence.

The cabbie notices. "Sorry about that, lovey. This follow that cab business never turns out well, should have guessed it; never does in the fillums—or in real life for that matter. To think I've been waiting for it to happen for twenty years. He should be hung, drawn and quartered in the Tower of London for what he is doing to you, darling. Are you going to be OK, love?" The cabbie rightly assumed that this man is probably a love interest of his fare or was!

"Yes—thank you. You never know, it might all be innocent. We are pursuing a case you know, like in the movies you mentioned. This could be him working on a vital lead. Yes, it's probably that," replied a thoroughly despondent Tina.

The cabbie looks at her like he thinks Tina is having a mental breakdown right in front of him or just gone pain potty—a case, really?

"If you say so, miss. Yes, he is on a—case and she is the—vital lead. I'm sure that is what it is. Anyway miss, I need to shoot off, don't worry about the fare, it's on me, you take care now."

"Thank you again, sir. You're a good 'un," said Tina and then she exits the cab, which leaves.

As the cabbie drives away, his thoughts are still with the situation he has just left behind. "If that's him working a case, then I'm a super spy like James Bond in disguise. Poor girl, I hope it works out for her in the end but at least, she knows about it now." He disappears off.

Tina, meanwhile, is standing outside the restaurant looking in, but conspicuously. Luke has his back to her. The restaurant is busy.

Inside, a waiter approaches Luke and Sophia. "Are you ready to order, sir, madam?"

"We certainly are, John. The lady will have the broiled chicken, with the sautéed potatoes and the garlic mushrooms with all the veg and trimmings that come with it. For dessert, she will have the Tuscany apricot and apple pie with a dash of American cinnamon."

"An excellent choice, madam, so nice to grace us with your presence again," said the waiter. Sophia smiles.

"As for myself, I can't see it on the menu but I'm gagging for some F and C, that's greasy fish and chips with mushy peas with a good dollop of curry sauce as well, Asian style, not the Chinese one with all the bits like fruit and sh—stuff in it. For afters, I'll have a banoffee pie, freshly made I hope, not the frozen variety in this top-notch swanky joint. Oh, we'll also have the house wine, one bottle please."

The waiter looks at Luke rather stuffily. "Fish and chips is NOT on the menu, we do not do battered fish in our establishment, sir, try one of the numerous takeaways for that. We do, however, have Dover sole, not battered but slowly baked in seasonal herbs with a hint of lemon. I'll try to persuade our award winning chef to mash up the peas as you so desire. However, we do not do and never have, curry sauce here, whether Asian or Chinese containing the fruity bits."

"Oh you're missing out, John. Tell your chef, if he wants to win another award, get some proper mushy peas, with a bit of sugar in it and some authentic curry sauce knocked up back there in the kitchen."

"I'll—bear that in mind—to mention it. Your meal will be ready shortly, it would be even quicker but we like to make everything fresh with quality ingredients in our 'swanky joint'. Thank you for choosing Mayfair Grill. By the way, my name is Roger," said Roger the waiter and goes off.

"Thank you, Garcon," said Luke to the departing waiter. "I like this rest—" Luke could not finish his sentence as he sneezes, a very loud sneeze it is. Other guests look at him with displeasure. "Whoa, that was a sneeze and a half!"

Sophia mumbles to herself, "True northern scum!"

"What darling?" asked Luke.

"I said, you are a true northern chap! Twenty-four carrot, with your fish and chips and curry sauce dollops."

"I am—in fact me and Ti—me and—a friend of mine are often accused of being too local in our ways and lifestyles and that's other northerners saying it to us. That's why this trip to London will do wonders for us—me. See how the outside world live their lives."

"Is that why you have come—to London? What have you found out so far about us down South—Londoners?"

Luke makes a circle with his thumb and index finger with the other three digits pointing upwards and out. In other words, a positive, contented sign. "Cushty bhari! Sophia. Can't fault it so far."

"So, absolutely no down sides, no negative, no seedy underbelly to London then? You can tell me sweet heart, don't hold back, I want the truth and nothing but. I might be able to offer some insider advice."

"Nope! No worries so far. London is lovely. Does not disappoint."

"Good, that makes me very happy."

"Well, this will make you even happier. What do you call a melon cut into four pieces?"

Sophia is in no mind for random, Christmas cracker type jokes but goes along with the pretend enthusiasm. "I don't, know sweetheart, please tell me what you call a melon cut into four pieces."

"A quarter-melon!" answered Luke with genuine enthusiasm as if he had just told the greatest joke in mankind. "It's the way I tell 'em!" added Luke but in an Irish accent, he knows his stand-up comedians from a bygone era. The benefits of a jobless day time television education—stuff of life, ain't it?

Sophia, as usual, fakes a laugh. "Oh that's is genius, darling! So funny! I can tell we are in for a superb evening." Sophia is not beyond a sarcastic remark.

Tina is still outside but has moved a little away, leans on a bin, still deep in a troubled mind-set. A single tear is rolling down her left cheek.

Inside, Luke and Sophia are enjoying their meal. First course is about finished by now.

"The food is truly gorgeous here, don't you think? This is why it is my favourite restaurant," confessed Sophia.

Luke looks at Sophia. "Not as gorgeous as you are, my lovely." He lifts Sophia's hand and plants a peck on the back of it and makes a noise as well.

"Luke! People are here. Some in this restaurant tonight might be deciding on matters that affect our economy come tomorrow morning. Real powerful people."

"Let them, I don't care. Why are girls always bothered about what other people think? When they see us all happy and that, they'll ask the waiter to have what we're having, innit. Good business for them, might even give us a discount. A little bit of love is always good for the economy."

"Listen Luke my darling, I've been thinking. I want to visit where you are from, up north. I want to meet your family—your parents. I got tomorrow free and the next few days. I really want to go visit your neck of the woods. What do you say to that?"

Luke stops chomping on his food. "Up north? What on earth for? It's—grim up north—compared to down south. You won't like it, guaranteed. People up there think Bird's Eyes fish fingers as gourmet food. They have feel good tours in Marks and Spencer or Waitrose without actually ever buying anything because they think that is where the posh people go. Buying something in those stores only happens if it's someone's birthday."

"But I still want too, let's go—tomorrow, pretty please."

"Sophia—let me think about it—you surprised me. Let's not rush."

"OK, but don't think too long, darling."

"I won't, promise. Now, let's eat, enough talk." The dining duo, by now, are onto their desert.

Tina is back at the window again looking in. She is fuming by now. All the thinking time leaning on the bin did nothing to calm her. She is enraged and finally goes in. She walks over to an anonymous couple near the doorway and picks up a jug of water, they just stare in astonishment. She walks over to Luke and Sophia's table. They both stop dead and look at her, Luke is well and truly shocked, Sophia's expression is one of someone who could not care less that they had been found out.

"Tina! What are you doing here?" asked Luke.

"Doing? I'll tell you what I'm doing here. A little non-secret, zero black ops, non-covert mission of my own." To that, Tina pours half the water in the jug on Luke and the other half on Sophia. They react with shock and fright.

"What on earth? How dare you, you gutter bitch!" shouted Sophia.

"Tina!" shouted Luke.

"Enjoying yourself lover boy with your bit on the side, this hooker. Spent our money on her and this meal, sorry, Mr Haversham's money? Banoffee pie, hmm—nice! But why, you've already bagged yourself a large tart?"

"I beg your pardon! What did you call me? I am a woman of high class, Luke is my date so I don't know who the hell you are, but you'd better go before I call the vice police," threatened Sophia.

"I called you a Tart! With a capital T-A-R-T, can't you hear me over those rose gold-tinted earrings," yelled Tina.

"Luke, darling! Are you going to let this—peasant pig talk to me like this, do something? Did you not pay her—five pounds or ten pounds going rate fee? I don't blame you if you didn't, she's priced herself far too high." Sophia said this with a bit of self-satisfaction.

"Listen, Sophia—I kind of know her—" said Luke but was cut up by Sophia.

"Correction, Luke sweetheart, did know—THAT! Now you know me! There is simply no comparison. Get rid of this—creature feature lady of the night, it's time you said, 'get stuffed' to this turkey. The only culture and breeding she knows is the damp mould patches in her rundown council estate house," insisted Sophia.

Tina looks at Sophia. "Yeah! And the likes of you probably get yours from bio yogurt pots! (Looks at Luke). And what's this, "I kind of know her" bull, lover boy?" replied Tina.

"Girls! Girls! Let's all calm down!" pleaded Luke.

Roger, the waiter comes over. "Excuse me, sir, ladies. I have to request you keep the noise down, our other guests are quite perturbed by the scenes here."

"It's OK, John. We can sort it out, no worries," reassured Luke. The waiter goes away after saying thank you, half convinced that it might be sorted out.

Sophia, now much more composed and calm, says, "Luke, give her some money, it's always the same with these kinds of people, always on the take, always seeing what they can squeeze out of clients. Probably got five illegitimate brats at home starving and wondering where each of their fathers are? (She giggles).

You've bettered yourself now by associating with me. Go on Luke darling, pay her some charitable pocket change, so she can actually pay for the baby food and nappies at least, instead of stealing them."

"Excuse me, Penelope, I've never nicked anything in my life! There's only one Nicola, the knickerless nicker present here; it certainly isn't me, I've got mine on and you can't miss 'em, as they are as large as a ten litre storage box. (A few customers giggle, especially three members of a family of four rather plumpy people, the mother does not find it amusing and gives her husband and two kids the mean eye. Tina grabs the necklace around Sophia's neck lightning fast).

And you're the whore here, love. Whose husband bought you this, eh? How many night shifts with rich old Hooray Henry and his country club pals did it take to earn this? Your kind make me sick!" Tina then lets go of the necklace.

"Tina, Tina, I can explain everything, just hear me out!" Luke pleaded.

"Waiter, waiter, throw this freeloader out. She is disturbing, interrupting our dinner," shouted Sophia. The waiter starts coming over again.

"Oh no, I am sorry! Don't let me interrupt your romantic dinner. Go on— carry on with you lovely meal. (Tina then pours some wine over Sophia from the bottle, following it up by throwing some left-over veg on her. Sophia's mouth is wide open in shock and disbelief. Tina then stuffs a sautéed potato into her mouth).

Bon appetite Queen Antoinette! Luke! I'm going to our special place now. Be there like real soon or we're history. (Tina then grabs the empty water jug, abruptly turns around and heads to the couple's table she took the jug from and puts it down). She stole my client, what a dirty low down stinking bitch, don't you think? I really wanted to dine here tonight with that gentlemen service user. He pays top dollar for services rendered an' all."

The couple look at her in shock freeze mode. Tina then quickly heads off before the waiter can get to her. He follows her to the door and stays there to make sure she gone, not just the premises but the vicinity as well.

Chapter 23
Wounds to Heal

Tina is sitting on a bench on the banks of the river Thames, in the urban city centre area. The moonlight is shimmering on the surface of the famous river and the stars are twinkling in a clear sky. A perfect moment if it was not for the sad events she had just been a part of. She is sobbing.

A few drunken yobbish youths head her way, they see her and all have a mischievous look about them. They get to Tina and see her crying.

"Crying are we, love? What's the matter, the Blob has ditched you for a thinner Blob? Well, what can I say, shit happens?" said one of the youths and laughs.

"Don't get too close, Robbo, she might eat ya'!" said another youth.

"Get lost, dick heads!" replied Tina without a hint of being scared of the louts.

The youths react to being called dick heads and at least one looks like he wants to turn verbal insults to a physical assault. It is easy to pick on and bully girls.

"It the filth! Coming this way, time to bounce homies," shouted one of the youths and they all run away. A Bobby on the beat can be seen within the vicinity but he is not too close. When you are drunk, it skewers your judgement, especially distance. This thankfully, leaves Tina all alone with just her sorrows to accompany her again.

After a while, Tina looks to one side and sees a figure coming her way. She looks sharp and a smile appears on her face but then quickly disappears again—like it has been overruled. The reason for this short-lived smile? It is Luke coming towards her, conjuring both love and hate feelings within her.

Luke finally reaches Tina and sits next to her on the bench, initially saying nothing.

"You came?" Tina stated after the very awkward silent period.

"Yep! Of course, I came, my princess," replied Luke.

"You came to me!"

"Yes, yes, yes! Look Tina, I'm truly sorry for all this. Right now I feel so gutted, so bad, so mean, I've even fallen out with myself over it. I'm begging you, please forgive me for everything, darling. I would say I have come to my senses but and hear me out before you say anything or react badly, I haven't. Because I haven't lost 'em in the first place, if that makes sense."

"What! (She then says to herself). Calm down, Tina, calm down. (Says to Luke). I'm already confused, don't make it worse for yourself Romeo, what are you trying to say to me? If it's a load of cobblers, I'll swing for you, I really will, be warned."

"Fair point. Let me explain. That—girl—woman isn't—wasn't—never will be my fancy bit on the side. I mean come on, me and her, we're poles apart, planets apart?"

"What was she then, something you bought from a tourist gift shop? Only the kind of gift one does not take home to show to the family or your existing girlfriend for instance."

"She was a plant—a spy for that slimy Sir Marcus. I'm almost certain of it. I first saw her—well, she first saw me back in that cafe—you and I had breakfast in a while back, the one where I asked about the coffee.

She showed a strange and suspicious interest in me, which I found really odd. Anyway, to cut a not too long story short, I played along just to get any good information out of her, links back to Bainbridge and Isabelle and that."

"So, what you're saying is she was playing you, but all along, you were playing her, at her own game? A game you seemed to be good at playing and enjoying."

"Precisely! But I didn't enjoy it. I mean, come on Tina, would an upper-class skirt like her ever look at me? Let alone, an instant attraction in a back street greasy spoon cafe. I sussed her out from the word go, then my suspicions were further backed up when she suggested we go back up north, you know, like leave London tomorrow. And the fake parents! What an amateur set up they were? They were actually quite funny, you would have laughed if you were there, Tina."

"Sounds like you've had quite the time, investigating this lady friend. Even been invited home to the parents, fake or not. Things move quickly in London.

Maybe that's why they call it swinging London. A good place to break even the strongest relationships and hearts."

"Well, nothing is broken between us, our bond is stronger than—bonds in a diamond structure, if I remember me school chemistry right. And like you just said, it was all in the name of the case and nothing else."

"Did you find out anything, from this posh tart, since you've had plenty of case time on it as we both know?"

"No, not really, but the fake parent's place, it's another address we could maybe follow up on. I don't think Isabelle will be there though."

"There is one thing, I—you need to explain to me before we put this sorry affair to bed."

"What, my sweet heart, fire away?"

"Why did you keep it from me? Why cut me out? We're partners in this, I would have understood, given you my blessing even—kind of—maybe."

"We are partners! But, call it spur of the moment or blurred vision, whatever, I made a decision not to tell you, which I now know was wrong, really wrong. Maybe I thought that if you did not know, my deception and depiction as a cheating boyfriend would play better, more convincing to her. I needed to look like I was totally smitten with her, a nobody dating a somebody, things like this don't happen in places up north.

I'm not going to meet the Duke of Wellington's great, great, great, great granddaughter on the night shift at the local bread factory, am I? And, if it does happen in swanky old London, then it's probably false, for reasons other than love. Like this time, she was stringing me along, part of an evil plan. Besides, I reckoned if I'd told you beforehand, you'd never have agreed to it. What sort of a girl would say OK to her fella asking to date a hot chick and have the cheek to call it work? Too improbable."

Tina, sitting and patiently listening to Luke, breaks into a smile and laughs. "Come here, my lovely. (She hugs him). You're not a nobody, you are a somebody, worth ten times the likes of her and her kind. You're forgiven but don't let it happen again. If we are to make our business work and more importantly, our relationship work, we must work as a team. No lone wolf shit— unless we both agree to it."

Luke, appreciating the hug, is beaming with joy. "Agreed! No more lone wolf shit, unless we both agree to it, just as you said."

"Yeah! I felt like hitting you—really hard when I saw you walking towards me. I was contemplating whether to hit you on the head or your cheating balls. Now I just want to kiss you."

"Glad to hear it, again. Listen, let's forget about the case for tonight and go back to the room for some making-up time, you feeling me?" Luke used words once spoken by Pops.

"I'm feeling you, literally. Although, the amount of time we don't spend on the case is all costing our paymaster client. We must update him one of these days, otherwise he might think we're amateurs or cowboys or scammers and we've skipped the country or something like that. Not good for a fledgling business."

"You're so right, I gonna ring him tomorrow, first thing. Tonight, let's work on our own critical case. One I defo know how to solve because you and I go way back."

"True, we do, but no more funny business or we ain't gonna go way in future! I really did want to hurt you, you know, both physically and emotionally, like you hurt me. I wasn't kidding."

"What can I say or do more, if I had a hat, I would have eaten it, right in front of you, here and now. Like the great Stan Laurel did from Laurel and Hardy."

"Oh, I was thinking, more—Charlie Chaplin."

"I'm with you, you'd have wanted me to do the fork and roll dance? Sure, I could've done that no probs."

"Not quite, slippery Simon, you wouldn't have got off that easily, I was thinking of the other one. I would get you to boil your leather shoes and eat them, laces an' all. None of the ones from Primark either, but your best ones from Next, that you got for your last birthday from your mum." Luke frowns, Tina smiles.

"I bet you didn't know that just like Michael Jackson and Moondance, Charlie Chaplin only made the roll dance more famous, it was actually invented by Fatty Arbuckle a few years earlier," Luke said all knowingly.

"Did Chaplin invent the boot eating gag?" asked Tina, thinking Luke might be thinking he's got the upper hand in this minor verbal tussle.

"Probably, yeah!" said Luke a little bit unsure.

"Then I win! Now, let's go home," firmly said Tina.

Luke is standing in a devastated, ruined London. Total destruction of a once mighty metropolis. There is a war on—a war between humans and aliens. The aliens, armed with far superior equipment and weapons are victorious. At this point in the conflict, they are mopping up the last bits of resistance in the UK.

The British Prime Minister is surrounded by all his aides and some military types, probably discussing unconditional surrender but so far, the invaders have shown little mercy or clemency to humans. Surrendering by the humans is the last ditch tactic left to hopefully have a chance to stay alive and avoid extinction and maybe live to fight another day. But the aliens seem to know this too so their policy has been to kill on sight! Total extinction!

Luke approaches a teen boy, gangster type looking. "Hey! How's it going little man?"

"It's bad bruv! Everything is gone, fam. We've lost, they've won. Nothing is left, totally bombed out, all hope has gone man. You know what, there is not one place left that sells Nike trainers anymore? Life is over, fam!"

Luke sees the Prime Minister's group and goes over. "What's the update on the situation, Prime Minister Sir?"

"Looks around you, young man. In a word, hopeless. No politicians' speech is going to fix this. Human life on earth is under real and present danger of becoming extinct, son."

"That bad, eh?" expressed Luke.

"You know what's funny in all this mess, it takes an apocalyptic event to get a politician to speak frankly and truthfully? Refreshing, isn't it? One positive is, the opposition can't blame me for this or my government's policies for once. I can't even stand here and belt out a heroic fight back speech and lead one last victorious battle against the aliens like in Hollywood films, no hero of the hour to call upon. God, I wish I could."

Luke has a smile on his face that suggests he has had an idea. "No sir, not like the Hollywood movies—but maybe more like small screen television! Excuse me sir, permission to try something."

"You don't need permission from me any more my son, society has broken down to a state of nothingness. Do whatever you want to, with my—our blessing. We've thrown everything at them, nuclear weapons don't even scratch the damn metallic paint on their shiny spacecrafts. Their force fields won't even let in the littlest microbes like bacteria and germs, so no hope there either; no 'War of the Worlds' solution to hope for. Like I said my man, this ain't the movies or a sci-fi novel. What have you got in mind young 'un, just out of curiosity?"

"I'm going to Captain Kirk 'em, sir. Don't worry Mr Prime Minister, Luke Woam is here to save the day, I've gonna have to flowcha now!" Luke replied and goes off towards the aliens.

The supreme alien leader is on the ground, probably revelling in the triumph of total and utter victory; the biggest knockout blow the world has had since the dinosaur destroying comet hit us approximately sixty-six million years ago. He is also surrounded by the usual stooges that linger around important dignitaries.

They are all wearing spacesuits with breathing equipment attached, their faces can easily be seen through the large clear glass visors. All of them, including the leader react when they see an unremarkable lone earthling figure approaching them. They let him come quite close, as they can see he has no weapons on him, plus he's looking very anti-threatening.

"Hello, alien beings, greetings from the few humans you have managed not to extinguish. My name is Luke Woam. I want to talk to you, please."

The aliens look on with amusement and astonishment, the leader speaks in alien to an aide, probably a translator. Then this aide addresses Luke in English. "The leader wants to know what is it you want to talk about, your imminent death in a moment from now, maybe?" The translator's voice is slightly electronic sounding due to being routed through equipment.

"That may be, but I just want to say something before you zap me. I am begging you to reconsider your actions. What I'm saying is, we don't need to fight with each other, we can greet each other not as mortal enemies but friends. Co-operation between species is more important than conflict, over time we can learn to trust one another, to find new ways to work alongside each other. All the knowledge you've gained can be shared with all our knowledge and together, with every other species in the entire universe, we can build a better life, a better world, a better universe, not just for now but forever more.

Create a long lasting bond that will serve not only us but our children, our children's children and so on. Together we are stronger, we become one, we'll have a society where peace, love and harmony between cosmic neighbours will thrive and prosper like never before. Fighting only leads to death and destruction. All it takes to achieve total paradise, a rock solid determination to endeavour towards harmony and peace and co-operation, is a simple yes. So, we're asking you, pleading with you, let friendship be victorious today and forever more."

The translating aide finishes translating all that Luke had said to the leader. Everyone, especially Luke, is attentively waiting in complete silence for a response. The alien leader's face is emotionless at first, then he breaks out into a smile, next he says a lot of dialogue to his translator. The translator is nodding furiously.

Finally, the translator faces Luke. "Our leader has been moved very much by what you have said. He agrees that friendship is the key to expansion, not war and conflict. We will cease all hostilities with the people of this planet called Earth immediately and work out ways to co-operate in a peaceful way. Our Supreme leader wishes to express our sincere apologies for the destruction caused to your planet that was done before we learned the errors of our ways. We apologise humbly. He also wishes to state that he likes his space suit temperature lukewarm, the weather here is not to his liking."

"On behalf of my people, I accept your apology and salute your momentous decision. Don't worry about the destruction, buildings can be rebuilt and they will. Let's just look forward to a new era of human/alien co-operation and friendship." Luke feels proud of this monumental moment in world history. He IS a somebody! In fact, he feels so noble and majestic and daring now, he has his eye on a rather nice looking female aide standing in the group in front of him. He goes forward, lifts up her visor and kisses her, a long sexy kiss, Captain Kirk style, before sliding down the visor again.

The female alien is stunned but looking rather pleased with the whole episode. Just like our earth man Luke, she probably thinks of it as doing her bit for intergalactic peace relations—make love not war, for once! After the kiss, Luke decides to head back but not before a last parting word, "Well, your supreme leadership, I have to go back and tell my people the good news, so I guess I'll have to flowcha!" Luke goes off with a big smile, having peacefully conquered the invading aliens and a sexy alien female to boot. What a man, what a man, what a maaan!

The alien leader says something to his translator. The aide replies in alien language, "Sorry my supreme leader, I don't know what 'flowcha' means, we have never come across that word in our fifty years of careful observation of this planet and all its known languages." The leader says something else to the aide to which the aide replies, "Of course my leader, we will at once add it to our records as a word of great importance."

Back with the Prime Minister's group, they witnessed everything and are pleased that 'their man' is still alive and breathing, plus walking back to them looking rather happy. The cross culture kiss did not go amiss either.

"Good God, man! Tell me he didn't just smooch one of the aliens?" asked an amazed Prime Minister to anyone in the cohort who would answer him.

"He did sir, now he really did Captain Kirk 'em. But I'm sure he did it purely because he felt he needed to for the good of humanity, just doing his patriotic duty. The wooing and seducing of the scantily-clad attractive alien females into submission always fell to Captain Kirk unfortunately, lucky bugger!"

Chapter 24
Back to It

Luke awakes feeling all happy and with a reinvigorated zest for life again. He has not felt this good for a while, not since just before Tina made a surprise appearance at the restaurant or less interesting but still significant, when he found out he had got a job. Tina also begins to stir to life in bed next to him.

"Hmm, I feel good. I feel as snug and cosy as Charlie's four grandparents in that teeny tiny little bed in the original and best 'Willy Wonka and the Chocolate Factory' film. I feel as good as if I had found all the five Golden tickets myself and during my private and solo tour of the factory, was told by Mr Wonka himself that I was the sole heir to his business. We sure needed that bonding session," buzzed Luke.

Tina laughs. "What a tosspot, have you been on the magic mushrooms or summat? I'll have you know there is nothing wrong with the bond from my end, Casanova. As far as I am concerned, it isn't and never was broken so isn't in need of a mid-relationship fix, until someone decided to break it!" replied Tina.

"Come on, Tina, cut me some slack will ya'. We've discussed that and put it to bed literally, bed being the operative word, I hastened to add." Luke puts on a cheeky, flirtatious smile.

"Yeah, OK. Now that we are working as a team again, what's the plan of action? The enemy have definitely made their move, I say we up the ante and start getting bolder."

"Just what I was thinking. I think we need to make another unauthorised visit to Sir Marcus' house, like inside instead of wasting time eyeballing the outside. He knows by now that we haven't called the police on him. So that might make him a bit less cautious, a bit more careless. Maybe he thinks we are some two-bit outfit who can be and have been, run out of town, with a flimsy plan like using that—ugly, femme fatale sort."

"We are a two-bit outfit, literally so. But we ain't scared or running, we're northerners, if anything, we are more fired up. I've got a haunch Isabelle might have been moved back to Bainbridge's house, going on what you just said. So, let's get ourselves over there lover boy, haste not waste."

"Really? Moving Isabelle back to the scene of the crime, you think so? But why would he do that?"

"What crime thrillers were you watching at home, whilst never having a job? It's called 'hiding in plain sight' Hercule. Bainbridge knows we've checked his place out and established she's not there, so he'll reckon that's the last place we'd look. But, we're too clever for him, his place is first on our list. We might be small time but we're a crafty two-bit outfit, too wily for that stuck-up toff, that's for sure."

"A bit like, between us, we know a little of everything, but much of nothing but we get by. Something like that, eh darling?" added Luke.

Tina just looks at Luke and says, "Hmm." She wasn't too sure what else to say to that. She got it right though, a little says a lot!

In Sir Marcus' house, Sophia and Sir Marcus are discussing the previous day's incident over breakfast. Butler Benson is busy being here and there, in and out, on his daily duties.

"I think we can safely say that our plan is out for a duck," conceded Sir Marcus.

"I wouldn't be too sure, darling. Although Mr Soppy Bollocks did leave to go after that—Gorgon, I know the damage is done, we just need to let it simmer and then come to the boil any time now. Let the smallest cracks become large and destructive," replied Sophia. "Trust me, sweetheart, you can rely on a woman's instinct, never fails."

Sir Marcus laughs. "My little pumpkin, if you only knew how these northern degenerates really behaved like. You really do need to venture out of merry old London sometimes—to the provinces. I'm sure I've mentioned it before to you that for them, affairs are part of their dysfunctional DNA make-up. A typical day consists of drinking, drugging up, arguing, swearing and fighting. Throw in a bit of house fire where they squat and that really rounds up the average day.

People like them break up and make up ten times a day with copious amounts of cheap alcohol and drugs involved at each stage. In fact, having multiple partners at the same time is a badge of honour for them and let's not even go into identifying the different fathers of the batch of kids each woman has up there and at least half the batch are mongrels, fathered by men from the dark colonies. I fear the two have already made up over a joint of cannabis and supermarket booze, no doubt. No, if anything, they'll be more determined than ever, probably start by coming back here to probe some more, trying to catch us unawares."

"What are you saying, we are defeated?"

"Never! Us Bainbridges never throw in the towel in a fight. My ancestors fought alongside William, Duke of Normandy. They were fighting the peasant Saxons back then too, just like we are now."

"Are we going to fight them? That is so primitive! I'm a lover not a fighter, darling."

"No, my delicate flower, it's what's called a figure of speech. And spare me the cheesy song lyrics. Just like my ancestors, I will use foot soldiers, expendable assets. It's time for that idiot Pops and his monkeys to earn their money. One thing is true, wannabe private Dick and his large side kick haven't notified the police because they know it's futile, a waste of time and they don't want to get on the wrong side of them. That is to our advantage."

"Why don't you just get rid of that damn girl you've got. Why is she still here? More trouble than she's worth, I'd say."

"Never to that too. Living in London is not cheap, my dear, you should know that. This girl is worth a lot to me, a ruddy fortune. She is quite rare you know, somewhat vastly superior and upper-class than the usual trash that Pops brings our way, especially from up north, some you can't even give away for free.

She is good business and when I do sell her, the beauty being all the money will be tax-free! Hardly going to declare her on the tax return forms, am I? (He laughs). Benson! Benson! (Sir Marcus shouts, knowing that Benson will be lurking around somewhere nearby). Call the monkey brigade, tell them to get over here right away!"

Benson appears in the room. "I heard you sir, you want me to call the King's Cross clowns." Sophia smiles at his description.

"That's right Benson, good hearing for a man of your age, I must say," replied Sir Bainbridge.

"Are you sure, sir, using them? Their single shared brain cell gets less used than the five pack cloth handkerchief set your father got as a present way back in 1963. Christmas cracker jokes are more sophisticated than them."

Sir Bainbridge has a chuckle. "Oh, those ghastly handkerchiefs, I remember them, I don't know why on earth my father kept the set. Didn't I ask you to wrap it up as a fuddle gift in the eighties sometime? Let's face it, fuddles were invented so people could get rid of all their unwanted and unloved items, like handkerchief sets."

"I did sir and you did indeed fuddle it out. But the recipient found out who gave it to them somehow and returned the damn thing to us and did not even want any money instead or exchange gift. I chose not to inform you of the trivial matter at the time, master."

Luke and Tina are sat on a bench in the city centre, both eating an ice cream.

"Expensive but really rather good, innit?" stated Tina.

"Yes, it is. I'll tell you what, the dearer waffle cone is always worth it, the extra pennies—well extra pounds down here," replied Luke.

"So, what's happened to our determined plan of action, gone for a Burton?" asked Tina. "Even though it was me banging on about not wasting time, so, I don't know why I just said that?"

"Nope! But no point rushing matters me thinks, I'm not just all hunky good looks, you know. The way I figure it, old Bainbridge will think his plan has worked, that we're on our way back home after our big, big bust up over that posh tart. Like we jointly sussed, the last thing he will be expecting is us popping up at his place, being all clever and that.

You see, these rich folk have way more money than sense. They need help figuring out which shoe to put on which foot, the nearest thing they come to a crisis is when their preferred medium-rare sirloin steak arrives on their plate as well done, it's the end of the world stuff for them, innit."

"That's team work in action, Jimbo. Two great minds at work, working together as one! I can see it too. He's probably out celebrating his cunning victory right now."

"Even better news for us. Less in the house for us to avoid, maybe just that crusty old butler. Things might be turning in our favour so who needs the help of lucky charms any more, we've got us!"

"Now that we are possibly facing real dangers, like powerful evil men and considering we are going to be doing this kind of work for the foreseeable future, don't you think we should take precautions?"

"Precautions? Like what, you not getting pregnant, contraception?" asked a baffled Luke.

"Give over, you dick! I mean like bullet-proof vests and pepper spray, you know, stuff like that. In the future like, when our business grows."

"Kevlar vests? Sweet pea, we're based in England, the north but still England, not South Central LA. Besides, you've seen the movies. Every time the hero cop, be it man or woman, dons a Kevlar vest, they end up always getting—"

"Shot to shit!" said both Luke and Tina in unison.

"Damn right girl and always in the heart area so pretty much would have been fatal. However, if they don't put on a vest, then they just get a—"

"Flesh wound!" both said in unison again.

"Damn right again girl and always usually in the arm, the non-shooting arm. A tiny scratch of a flesh wound usually that they quickly shrug off to go on and kill all the bad guys. So, tell me woman, do you not agree that Kevlar vests are bullet magnets in the movies and therefore dangerous?" asked Luke.

"Yep, they are kind of, strange innit."

"Besides, Kevlar vests are really expensive," informed Luke.

"You know what, sticking to movie folklore, instead of pricey vests, we could buy ourselves a chunky cig lighter each and put it in a pocket over our heart area; they always stop a bullet in the movies. A lot cheaper and smaller."

"Yes! Or one of those old fashioned, posh mans' metal pocket whiskey flasks. They also always stop a bullet too," burst out Luke.

"Wait! What about a big fat wallet, that'll work too?" suggested Tina with great joy.

"No!" said both in unison.

"Our wallets will never be that big or fat!" said Luke sombrely.

"Heroes never truly die in movies anyway, vest or no vest. Even if they do die in the first film, they always come back alive and kicking in the sequels," concluded Tina.

"Yeah, if the bad guys nuke the hero with an H-bomb, he'll—or she will—only toast some marshmallows on the heat of the mushroom cloud whilst surfing all the way to the evil lair on the back of the shock wave," added Luke.

Both laugh again.

"It makes you think though, doing jobs that are dangerous, we might never see Bolton again if it all goes wrong," lamented Tina.

"Down here in London, they might say that's a good thing, bloody snob nobs, that they are," replied Luke. They both laugh yet again.

"What I really could do with is a bloody sports bra right now," said Tina.

Luke smirks. "You can say that again, now I can see why they've been invented."

Back at the Bainbridge house, Pops and his three-man crew are waiting in the main room along with Benson. In comes Sir Marcus. Sophia has long since gone.

"Right you lot, I've called you here to watch over my house. All you have to do is deal with any unwanted visitors, intruders, specifically a skinny little runt with a northern accent and maybe his fat girlfriend. Use as much unreasonable restraint as you want on them, I don't mind. (The four of them just look at him blankly). Beat them up as much as you want! Get rid of them!" The four nod with joyous agreement.

"Oh them two, well it's about time boss, you've made the right decision letting us handle it. We're experts at disposal of trash. Luke Woam will be ice cold soon," replied Pops when he fully recalls who Sir Marcus is talking about.

"My boys know them already but I thought you sorted them out, history. That gorgeous bird Sophie did her thing to him. (Pops makes a hugging and kissing movement, his three mates laugh at this). You should see her guys, she's the most beautiful bit of skirt I've seen all year, apart from on the telly, of course! And get this, I was sitting next to her in a car and she was chatting me up 'cause she couldn't get enough of me." All four laugh again, Pops react with pride to the new found respect from his chums.

Sir Marcus and Benson look at each other with total disbelief.

"Not underestimating my opponents is how I got to the top, you fool. Leave the assumptions to me. All you four have to do is house sit, sit and hopefully have to do nothing, you must be good at that. I am going out for a while. Benson here, will be around, if you need anything call him, you are not allowed to just wander anywhere around my house any old time you wish.

Oh, you lot are only allowed to use the toilet for a number one and be clean about it, lift up the toilet seat. For a number two, go to the local fast food restaurants just a short walk from here. I'm off now, I'll see you later." To that, Sir Marcus goes off.

Luke and Tina eventually make it to Sir Marcus' house and wait outside the back of it, just far enough away not to stand out.

"Listen, Tina love, I know we have agreed to total team work but it would be better if I went in alone. I could slip in, move about stealthily, search and slip back out easily. If I get rumbled, being on my own will also work better when I need to scarper. What do you say, partner?"

"I say, a lot of that sounds like a carefully worded dig at my size and weight, yet again! Tell me, it ain't so?" firmly replied Tina.

"Of course it isn't, honey bun. Come on, you know what I suggest makes sense."

"Yeah, I know. A deaf person can tell you that. Off you go and Luke, my love, be careful. First sign of trouble, get the hell outta there."

Luke acknowledges this and proceeds to go towards the house. In no time at all he is at a window. This window is an old framed sash fastening one and Luke prises it open easily.

"Forgot to lock the window, Jeevesy old boy? Not doing your job properly, no 'butler of the year' award for you, sir."

Luke drops into the inside of the house without making much noise. He slides most of the window down but carelessly leaves a small but noticeable gap at a point where resistance to the downward motion appears. Now, the search can begin in earnest.

Luke can hear voices from the room Pops and his crew are in. He recognises Pops' voice and realises that his gang are present in the house too. "Shit! Shit! The four of them plus Jeeves, I didn't plan for this!" Nevertheless, he ploughs on and sees the path to the stairs is clear. He runs silently to them and goes up. Once up, he bypasses the master bedroom and instead goes to have a recce in one of the smaller bedrooms.

He goes in and his eyes light up immediately. For, lying right in front of him, on the bed, is Isabelle. He almost yells with delight but does manage to contain it. He rushes over to her. Upon examination in the first instance, he sees that Isabelle is not moving, just looking like she is sleeping. Luke stirs her and gets a groggy response. "Drugged! Of course." He continues to try and bring her around but Luke knows he is onto a loser with that.

Meanwhile, trusted butler Benson is, as always, on his house duty rounds. He pops into the room where Luke gained entry. The cooler temperature, noise and the gusts of wind all alert his attention to the slightly ajar window. He goes over and closes the window fully with a bit of force. He then stands there, pondering for a few seconds, thinking whether he had simply not shut the window on a previous occasion, which is out of character for him or something more worrying, like it was a means of entry for a possible intruder.

Pops and his crew are enjoying life in the fast and luscious fruitful lane. All four have drinks and all manner of quality foodstuffs on the table in front of them. Christmas come early for them!

Tommo puts a whole fried egg in his mouth and chomps away. "'Ere Pops, you certainly have all the right connections, bigwigs like this—what's his name—Burberry or Blackberry, something like that? You done well."

"It's Bainbridge! He's just another satisfied client of mine, one of many. I have all sort of clients, from ordinary geezers wanting to have a pop at some young pussy well away from the gaze of their clapped out wives, to royals and millionaire rich gits. I aim to please, that's why they keep coming back to me, five-star service, innit," boasted Pops.

Chayse drinks tea from a cup but holds the handle with only his thumb and index finger. "Frightfully nice cup of tea, Lord Pops, can you pass me the cucumber sandwiches and a jolly dollop of caviar, please." He laughs as do the others. There is no caviar present or cucumber sandwiches.

Tozzy picks up a magazine and looks at the front cover. "It says here, "Viscount Godfrey" on the front cover, must be this toff, dressed in all the pantomime gear. From now on, you can all call me Vis-count Tozzy." Obviously Tozzy does not know how to pronounce the word Viscount.

"In that case, I'll be—Earl Mozzy. Awfully nice to make your—acquaintances, your highnesses, Vis-count Toss pot!"

To that remark, Tozzy throws a small chunk of food at Mozzy.

"If you losers are all that, then I must be Lord king, Duke, Prince, General, Admiral, Super king, ruler of the world, Master of the Universe! (The others agree without contention). What I really am though, always been, is a mighty stallion, king of my own newly conquered super large herd, the alpha bleeding male.

I can bide my time in this cosy little set up we got here. You see chaps, old Bainbridge is only a year or two away from becoming a mule, I saw on telly that mules carry no seeds in their sacks—completely blank—sterile, like seedless grapes. I do wonder if they still get urges—you know—to do it—makes you think, don't it?

Anyway, with me, a stallion and his Lordship, a frigging mule, I'll be right in there pretty soon. Even those little blue tablets won't do much for him, might seek advice from that old codger butler of his, about wrinkly limp dicks. (His three chums laugh at this). It is written my friends, in my case, graffitied somewhere on a wall, that Sophia will be mine one day, I might even nobble the lady of the house, have a pop at her, Bainbridge's bit on the side as well."

"Then rightly so, this is the life boys, we have struck gold, super lucky," said Tommo, "but let me tell you my brothers about this guy who had the shittiest luck in the world. I knew him from way back in primary school. His name was—Kingston—Saul. Yeah, that's it, Kingston Saul.

Now young Kingston and I shit you not, he was black, well half black, probably still is (he laughs as do the others), but get this, he was black and a quarter Jewish, a quarter Paddy Gypo—and a fag—a right proper gay boy, what a combo to have! (Laughs very loud). I mean, if that isn't suicide stuff then I don't know what is, I give up." All four burst into raptures.

"What a mega bummer deal? A mongrel black, Jewish-Gypo, faggot gay boy! Forget suicide, I would have shot him myself back then and that would be doing him a favour!" confessed Mozzy.

Pops laughs and says, "In primary school? What with, your water pistol or would you have beaten him to death with your lollipop?" They all laugh together.

"What did he bring for his packed lunched? Kosher monkey meat bagel sarnies with a side of the old boiled Paddy potatoes?" joked Chayse, he did not want an answer. They all laugh again.

"And a ganja reefer to spark up at playtime no doubt, essential life stuff for them ain't it?" added Mozzy.

"'Ere Pops, do you reckon Lord Bumblebee snorts coke, maybe has some stash hidden in his neatly folded pyjama, sock and pants draw? They're all at it, aren't they, the rich folk," asked Tommo.

"Dope! I don't think so, maybe in America but not here, they're more sensible over here. I know they say, 'no dope, no hope' but in England, they get off on making money, legally stealing it with the help of the government and the feds from poor people like us. Only then do they dabble in a line of dope as a reward like, 'cause nothing is left to chance with them.

Why do you think we lose big time in the gee-gees and Bainbridge and his pals win wads of dosh at the posh race courses? They only wear those silly top hats to carry home their winnings," replied Pops. There is quiet amongst the motley crew—almost as if they are actually thinking deeply about all this.

"Guys, I need to take a royal dump. Do you reckon old Duke of Dork really meant what he said, that we can't use the bog to bust out a log?" asked Chayse. "Are the toilets too posh for the likes of us?"

"Just do it! He won't be back for ages, the pong will have long gone by then," advised Mozzy. "After you've used it, the posh bog will really be out of bounds for the rest of us that should please the squire."

"Why don't you drop one in the garden, keep him happy and fertilize the garden at the same time. We can say the butler did it, it's better than him murdering someone innit," joked Tommo. They all laugh again.

"Listen, guys. I've thought of another one, we can all be, Thunder, Thunder, Thunder Cats!" bellowed Chayse with great glee.

"Nah!" came the unison reply from the other three.

Back with Benson, his pondering time is over. He decides the slightly ajar window must be the result of an intruder and rushes off—his destination, the room with King Pops and his newly anointed noble knights. He gets there as fast as his old legs can carry him, bursts through the door and goes right up to the sitting down, well fed and watered foursome.

Pops looks at him. "Ease up there, grandad, you'll give yourself a heart attack. Blimey, we were only kidding about dropping one in the garden. Have you got us bugged or summat?"

"What? I got news for you lot, the guy the Master told you about, I think he is in the house. Go hunt him down, try upstairs first. That's where the girl is right now. All the doors in the house are locked, so he can't get out. Now go, move yourselves! He's here, I tell you," yelled Benson.

"What do you mean, Flash Gordon is here?" remarked Tommo, mimicking the voice style of the evil lady dressed in black in the Flash Gordon film. "I've always wanted to say that at the right time." He smiles like it has given him some long overdue satisfaction. Little did he know that the actual words are, 'What do you mean Flash Gordon is approaching?'

Chapter 25
The Chase

Luke needs to think fast. He knows he is on a timer, whilst in the house as old jobsworth Benson, will come upstairs sooner rather than later. He says to himself, "What do I do, she can't walk or move for that matter. I certainly can't carry her. Leave her? Shit! I have to leave her as she is."

Luke gently stirs Isabelle again, "Listen Isabelle, if you can hear me, I want to help you but unfortunately, I must leave you here for now, OK. I promise to come back for you. Just stay strong, princess." He then goes over to the door and opens it. He can hear a commotion downstairs, so goes into the landing and sees Pops and his crew coming up the stairs. "Oh bugger with nobs on!"

Pops sees Luke looking down at him. "It's him, that slimy twat we're looking for, let's get him and punch his lights out. He' alone, he hasn't got his gang with him." Pops added the last bit even though he knew it was not true about having a gang.

Luke needs to do the opposite of what he did earlier on—get out of the house quick time preferably in one piece. He looks around the hallway doors. He thinks quick, he remembers seeing a sturdy looking waste pipe running down from the frosted toilet window on the outside, the window itself was also sash opening.

He looks to locate the toilet, it is just down the corridor and heads straight for it and goes in and locks the door. That should buy him some extra time. He runs over to the window and manages to slide it open and looks out and to his great relief sees a nice solid looking old fashion iron pipe easily within reach distance to one side. As he is climbing out of the window, he hears loud voices outside the door and then hears attempts at forcing the door open. Luke ignores that and climbs onto the pipe grabbing on for dear life.

The pipe, probably Edwardian era, looks like it was made to last a hundred years—only problem with that is, it has most likely been a hundred years nearly since it was fitted. At least it is not one of those modern thin plastic ones. Well, beggars can't be choosers and Luke shimmies down this fat (but thankfully still) solid pipe most unlike a pro, he very cautiously and jerkily makes his way down. He has probably done this countless times in seconds flat, whilst wearing full body armour and countless weapons slung on his back—in computer games, but never for real, no! Eventually, he makes it to the ground, both feet firmly on terra firma.

"Oh thank God! Thank Allah! Thank the Sun god!" He looks up and sees the sticking out head of Pops looking down at him.

"You won't get away from us, shit stain! We'll get you, you'll see," shouted Pops. He looks slightly back into the room. "He's out at the back of the house, quick, let's move." Pops disappears from the window.

Luke runs away from the house towards the approaching Tina, she had seen Luke a bit late, exiting the house in the most unusual way, descending down a pipe. This obviously got her worried.

"Luke, Luke that was kind of real dangerous, guess you were rumbled in there."

"Yeah, and now, they're after me—us. We need to get the hell out of here right now. Come on!"

Luke and Tina run off, Luke looks back and sees Pops and his three stooges suddenly appear from a door in the rear of the house and run in their direction. Luke and Tina, being of this computer games playing, tech device savvy, burger loving generation, run away but not exactly like a bat out of hell! But that cuts both ways, Pops and his boys are hardly candidates for a cross country slog either, they have just spent a good deal of time stuffing their bellies with food. Kids and young people!—they're just not fit and healthy these days.

The chase is on—Luke and Tuna run down some main streets before turning down a side street. One thing both have on their minds as they are running, a vital requirement for this line of work it seems, is having excellent stamina and fitness and a good pair of running trainers. Something to work on in the future.

Pops and just one goon also turn down this side street—where are the other two goons? Anyway, Luke and Tina continue running down this side street, up ahead it narrows considerably as scaffolding, lorry size storage containers and safety fencing are in place on the buildings to the right of them. To the left of them is a high unscalable wall.

As the two run down this narrowed sectioned they see a road tarmac leveller heading straight for them. The other two goons are in the cabin, looking at them and laughing. So, Luke and Tina are now in a bit of a serious pickle. Behind them is Pops and one goon, in front is a demon road roller, driven by two maniacs, about to make them a permanent part of the road.

"How the heck did they get ahead of us?" gasped Luke.

"Oh Luke! We're done for. Finally, our luck has run out, deserted us when we needed it most. I love you, just wanted to let you know."

Luke does not answer straightaway, instead, on hearing the word 'luck' he grabs the lucky charm around his neck in his hand. "I wish for an escape route, we need a miracle escape right fricking now!"

Tina looks on in a bit of a confused state. Has Luke gone mad, a last minute breakdown, is he really pinning his hopes on the one thing he has always dismissed as superstitious nonsense? A flash sparkle comes from the lucky charm, unseen by both.

The roller is very close now, it will soon do what it is designed to do—flatten everything in its path, living or not.

"Luke, we're not getting out of this one in one piece or if we do, it's going to be one big flat piece of pavement pizza!" said a distressed Tina.

Suddenly, a gust of wind blows a large bin sack in the road slightly to the side of the hapless and helpless twosome. A man-hole in the road reveals itself to be underneath, then the cover lifts up to reveal a sewer worker man pop his head up from under it. "Oh dear, Stan, we've got the wrong one, this isn't the one we went down from."

Luke and Tina's faces light up. There, in front of them is an escape route, a miracle escape route.

"I don't—frigging believe it! Let's go!" yelled Tina.

The two waste no time bombing it to the man-hole. They almost push the worker down the hole. He protests but then just descends. Luke lets Tina go down first—what a gentleman, eh? She quickly disappears, Luke looks at the roller, it is so close now, he can smell the diesel and even feel the heat coming off it—but the worst is the sound of this behemoth death machine with its killer roller.

Luke shoots down the man-hole and just manages to mostly slide the heavy cover snugly in place but the last part of it is done by the roller's crushing forces.

The thud of that almost knocks Luke from his foothold on the rung of the side ladder of the descent well.

In no time at all, all three, Luke, Tina and the stunned workman are at the bottom with Stan.

"Ere, what's your game, you two? You can't be down here, authorised personnel only. It's not one of your tourist sites you know, you must leave now or I'll call the police!" said the first worker, who was at the top a moment ago.

"Not tourists, Eric, it's more likely to be one of those stupid university student stunts or dares or whatever they call it, they get sillier and more dangerous every year," added Stan, his colleague.

"Sorry mate, we're being chased by some muggers and this—well, presented itself so to speak and we took it. They had knives on them. We could have been killed. Now, we will leave, just point us in the right direction and we'll be all too glad to get out. So long as it's a man-hole far away from this one."

"Muggers you say, oh alright, follow us to the one we should have come out from anyway, nowhere near here, is it Stan?" Stan shook his head without speaking.

"Excellent, my friend, lead the way. Let's flowcha out of here! (They all begin their sewage tunnel trek, not exactly a walk in the park!). You know what Tina, one could say, we got out of the shit by being in the shit!"

"Give over, you joker! That's a shit joke!" replied Tina.

"Yeah, it's a stinker!" carried on Luke.

"OK, time out. Change of topic otherwise you'll keep on and on. I'm thinking there must be easier ways of earning a living than this malarkey. We very nearly got Ikea-ed, back there, my life flashed before me," said Tina with genuine emotion.

"Ikea-ed?" asked Luke.

"Yeah, Ikea-ed. You know—flat-packed. No one would have been able to screw-driver or Allen-key us back together again, no standing tall and proud. Thus, endeth the tale of Luke and Tina, died young and penniless." Tina and Luke chuckle, better than crying I suppose.

"What else can we do instead, no one is just going to hand us money because it's us? We're not blessed with any talent or star power. Sticking to Scandinavian things and money for nothing, you know that band Abba, they were offered a billion pounds to reform. A billion pounds! Just to do what they love to do. Now that's easy money.

They should reform and tour, eight billion people would have the pleasure of experiencing then once again. If I ever meet the two bearded fellas in person I would say to them, "listen Benny and Bjorn, we don't care how you look, perform or sound, just as long as you two can still play your instruments, the two ladies can still slip into those sexy outfits and sing too, then everyone's a winner, you boys have got to say yes". It makes a huge amount of financial sense, everyone takes it all; the Abba four take umpteen truckloads of cash to the bank and the rest of the world's population take pure musical heaven into their cherished memory banks."

"Oh! I just remembered. What was all that about, up top, just before we very nearly met our fate? I distinctly remember you putting all your faith into the lucky charm, the cheap and tacky trinket of false hopes, according to your Oxford dictionary description."

Luke does not answer straight away, he knows he is guilty of said actions. "OK, it was an unusual situation, wasn't it? I mean, who in their lives nearly gets run over and killed by a very slow moving twenty-tonne heavy plant machine. Near death incidents makes people—"

Luke gets cut up by Tina. "Hypocrites?"

"Well—that might be a tad too strong a word, my dearest. I was thinking more like kind of deviate from all forms of basic rational thinking. It makes them believe in—cheap and tacky trinkets of false hope!" Tina just looks at Luke, Luke looks at Tina, the silence is loud and speaks a thousand words!

Up above the miracle escape man-hole, Pops and his crew get the roller out of the way. They try to prise up the man-hole but it is firmly pressed in place and there are no good finger grab points, you need a special lifting hook.

"Fluky bastards! This is a right piss pot and a half of a situation! How can someone have so much fricking luck? Where do they get it from?" shouted Pops.

"We'll get them next time, Pops, nobody has that much luck. It'll be third time lucky—for us! Bad luck will strike them down with a vengeance, guaranteed," stated Tommo with confidence.

"Like yah' poofsta' friend Kingstaan, from waay bark maan," replied Pops in a Jamaican accent.

Chapter 26
Not Another Protest!

Luke and Tina emerge (sewage free) on the ground level streets of touristy London town. It feels good to them to breathe air that is not reeking of human faeces and all manner of rotting organic matter. Instead, they are breathing the only slightly more pleasant modern urban city traffic air—much more normal, familiar and acceptable. The footfall in the streets is much more than usual, even for London, the two finds themselves on streets near the very popular urban sprawl of Trafalgar square.

"What's going on, Luke? Why is it so manic here, police everywhere?" asked Tina.

"Look at all the hippies and young student types. Must be yet another demonstration or protest in the capital. I'm glad there is though, with so many police about, if Pops and his gang find us or even manage to see us in these crowds, they're not going to ambush us, are they, safe as houses me reckons?" replied a happy Luke.

"On the topic of safe, I also reckon we should maybe operate nocturnally, sleuth about on a night time."

"Night! We'd lose half the day that way. And it's scary at night. The same street goes from PG to X-rated just because of the amount of light it has or hasn't."

"Yeah, but operating at daytime, easier targets, we keep getting our heads bashed in—or nearly. It's like fish in the ocean. A lot of them only come to the surface at night time when it's much safer."

"That's because the fish are smart, they've learnt, haven't they? When they come up top in the day time, people keep making fish fingers out of them."

Tina giggles at this comment from Luke. "Worth thinking 'bout though, in the future, like."

"Maybe a bit of both, as and when needed, in the meantime, keep the st quo as they say."

"Yeah, I suppose,"

As they walk past the hectic, crowded scenes, a student type hippy approaches Luke and Tina. "Excuse me please, you two are young, we're doing a demonstration, cum harsh protest, cum riot if the police get out of order in trying to subdue us or restrict our right to free speech and protest. So, I was wondering if you'd like to join us by waving some banners for us?"

"What you protesting about, what are you rebelling against? And please don't say, "I don't know, whadaya' got?" to me," replied Luke, pleased with himself about knowing some movie trivia and being able to use it for the right situation.

"I was gonna, but now I'm not. Anyway, we're letting the government know about student feelings on cut backs in education, extortionate university fees, demise of student grants, about politicians butchering and medalling with higher state education in Britain. We're letting the establishment know in all the usual, normal student ways of course. Plus, anything else we can think of."

"Listen mate, I couldn't get out of school—education fast enough. Uni was not an option, I discussed with my careers teacher. If Tina and I go to Oxford, it'll be Oxford Street, not a street in Oxford. I sympathise with you geeks and nerds but I'm not one for being pressed gang into your cause.

Us two (he points to Tina and himself) have more pressing and immediate cut backs to our lifespan issues to deal with right now. So, Sorry about that, Bartholomew mate. But good luck to you and your mob, happy protesting or rioting, whatever tickles your pickle."

"That's alright, pal. Just leaves more petrol bombs and traffic cones to chuck for the rest of us! See you," answered the student hippy and he went off.

The two walk at good pace through the busy streets, all the time getting further away from the demo mob and the riot police.

"Isabelle, oh Isabelle, why did you have to make our first case so complicated? Why didn't you just run to your nearest smack head boyfriend's digs like all the rest probably do? Or run off with the paedo fairground worker when the fairground is in town, I mean how hard is it to track a fairground posse? Or, better still, run away to Blackpool, at least it has a beach and the only scariest thing there is the Pepsi Max," complained Luke.

... then we would not be paid so much, probably about a hundred-
ps!" replied Tina.

s the same the world over; the bigger the risk, the bigger the pay. But
...r mind all that, let's work out our next move. Oh! I've been meaning to
...nention something to you but been putting off as it might sound kind of bizarre.
It's been going round and round in my head since our little talk in the stink
tunnels."

Tina perks up a bit on hearing this, whatever could Luke mean? "Go on then,
I'm all ears and all for bizarre."

"You know this lucky charm of yours, well I think I might be changing my
stance on it, yeah—shock jock and a half! I think it might make you believe, it
is responsible for bringing good luck when you need it most, like make you feel
better having it than not having it. You know what I mean? The luck could well
be just blind coincidental luck, but in times of extreme stress, I now know I
would rather have it with me than not. Have something to pin your hopes on
other than God."

Tina looks at Luke for a few seconds without reaction or emotion. Then she
bursts out laughing. "Have you become a believer? What's brought this on? A
believer of lucky charms? It's about bloody time."

"Lots of times—well a few times, really. That's what I've been thinking
about. In fact, I wished for an escape back there with the roller and low and
behold, a man popped up from a man-hole and saved our hide. There were other
times as well but I'll tell you later."

"Well, it was five pounds super well spent, wasn't it?"

"Yes, yes. But, like I said, it might all be just very fortunate coincidences,
just good luck, in general, but I'm glad you bought it and let me wear it. You
wanted to hear me say that from the beginning, well now you have heard me say
it. I am becoming a believer of sorts, just like the cornerstone of religion."

"Good! What's our next move now that things are getting hot? Whatever we
do next is going to be crucial."

"Let's review the facts. The girl, Isabelle is in the house but drugged up. Sir
Marcus wasn't there when we were there not so long ago. The goon squad are
out here somewhere looking for us, at least for a while longer. I think we need
to strike whilst the iron is hot. You take a taxi to Bainbridge's house and wait for
me outside there, whilst I nip to the chemist and seek advice about how best to

revive a drugged up person, any over-the-counter wake up potions I can get hold of. We need her fully, physically alert and mobile."

"Why can't we just stick together, if it's not a silly question or suggestion, this is not a movie, you know?"

"No, it's better we split up, in case we run into Pops and his mates. Now, time is of the essence here. There's a cab over there, you set off, I'll catch you later, love, if I've not been arrested first because the chemist people have reported me for asking about knock-out reviving potions. Stay safe," said Luke.

"You too, my love. Oh, you're getting better at indirectly saying I'm in no shape to run from the baddies, but I'll—I'll forgive you again. I can't be bothered bloody running anymore or arguing with you," replied Tina. The two go their separate ways.

Luke is walking with determination in search of city centre shops in high end London. He is seeking out a pharmacy establishment. He is deep in thought about everything that has happened so far. He is conscious that the case of the missing girl is most likely nearing its conclusion one way or another. His awareness of his immediate surroundings is, therefore, not, let's say, up to military grade.

Pops and his mob of three, are sitting snugly in a line on a bench. In these modern times where the world's cuisine is right on your doorstep, the three are eating that all too British fast food dish of fish and chips, each one covered in mushy peas all contained in card board cartons. Looking for Luke and Tina has temporary been put on the back burner. Delicious food takes priority.

"You can't beat good old British fish 'n' chips. It's the business, lashing of mushy peas and you're in food heaven. Mind you, charging us fricking nearly nine-pounds for it is daylight robbery. Who do they think we are, Chinese, Arabs, Yankees?" retorted Pops.

"Yeah, they should have lower rates just for us proper English people. After all, London is ours, sometimes I go a whole day and I don't even hear anyone speaking English," added Chayse.

"You got a point there, Chasey, with all the foreigners living here and all the tourists, are there any proper white English people left in London, tell me that? I count the Irish as foreign too," further added Tommo.

"Well said, Tommy boy. You know that McDonald's advert on telly that says it only uses British and Irish potatoes in its fries. Well, to me Irish is foreign, they are using bloody foreign Irish potatoes, why can't they just use British potatoes instead of paddy ones?" replied Chayse.

"Those Paddies though, they do know a thing or two about spuds. They're champion potato munchers, it's their national vegetable. Maybe that's why McD's use—foreign—Irish potatoes," contributed Mozzy.

The non-multicultural accepting gang of four continue devouring their patriotic national dish with relish and hardly take time out to look up at their surroundings. Luke, absorbed in his own world of deep thinking is still oblivious to anything around him. So, it is unfortunate (like an unsuspecting tourist wearing a loose coat with deep pockets in an underground train carriage full of skilful pick-pockets), that he just happens to be walking towards the bench where Pops and his mates are busy stuffing themselves.

Pops stuffs a few pea-smothered chips and some fish into his cavernous mouth. For just a moment he happens to look up, then it hits him. For there, seemingly gift wrapped, is his quarry, his prey, idly walking directly in front of him. Pops' industrial spec mouth grinds to a halt as 'no idea' Luke eventually walks past him and beyond.

"Bloody fricking hell, that's the dipshit we're after. (He turns to look at his mates). Guys! He's right there, that Luke the puke guy. Let's get him!"

His three mates are a bit reluctant to get into battle ready mode, not only are they eating tasty hot food but expensive food at London prices.

"Come on, you dozy pillocks, move your arses!" ordered Pops.

His 'elite' troops moan and groan but lethargically get up from the bench, they all put their fish and chips cartons down on the bench. As the four are about to set off, a street cleaner nearby is giving them a dirty look. The four go up to him.

"'Ere mush, those fish and chips on that bench are ours and we definitely want them, so don't go getting any smart ideas about trashing them. We are just popping away for a few seconds that's all, important business and that. Leave them alone, got it pal?" growled Pops in a very persuasive and threatening manner.

The cleaner looks at Pops then looks at the bench a little way away. "You mean those fish and chips over there mate, rest assured, I won't be touching them, sir." The cleaner is grinning like he knows something the four do not.

The four look back towards the bench, quite pleased that the street cleaner is so amiable and compliant. What they see is not so pleasing though. For a gang of proper (as opposed to fake) homeless/beggar type looking elderly tramps are eating (and coughing/sneezing) away at their prized and pricey lunch.

"For frig's sake!" yelled Pops. He looks at Luke gaining more distance over them. "We'll do those tramps later, let's get our target first." They all run in the direction of Luke but they unwisely, maybe because of the sheer disappointment of losing their expensive lunch to a bunch of vagrants, make quite a bit of commotion.

The noise being made some way behind him, makes Luke snap out of his day dream world. He looks back expecting to see anything other than what he actually does see—Pops and his stooges running fast towards him. Once again and for the third time, he finds himself being chased by (and him running away from) Pops and his thugs.

"Oh shit with sugar on top! I thought London is meant to be a big metropolis, more like a small bleeding village?"

Luke now also runs off, dodging tourists, tourists and more tourists, as yet another 'run for your life' chase begins.

Luke, as always, takes to the side streets as they offer more hiding places and protection. He runs down another side street that serves as the rear traders' entrance and deliveries. Up ahead, he sees a door being opened and a little, skinny Bangladeshi restaurant worker appears with a bag of rubbish to bin, the worker first props the door so it stays open This worker goes over to the bins, he has his back to Luke and the door.

It does not take a genius to recognise an opportunity that presents itself on a plate with a sliced lemon on top for good measure. Luke swiftly flies into this doorway and very quickly closes most of the door (just leaves a small viewing gap), all before Pops and his mates appear on the scene. Luckily, for the chased, the chasers run by without a clue. Luke breathes a deep sigh of relief. However, just then, the Bangladeshi worker opens the door and gets a shock when he sees Luke standing there.

"Hey! What you doing there? This is private property, you leave now!" shouted the worker in an Asian accent. It is loud enough for the running crew to stop dead in their tracks and start heading fast back to the door, they are only metres away.

"Sorry mate, wrong door, it must be the next one down," replied Luke and comes out of the entrance and immediately looks to his right. He sees what he hoped he wouldn't—the goon party almost breathing down his neck.

"We've got him!" shouted Pops in a very satisfying way. Also, he is probably glad the chase did not last long.

Luke, again had fast, make or break, thinking to do. Run or—close and lock the door where he is standing? He decides to do the latter. Luke pushes the angry worker out of the way into the street where he falls over and he bangs the door shut. It is one of those Yale locks so Luke hopes the worker does not have a key on him. Most workers normally do not, as they just make sure the door cannot close by propping it open or jarring it, just as this worker had done. He then starts to move some cooking oil drums against the door.

Outside, Pops tell Tommo and Mozzy to go around the front of the restaurant to block Luke escaping that way. He turns to the worker who has now got up. "Tell me you have a key for the door Gandhi!"

"Yes, yes, I have key. I open," said the frightened worker and he indeed produces a key and unlocks the door and pushes to open the door but it does not budge much. "It is not opening, something behind door!"

"Out of the way, Gunga Din!" ordered Pops and pushes the small-framed, eight-stone worker out of the way but a bit too hard as he falls over again, bangs his head and gets knocked out. Pops and Chayse looks at him and laugh. Pops then starts pushing hard on the door himself.

"Help us out, Chaysey you lazy twat! Push hard, give it some welly."

Together, the combined forces are too great for the barricading oil drums and the door gives way. Pops and Chayse run inside. They go through the corridor and beyond.

Luke makes it into the customer seating area, he is just about to head for the main front entrance door when he sees Tommo and Mozzy enter the premises. He looks back and hears commotion and voices of Pops and Chayse behind him. He is trapped! He looks around and sees steps going upstairs. He darts for them and goes up. On the first floor, he sees more customer seating tables and toilets. No real escape or hiding places here.

He sees some more stairs and go up again before his hotly pursuing foes can get to him. Nothing doing on the third floor either except a mostly empty unclean floor space with absolutely no hiding places. Luke goes upstairs again but he can see it is the last set of steps, end of the line after that, nevertheless, he goes up and almost falls through the door at the top into bright daylight. To his little surprise but huge disappointment, it opens up to a flat roof, with nowhere else to run, except maybe, run out of options.

Luke runs to one end of the roof, edge of the building and looks down. It is a long way down, no way anybody can survive a fall from that height. He turns around and sees Pops, Tommo, Mozzy and Chayse bursting through the roof door much like he did. They all look around but it does not take more than a few seconds for them to locate Luke's whereabouts, conveniently standing where they would want him anyway—the dangerous edge. The roof entry door slams shut and it is one of those where it can only be opened from the inside.

"Finally, we've got him cornered. Been waiting for this a long time. Come on guys, time to conclude this sorry ass business deal that's been giving my arse an itch. One of those fricking arse itches you always get in public places where it's impossible to scratch the damn thing," said Pops as he and his goons walk in a rather slow pace now that their prey is close and seemingly trapped. They get within a metre of Luke and form a semi-circle around him.

"Don't do anything stupid boys, this doesn't involve you lot, my beef is with your boss, your buyer, Sir Bainbridge. All I want is the girl back, that's all. We can resolve this without any malice or resorting to skulduggery," pleaded a nervous Luke, rather (hopelessly) hoping a pep talk about morals and common sense will penetrate the thick skulls of his opponents.

"Malice, skulduggery?" Laughs Pops. "Who uses words like that nowadays? Mind you, who has a piss take name like Luke Woam either? I have my Paninis lukewarm. (His chums laugh). We're not going to malice you or skulduggery you, we're simple folk down here in the south, we're just going to chuck you off this here roof. It's the London way!"

"That's an offence, you're talking of committing a murder! I'm making a citizen's arrest on you four, so, put your hands up and follow me to the police station. Right now!" firmly said Luke and puts his right hand into his pocket lightning fast, causing Pops and his goons to worry and flinch back, as if they were expecting Luke to pull out some sort of a weapon like a knife or a hand gun. In actual fact, it is only a couple of tissues which Luke proceeds to wipe the perspiration from his forehead.

The four goons, realising the immediate situation is not as dangerous as they were envisaging, burst out laughing, to Luke's confusion.

"Give me that! (Pops snatches the tissue bunch from Luke's hand and throws it over the edge.) Oh, we're quaking and a trembling in our boots, Rambo! We're gonna cry all the way to the chip shop! I'll tell you what is going to happen, even though I let the cat out of the bag and told you a few minutes ago but you were clearly not listening. We are going to throw you of this bloody roof any second now.

So far, you've had so much fluky good luck and fortune, I wouldn't be surprised if the shit in your pants that you're shitting in right now, comes out pink and smelling of roses. Well, I've got news for you, private Dick, luck won't save you this time, you'll be needing a miracle ripped right out of the pages of the bible to save your ass. Got any last words, to jot down in your little black flip flop case book like, if you need a pencil just ask?" Pops and the three goons laugh.

"Just two, yippee-Ki-Yay. Why don't you guess the second word? You can look at each other for a clue as to what it is," replied Luke. In his last moments, his film trivia knowledge does not desert him. Plus, he can be as daring as he likes with his words, his fate is sealed it seems.

Pops and his crew stop their smirking when they hear Luke's reply, they do not get angry over it; after all, they are ready to enact their punishment, the ultimate punishment anyway. Or maybe they could not figure out the second word between them.

"Push him over, guys. This is what's known as case closed, prick Dick."

Pops lets his goons commit the actual offence, which they willingly do. Luke is pushed off the roof edge and down he goes. Of course, Luke protests as he is being pushed but he is no match for three men.

The four goons gloat at the falling Luke. "Let's see if he sprouts wings and flies off like a bird before he hits the deck? It's about time decent folk like us got some good luck! Oh, damn! I forgot to get my book back off him. Never mind, I'll get it when we go down, it'll be easier, he's hardly going to object, is he?" mused Pops and chuckles.

Luke feels the mad rush of wind in his face as he is 'dive-bombing' towards terra firma. It will only be a matter of seconds now. Crazy thoughts enter his head like suicide jumpers and their last moment/feelings/senses. Then quite strangely, the topic of gravity and Newton and a numerical value of 9.81m/s^2 flashes in his head. He is, even when plummeting towards his death, is annoyed that a science lesson would be his last thoughts. What is really annoying him though, is he never remembered these things at school or exam times, now it is all pointless. Then—it comes to him. The lucky charm! Yes!

This is the critical time to really dump the slightest bit of scepticism once and for all—well, the last seconds or so of his life. He has to believe in it like devotees at Lourdes do. This is the extreme moment of stress he was on about to Tina; rather have it than not! He grabs the charm in his hand and shouts, "I wish

I survive this fall, something to break my fall, instead of my bones! I need a miracle now, now godammit, now!" Luke, still manages to quote movie lines even in the dire situation he finds himself in. A true movie fan to the end.

Pops and his mates are still looking down, they are not the types to be upset with a bit of bloody gore, in fact, they are revelling in the spectacle. Then, as they look, a medium sized open flat-bed truck suddenly turns a corner and drives towards Luke and stops directly underneath where Luke would impact the ground any second from now. What is even more amazing, it is loaded twenty deep with industrial sponges, probably for the furniture industry.

Luke lands smack in the middle and bounces off and lands, also amazingly, on discarded empty boxes conveniently stacked a little distance away. He survives! He is unscathed! He gets up with only a bit of a slight daze. He looks up at the four rent-a-villains on the roof. "Hey guys, nice hanging with you, it's been a blast for me but I really must flowcha now, got a bit of unfinished business with Sir Marcus Bainbridge. I'll tell him you said, "hello". Oh, be careful standing there, you might fall off!"

He hurries off. The sponge laded truck drives off as quickly as its fortuitous arrival. The four at the top, especially, Pops, shout with great anger and annoyance at the top of their voices at Luke.

A minute or two later, Tommo runs over to the roof door and finds there is no handle to open it on the outside, the door is not only locked but solid, after all, it is a security door. They are trapped on the roof. "Guys! I hate to have to tell you this but—"

Chapter 27
The Rescue of Isabelle

Luke, with determined haste, is now in sight distance of Sir Marcus' house. He knows that Pops and his goons will also be heading this way, in a little while of course.

Tina is waiting outside the house, just as Luke had asked her to.

"Come on Luke, where are you?"

Suddenly there is a voice behind her, "Here I am, since you're asking." It is Luke's voice, he has arrived on the scene without Tina noticing.

"Thank God! Nothing happening here yet, all is quiet. Where are the things—stuff for Rachel, the revival juice? Glad you weren't arrested," said Tina.

"Ah! Ran into a slight problem back there. Pops' gang eyeballed me and gave another of their famous chases. Anyways, I managed to shake them off for now but they'll be blundering their way here real soon, or even as I speak. Although, I sincerely hope not so quick as that, however, we do have to move quick."

"Good, 'cause it's all boring so far here, no movements either in or out, just occasional sighting of that busy butler from the windows. I don't think he ever stops, must be a robot or something, the real human one probably died years ago and Bainbridge must have replaced him with a machine."

"I'm beginning to like boring, boring is definitely safer. Also, if I ever get rich and buy a mansion, I'll want someone like Benson the butler, he does seem to do the job he's being paid to do, he's no slack Jack, that's for sure. Maybe we could have him on our team, robot or not?"

"Erm—no thanks. Running is something we've discovered the hard way is a skill you need for this profession; the ability to run a mile in five minutes. With Benson, no way, more likely being able to spit and polish five silver ornaments in one minute."

"Yeah, I was only kidding, sweet pea. Come on, let's rescue that poor mare Isabelle before the goon squad reinforcements arrive."

The two go towards the house, make their way to a back door which they find is unlocked, probably from the time Pops and his goons used it to exit the house (that Benson had not got round to locking yet). They go right in and waste no time going upstairs towards the bedroom Luke had seen Isabelle in—always weary of Benson, the super butler at all times though.

They quietly get to the door and open it slowly, with no creaking noise. Tina starts filming everything on her phone for evidence. Through a gap of about two centimetres they see the elusive butler Benson, holding a syringe in the air and ejecting the excess air and liquid from it in preparation for administering into Isabelle, who is making some murmuring (coming around) noises.

"Stop right there, jobsworth, your evil game is up," shouted Luke as he bursts fully into the room and runs over to a very much startled Benson.

Tina also fully enters and is still filming away. Luke pounces on Benson and they have an old fashion struggle, the syringe gets flung away to the floor. Since Luke is far younger and stronger than the much older Benson, the fight is hardly a 'Wrestlemania' must watch.

For Luke, it is basically like having a 'free punch' many times over. For that reason, it is over shortly after it begins. Luke, not realising his impact strength on a much older man, must have hit Benson a little harder than he intended to as he falls down unconscious. Both Luke and Tina look down at the still body of Benson on the floor.

"You haven't killed him, have ya', he's an old man?" asked Tina, perfectly reasonably under the circumstances.

"God! I hope not. Can't have done. Better check anyway. (Luke bends down and goes about checking for signs of life. He smiles a huge sigh of relief). The old codger is alive, just knocked out, that's all. (A relieved Luke gets up). You could say he's sleeping on the job, must be a first for him. Anyway, out there you was saying he's a bloody robot—a terminator—absolutely will not stop and that. I've stopped him."

"He is—only he's the terminator's grandad—old and slow." Both Luke and Tina have a chuckle.

Tina had filmed most of the events that happened before hand but not obviously the knockdown. "He'll be back, no pun intended! He'll live to serve his master in prison. Probably wash his Lordship's back in the shower."

"A well washed back is the last thing his Lordship will need to worry about when in the shower room. Come to think of it, even Benson here might need to worry, after a long stretch some prisoners aren't so fussy. Charge of the rear light brigade stuff!"

"Let's see to Isabelle, I'll film her a bit, whilst you get her," suggested Tina, remembering they were on borrowed time here.

Luke grabs Isabelle, who is better than before, much less groggy.

"Wha—what's going on? I feel awful. Where am I?" asked Isabelle. Probably the first time in a while she is not fully under the influence of anaesthetic intoxicants.

"My name in Luke, this here is my partner Tina, we're here to help you. You—we must get out of here, it is not safe for you or us to be here. (Luke supports Isabelle as he makes her stand up). Good girl Isabelle, start walking."

The three, slowly begin their journey out of the house. They get to the top of the stairs, make their way down until they are just a few metres away from the front door.

"Nearly there, you two. Just a little bit more girls," said Luke slightly in an optimistic mood.

The front door opens and unfortunately not by anyone from the inside. The three inside stop and look on with true dispiriting disappointment. Either it is going to be Sir Marcus or much worse, Pops and his mob. The answer comes quick. It is Sir Marcus accompanied by Sophia.

"What on earth is going on here?" shouted Sir Marcus.

"I've just untied and ended you sweet little business deal," replied Luke with great satisfaction.

Sir Marcus, after overcoming the initial shock, starts to dart off to the side but Luke manages to act even quicker. "Oh no, you don't, pal." He lightning fast passes Isabelle to Tina, who grabs her and he pounces towards Sir Marcus. Now, Sir Marcus is no Benson, he dodges and moves out of the way of the fast advancing Luke and runs towards a nearby room. Luke thumps hard against the wall to one side of the door. Sophia runs after Sir Marcus.

Luke steadies himself after that dizzying hard encounter with the wall. "That didn't go as planned. He bloody moved out of the way."

"What did you expect him to do, you wally? Get him, he's in there!" yelled Tina, supporting Isabelle on her left side and filming with her right hand.

Luke runs towards this room and goes in. He sees Sir Marcus loading a long-barrelled shot gun with two pellet cartridges. Sir Marcus clicks the gun shut thus enabling it ready for use, ready for its purpose—to shoot at his intended target. However, to shoot, you need to point, take aim and fire and all this takes time.

Sir Marcus is in this process when Luke again pounces on him, this time more successfully. The two tangle and wrestle away as a single body and in this tussle the gun fires, fortunately it is pointing upwards and only causes damage to the ceiling. It fires again in the struggle a second or two later. Again, the roof bears the impact. This dangerous situation is more than Sophia can stomach and she now feels her best interests lie well away from this room, well away from this house. She scarpers quicker than a house burglar running from an armed trigger-happy American homeowner.

At some point, the gun is flung well away from the two, a relief but it had spent its two round capacity anyway, so it can only be used as a metal whacking rod at best now. Eventually, youthdom triumphs again in this 'non-Titanic' fight. Luke, with his superior strength and agility, overcomes Sir Marcus, he punches the older man squarely on the face and this proves to be the decisive blow. Sir Marcus goes down like a sack of potatoes and Luke is the victor—but it is a Pyrrhic victory.

Luke is exhausted and shaky, this was an energy sapping semi-brutal fight that involved the discharge of a firearm—although thankfully harmlessly. This most definitely had not been a game fight being played on a console, 'game over' does not mean it is a temporary pause to stock up on drinks and snacks before pressing 'play' again.

Sophia runs past the watching Tina and the still groggy Isabelle.

"Hey! Stop you little rich bitch hooker! You're going down for this!" yelled Tina, as that is all she can do whilst holding onto Isabelle but Sophia is hardly going to listen.

"Hardly, you ignorant slapper. I'm not going down—I'm going out," yelled back Sophia as she makes a quick exit.

Tina now thinks quickly, she feels she needs to contribute more than just propping up the unsteady body of Isabelle in this incident, plus she heard two gunshots in a room in which three people went in and only one came out of. She puts Isabelle down on a nearby chair and runs over to the room with Luke and Sir Marcus in.

She only pops her head in to see the situation cautiously and with great anxiety. When she sees Luke standing and Sir Marcus on the floor still, she is mightily relieved and goes fully in and over to Luke. "Oh thank God! I heard shots and feared the worst, are you OK my love? You haven't killed him have ya'?"

"Yes! I mean yes, I'm fine and no, I haven't killed him, miraculously. Although he did his best to kill me I think, the bastard," replied Luke. "Just for the record, Tina my love, I don't set out to kill everybody I have a fight with. I just nearly got blown away by a double-barrelled shot gun, for real, no blanks."

"At least it wasn't a Mark II Lee Enfield British Empire rifle, eh?"

Luke makes a smug face. "That's not funny, Tina. I could be laying on the floor looking like a human colander."

"Was I being funny? I wouldn't dream of it! I'm mightily relieved that it's you being alright and his dickhead nibs being knocked out, laying on the floor. Anyway, moving on, quick update, I'm going after your ex, that posh tart, she's done a runner and Isabelle's just out there sitting on a chair, resting but recovering quick time. See you later, darling." Tina darts off without waiting for a response but not before saying, "Might want to reconsider that bullet-proof vest thing!"

"Tina, Tina—wait!" Luke shouted but in vain.

Luke looks down at the still body of Sir Marcus. "I've never had a single fight in my entire life and now I've had three in a matter of a short while. Now, what would a gumshoe do with two badass villains?"

A short time later, Luke and Isabelle, who is much more alert and physically independent and walking now, are at the front door.

"You good to go, Isabelle?" asked Luke.

"Yes, thank you, I'm good to go. You saved me, helped me, you and your— girlfriend, is it?" replied Isabelle.

"Girlfriend and partner. We are a missing person finder outfit. You father, your family, hired us to find you. Glad he did. You're safe now."

"Oh—my family—I bet they're really piss—annoyed at me for doing this. You know—I dread going home but also can't wait to get home at the same time."

"It OK, your family can't wait to have you home as well, that's a fact. I regularly update them—sometimes and they are really concerned about your welfare."

"That's good to hear. What have you done to—Lord Numbnuts?"

"Oh, him and his servant Benson are—let's say—incapacitated at the moment. They won't be going anywhere anytime soon. Not even the Grand Old Duke of York's ten thousand men can save Bainbridge's royal ass from what I have got planned for him.

Anyways, talking about going—we need to flowcha out of here pronto. My partner, Tina is chasing down that posh tart right now, she's certainly an indirect part of this ring of child exploitation. We need to find them sooner rather than later as Tina is likely to make chopped liver out of her—scrambled eggs out of her—pummel stone her, you get my drift?"

"Loud and clear but what do you mean?" asked a confused Isabelle.

"Hit her! Beat her up senseless! Northern style."

"Oh! I see now. There is a mismatch about the two, total opposites in more than one way."

"What do you mean?" This time it was Luke doing the asking.

"Isn't it obvious? Big difference in body shape and weight—looks, if you don't mind me saying."

"Absolutely not! There is no comparison. Tina has been called the 'Bolton Babe' in her time—mostly by me. Body shape, eh? She does makes clothes look good when she wears them, I must admit, looks even better without them but let's say no more about that. (He makes a raunchy expression, Isabelle tries not to think about it). You're dead right, Isabelle; Sophia has nothing on my Tina, in any way, shape or form. Anyway, it's time to vamoose, come on, let's flowcha." The two then leave the house.

In the fight room, Sir Marcus is conscious but laying on the floor, behind a sofa so out of easy sight, well and truly tied up so that he can only wriggle like a line-caught hooked fish, his mouth is taped up too with only a functional sized breathing hole pierced in the middle. Upstairs, Benson is tied much the same way as his master and out of easy sight, he is moving less than Sir Marcus, due to his age maybe.

Chapter 28
Now This is Wrestlemania!

Tina is indeed hot in the pursuit of Sophia. They run and run and run. Now, just like any modern urban citizens of today, only running a short distance feels like doing a marathon. It is like asking a modern day school student to write a small paragraph comprising of only three or four short sentences—they start complaining about hand fatigue and flicking their hands about as if in agony. Then it is not surprising that both ladies are very quickly cream-crackered, the duo's run slows to a quick paced walk. Tina is almost upon Sophia as Sophia finds out to her surprise when she looks back; all the running in the recent past has made Tina a little bit fit! The chase finds the two enter a building site that is in full swing—lots of activity and builders working away, a very common sight in London, the skyline is adorned with tower cranes.

Sophia runs into the typically muddy yard floor of the construction site and steps right into a shallow ditch filled with highly muddy water, which slows her down. Tina pounces on Sophia just then from behind and both hit the deck hard, right into the muddy pool causing it to splash and cover both of them.

In seconds, they look like creatures from the 'muddy lagoon', with only the whites of their eyes and teeth still white, more Sophia's than Tina's. Thus, begins a female mud-wrestling match that usually draws massive paying crowds in certain countries. Here, the builders, all of them, stop building and start watching this free entertainment. No one makes any attempt to stop the two mud-plastered female combatants from going at each other hammer and tong.

"Think you can steal my fella? Well, think again, Lady Chatterley, he doesn't go for sluts like you, whether cheap or expensive," shouted Tina as she grabs Sophia's hair and pulls her down into the muddy ground pool. Sophia is also screaming and yelling.

"Get off me, you peasant bitch! For your information, I had your grotty fella eating out of my hand, he saw a real woman in me and he wanted it! Hell! Look at you, he probably dated me because he just wanted to be with a woman for the first time!" replied Sophia, still managing to spit out acerbic comments. Sophia too, produces some neat fighting/wrestling moves of her own on Tina, despite her big weight disadvantage. Is it due to some neat moves she 'engages' in with her more demanding clientele?

The builders are enjoying this so much, some manage to rustle up refreshments such as drink cans and bags of crisps, but thankfully, no pot noodles. There are even some members of public, mostly men but some women too, rolling up and watching, maybe bringing back memories from past holidays in the far east? None of them stop the rumble in the urban jungle either!

The mud fest tussle continues as both in turn get the upper hand briefly, only to relinquish it a second later to the other. The battle of the north verse south is even, the 'Roundhead' is an equal adversary to the 'Royalist' or the 'Saxon' is an equal match for the 'Norman' or for the strike, the 'Briton' is equal to the 'Roman'. Luke's predicted assessment is not as accurate as he assumed—there is no chopped liver anywhere.

"Why don't you just do what you're good at, steal my jewellery and run off, buy yourself some burgers or a family meal deal bucket just for yourself?" quipped Sophia, as she wipes some liquid mud from her face area.

"Listen Godiva, I pay for my food with my own money, not with money from some woman's husband! Do you get Scooby snacks from the sugar daddies for extra special, extra dirty favours?" snapped back Tina.

"Oh you offensive cow, time to carve you up like a spit roast hog—you—ten-dollar Tallulah!" barked Sophia as she took offense at Tina's remarks.

"Oh yeah? And I'll crush you like a beer can, chew you up and spit you out, flatten you just like a takeaway carton, you spindly insect!" roared back Tina. Both then launch themselves yet again at each other. Tina's weight has the advantage here at last, Sophia gets rebound to the floor and Tina dives down on top of her.

The builders/on-lookers clap with delight to see such entertainment for gratis in a super expensive city, where everything has a price tag, only the air is still free, no inhaling tax on that yet!

Meanwhile, Luke and Isabelle, through logic, common sense and the noise of the crowds, home in on the building site. It proves a job getting past the people who are naturally reluctant to give up a prime viewing spot. With determination they get to the front through some gaps. Luke surmises the cause of this would be Tina and Sophia arguing or more likely in fisticuffs but he certainly was not ready for what he and Isabelle do see before them.

"Oh bloody hell! How on earth did they end up in a fricking mud-wrestling match?" Luke asked himself.

"I don't know but—go on—what's your partner's name, Luke?" asked Isabelle.

"Tina."

"Go on Tina, smack that bit—witch up!" shouted Isabelle.

"We've got to stop it, Isabelle, like right now, not cheer them on. You wait here," said Luke then he goes forward to the two warring individuals and stands just short of the mud pool all whilst being careful not to get splashed on. "Stop this right now! Tina get away from her!" Many in the crowd shout 'boo!' and 'spoil sport' but Luke ignores them and continues in his unpopular quest to end this public spectacle, something the crowd failed to do so far, by choice. Some empty cans and items get thrown at Luke but again he endures that.

Tina and Sophia are still at it blood and guts style—is it a desire to get one over on the opponent OR is it the adulation of being a 'star performer' in front of an admiring crowd, baying for blood in the arena?

Luke decides it is time for more assertive action. He needs to get down and dirty, he need to step into the mud-fest. This he does by moving in to grab Tina and pulling her away from her opponent, who backs-off too.

"Tina, we've got to go now."

"Yeah! I'm about done here anyway," replied Tina.

Luke looks at Sophia. "If I were you, I'd get back to my sugar daddy."

Sophia does not reply, instead, she waddles out of the mud pool and runs out of the site. The crowd half cheer and half boo as they are denied a bloodbath conclusion. Some are starting to disperse.

"Why did you let her go? Even gave her some advice?" asked Tina.

"I want her to go back to Bainbridge's house. I've an idea about how I want them to get their comeuppance. It's way better than calling the police, those types of people never serve any real time behind bars anyway. Even if they do, they end up spending about a week or two of a six or seven-month sentence inside, in a five-star cell as well. The only thing denied them is a steak dinner and a heated swimming pool. My justice for them is the common man's justice, way-way better, you'll see. But right now we need to clean you up, come on, I've an idea about how we do that as well."

Luke, Tina and Isabelle are standing in front of Piccadilly Circus fountain. Tina falls into it as tourists dive out of the way, many others look on in disgust. Tina swishes about like a toddler in a paddling pool, the mud has not yet hardened so it comes off easily. After a short furious splash about, Tina is now mud free but very wet, the fountain water has turned muddy. A good swap/transfer of mud and water from Tina's point of view. Some tourists, especially, the Orientals, are doing what they do best, filming and photographing away. For the second time today, Tina is the object of a crowd's adulation and attention. Loving it large!

"Listen up, girls. We need to act fast. Isabelle, we are going to have to leave you alone for a short while in a safe public place. Tina and I need to sort something out really urgently, then we will come back for you, is that OK with you?" announced Luke.

"Yeah, of course, you do what you have to, I'll be OK to wait," replied Isabelle.

"Good! Tina love, I need you to again head for Bainbridge's house and wait outside for me there, just like last time. You'll soon be able to change your wet clothes too."

"Yeah, will do, but where will you be?" asked Tina.

"I need to sort out Pops and his playmates first."

"What? On your own, how ya' gonna achieve that?" asked a worried Tina.

Luke grabs his lucky charm in his hand so that Tina can see it. "Say hello to my little friend," replied Luke, mimicking the famous line in 'Scarface' complete with the accent. "For reals, with a little help from this."

Tina looks at Luke holding the lucky charm in his hand and being overly optimistic and off the scale unrealistic. "I was hoping you were gonna say something about a little help from a secret army you've got hidden away somewhere, but hey, go for it!"

Chapter 29
All Stops for Pops

Luke hurries in the busy streets of London. As usual, tourists are his main obstacle, he thinks to himself as he is making his way, that in any short stretch of a London street he (or indeed anybody) traverses, he must feature in dozens of smart phone pictures as an inevitable, unavoidable and unwanted background filler. Then there is CCTV, also probably undercover security personnel posing as tourists watching us watching the world. There is no doubt about it, big brother is looking at us through many modern devices and probably the old fashion way too.

Luke figures that by now Pops and his goons will have got off the roof one way or other bar jumping off it. Most likely the restaurant worker will have come round from his unplanned 'nap' and opened the roof door and freed his 'attackers'. He probably did not even get a 'thank you' for this good deed.

Luke best guesses the route his adversaries would take to get back to Sir Marcus' house, so he goes that way. Sure enough, in the near distance he sees Pops and his crew approaching in his direction. This brings a nice smile to Luke's face. He grabs the lucky charm in his hand, the one he totally believes in now.

"Righty-o then, I really hope you don't have a luck credit limit as you only cost five pounds. If you do, then I wish we'd bought a twenty-pound charm instead. Keep doing your thing baby, I wish—"

Pops and his three goons walk fast pace towards some open space with a row of benches a little ahead.

"Hey! Look over there, it's those homeless tramps that ate our fish and chips," shouted Tommo.

One bench did indeed contain four tramps sitting on a single bench with their backs to Pops and his mates a little ahead. In fact, this place is the same place where Luke had walked past the four, whilst they had been eating their fish and chips earlier.

"Those dirty stinking tramps ate my lunch, our lunches," added Mozzy.

"They can wait, they'll be here when we get back. After all, homeless hobos can hardly go home can they?" laughed Pops.

"We need to get 'em back, you said we could get them back later Pops, now is that time, right time to do it," demanded Chayse.

"I know I did, but we've got urgent business to sort out right now, more urgent than a bunch of toe rag tramps," replied Pops. Pops clearly senses the desire of revenge in the body language of his troops and he needs to keep them on side. "Oh, OK then, let's duff them up but quick time, straight in, a few licks around the head and body and straight out."

The army of three cheer to this and the four of them head to battle, a one-sided battle. A bit like how the British Empire was won in the nineteenth century.

At the battle site of the bench, Pops and his three eager beavers dive straight in (true to their word) and take the unsuspecting tramps from behind, shouting obscenities at them as well. Punches and kicks fly everywhere but something is wrong, very wrong. What should have been an easy one-sided slaughter turns out to be anything but. The tramps reveal themselves to be undercover policemen and during the melee, more uniformed officer appear out of nowhere to apprehend the assailants. Soon Pops and his crew are all laid out on the floor being handcuffed.

"What the frick is going on? What are the feds doing here? Where the hell are the frigging tramps?" shouted Pops as he is being shackled. The other three shout obscenities to high heaven but this time to the police. A police man stands over them explaining why they have been arrested and then proceeds to read them their rights.

Back with Luke watching way off, his satisfying smile is larger and more pronounced than ever. He is still holding his lucky charm in his hand. "One rotten lot down, one more to go! (He looks down at his charm). Oh I love you baby, you—lucky, lucky charm!" He kisses it once and still looks at it admiringly. "I promise to get some expensive wood polish and give you a—a ten-pound makeover." He then goes off to rendezvous with Tina.

Tina is patiently waiting for Luke to get to her, she keeps looking out for either him or the dreaded Pops and his goons. As she looks for the umpteenth time, she smiles with great relief. For in the near distance, she sees Luke coming her way.

Earlier on, before Tina had got to Sir Marcus' house, Sophia had got there first. She stormed into the house, gaining entry from the unlocked front door and had shouted for Sir Marcus but received no reply. She then shouted for Benson and still met with silence. Since she was covered in mud, what did she care if the home owner was in or not, this mud had to be washed off as a matter of urgency and some fresh dry clothes. A quick shower would take care of the mud and the clothes would be found from Lady Somerton's no doubt immense collection. Sophia, knowing this house inside out, hurried to the bathroom and began the self-cleaning process.

Back outside, the two missing person finders take comfort from each other. "Luke! Darling. You're back—and not a scratch on you. Did you not find them anywhere? That means they must be on their way here then," asked Tina justifiably.

"Oh, they're on their way alright, just not here, thankfully," replied a smug Luke.

"What do you mean, sweetheart?"

"I'll tell ya' later Tina, my partner, my procurer of vital equipment. (Luke grabs and shows the lucky charm to Tina. She looks at him more than a little confused, what's a cheapish trinket got to do with anything with this situation?) Come on, let's get inside, I'm sure Sophia will be inside by now."

The two hurry towards the front door and proceed inside a little cautiously. Once inside, all is quiet to their relief.

"All quiet on the western front, but I think someone is upstairs, in the bathroom maybe, having a shower?" said Tina a little quietly.

"Sophia!" said both in unison and smile.

"I guessed she would be showering as soon as she got here. I tied and hid from view Bainbridge and Benson so she would neither have seen or heard them, nor probably bothered to look for them when she first got here," informed Luke.

"You're really getting into this role thing, aren't ya'? Move over dough and batter, its cloak and dagger now, mate."

"Maybe I was born to do this, my calling, I've found out what I'm good at."

"I don't know—you were rather good at being unemployed."

"Hey! I merely enjoyed being unemployed, not good at it. There's a big difference."

"OK, former unemployed of the month, every month, what are we doing here?"

"Oh, you're gonna love what I have in mind for Bainbridge and Sophia. Like I said before, way, way better than handing them to their friends—the police. The police down here just round up the innocent, they let the actual perpetrators like Bainbridge off, Scott-free. Follow me, we need to sneak into the bedroom, where Isabelle was kept."

"I'm all wet and muddy too, I could do with a shower and change of clothes too, a nice, expensive, evening cocktail dress, me thinks. Lord Snooty's fancy woman will have some clothes that should fit the bill nicely."

"Oh yeah, you do. But I don't think Bainbridge's lady friend's clothes will fi—" said Luke but stopped saying the full sentence on account of the dagger stare from his lady friend.

"Wise decision!" firmly stated Tina.

As they move more inside, Luke whispers very quiet to himself, "Even rich folk must buy some, one size fits all stuff, t-shirts or track suits and stuff like that surely, charity buys just for publicity like."

Chapter 30
Way, Way Better!

Luke and Tina stealthily go upstairs and go to the smaller bedroom that recently held Isabelle captive. They go in.

"Sophia's definitely in the bathroom? She might be all naked and that when she comes out, we are going to wait until she puts some clothes on before we apprehend her, right?" asked Tina, the spoilt sport. The way it was asked, it demanded only the right kind of answer.

"Exactly what I was thinking, let her put some clothes on first, then we apprehend her," repeated Luke. It is a good job we humans cannot actually read minds.

"I'm glad we think alike, same page. So, it's agreed, we wait for her in here." stated Tina.

"Yeah, also we need what's in here, the knock out drug they used on Isabelle to keep her under. Look, it's still there on the bedside cabinet."

Both go over to the cabinet and see a small bottle along with a few medical injections still sealed in their sterile packaging next to it. Luke picks up the bottle so he can read the label.

"Desflurane. Must be the 'go to' knock out drug these days. Erm, Tina, do you know how to inject someone, you know, stick it in the arm, like they teach you in a first aid course and such like?"

"They don't teach you how to inject people in first aid courses, silly. Like you, I've only seen it on telly or when I've been injected at the local clinic or hospital. You have to flick it with your fingers then squeeze all the air and excess drug out until you only have the right dosage inside the tube."

"Oh yeah! You have to get all the air out, as that can be dangerous. That's how the bad guys kill people in films."

"I take it you intend to inject Sophia with this drug?"

"Not just her, Bainbridge and old Benson too. Part of my plan, in fact, integral to it. Let's see how Sophia is getting on."

"Hold your horses, Randy Twinkle toes. Let's give her a few more minutes. Waiting some more is part of my plan."

In the forced waiting time (in Luke's case anyway), Luke decides to make headway with the knock out kit. He looks down on the floor. "Oh, the injection old Benson was going to use on Isabelle before I stopped him is all ready to use. (He picks it up). I saw him rid it of the air. We can use that on Sophia. I'll fill out two more for Bainbridge and Benson. Lucky, I can see how much to put in from this one."

"It's been on the floor, maybe it's better to use a new one," cautioned Tina.

"You're right, I'll prepare three new ones, discard this one once I see the amount. In fact, I'll half the dosage as I want them to be compliant and somewhat aware but not enough to object or do anything about it like struggling or escaping."

After some time, the two listen out for shower noises from their bedroom doorway and cannot hear any. Then they hear one door open and after a few seconds, a second door open and close quickly. Sophia is now ripe for ambush.

"She's had enough time to put some clothes on by now or at least still be in her bathrobe, we should make our move," suggested Luke.

"Eager beaver aren't ya'? But I agree. Let's do this, but I'm leading."

The two stealthily creep towards the master bedroom and wait outside the closed door. They look at each other and both just know when to burst through. This they do, with Tina leading as she desired.

Luckily for Tina and unluckily for Luke, Sophia had put some clothes on, some of Lady Somerton's casual comfort clothes. She is sat on the dressing table chair towelling her hair dry at this moment of interruption. She swivels around mighty quick.

"What on earth! How dare you break into this house? Get out at once or I'll call the police this second!" shouted Sophia as she stands up.

"Listen sister, you got this all wrong, sweetheart. This house is not yours, so you are also an intruder, an uninvited intruder. Plus, we are the ones who should be calling the police, not you darling! So, my little cherub, sit down, continue drying your dyed and falsely extended hair, but most of all—shut the hell up!" ordered Tina, in her element!

"People will know I'm missing, they will inform the police!" warned Sophia, probably saying things that she thinks she should be saying in this sort of intense situation. She slumps back down onto the stool.

Tina laughs. "The only people who will be looking for you are your clients, they will be aware you are missing—missing their appointments. Who they gonna call? Their wives? They'll just forget about your let down ass and move onto 'easy Ingrid', their reserve totty. Sorry to break it to you, princess but you're just a name on a long sordid list. You're a lady in waiting alright, waiting in a long queue. Now and again his nibs calls you up and throws you an expensive bone to nibble on. More doggy than pussy!"

Sophia makes a move like she is going to get up to fight by slightly getting up but then sits fully back down, Tina too makes an 'I'm ready for you' body gesture but luckily nothing comes of it either.

"OK girls, time out," said Luke. (He holds up an injection in his right hand). "Right Sophia, time for you to honour your new appointment."

Sophia looks at the injection with shock and horror. What did these two have in mind? They do not look like psychopathic crazy people but you never know, the most successful serial killers in history were skilled in looking like regular normal people.

"You two should know that I alarmed the house when I came in, you have triggered the silent alarm and the police are most likely on their way. You should be very worried, leave whilst you can," advised Sophia.

Luke laughs and says, "Silent alarm? Come on Lady Sophia. You can do better than that. There are times when I worry though, like if there was a deadly pandemic virus and half the world's population died out. What if both the recipe holders of the Coca Cola drink died? The survivors would never be able to sup the classic original dark nectar with their lips ever again. They'll be destined to drinking Pepsi for ever more. The police blue-lighting their way over here this second, that is not one of my or the good lady Tina's worry right know."

"Think you're clever, don't you? Two upstart ruffians from the north, London will finish you, end your pipe dream, we'll flush you away with the other turds in the sewage pipes. Both of you are finished, I promise you!"

"On the contrary mama B-I-T-C-H, we are near to wrapping up our first case successfully, 'Luke Woam—Missing Person Finder' is up and running. Of course, BEHIND every successful man, is a woman, me, my name is on the business card too, albeit smaller and less prominent but that will be addressed in the near future."

Sophia looks at Tina menacingly. "Behind and to both sides!" She then smirks, one of those smirks that is purely to annoy.

Luke has a quick guilty smile for just a second that he makes sure neither Tina nor Sophia see. For Tina it is a different matter, she ends her somewhat good mood on hearing Sophia's remark and tries to go for her but Luke holds her back.

"Steady on, Tina love, don't go getting yourself wound up, she's only trying to psyche us out, wind us up because she knows we've got her good and proper. Last act of a defeated and desperate pathetic person."

Tina restores her calmness immediately, she looks at Luke. "The lucky charm seems to have improved your vocabulary no end as well."

It is much later and Luke and Tina are walking away from the house, in the busy streets of London, it is evening time and therefore dark. Tina has indeed cleaned up and wearing some unisex type two-piece track suit with a t-shirt underneath—all a bit tight even though the jogger set was Sir Marcus' and not Lady Somerton's!

"You're a right, little devious, so and so nowadays. You've changed so much I'm having difficulty keeping up with you," stated Tina.

"Nah! I've not changed. Just broadened my horizons, I've escaped the confinements of being an unemployed, going nowhere man living in a two-bit woolly back town in the dreary north."

"Enough of the slander, Hooray Henry, we're going back to that dreary little town in a day or two, if all goes well," Tina said firmly.

"Sorry, I didn't mean it that way, we're northerners and proud of it!"

"So, what now? What's part two of our many-part plan? How we gonna follow what we set up back there in the house? You haven't told me yet, can't see much topping that."

Luke smiles to high heaven. "That, my dear, is the most fun part of the plan, that's why I've resisted telling you so far. (Holds the lucky charm in his hand). I need the help of this—your—nay, our lucky charm yet again, don't know how I got along without it?"

"You're really buying into this lucky charm thing, from dissing it like nobody's business to—believing it more than that gypsy Rosie Lee woman herself. You weren't kidding about it."

"Oh, I do, I do. Now, I really want two specialty clubs to be around that corner from us—"

As Luke and Tina turn a corner, there are a line of clubs to either side of them, part of the famous busy night life of the capitol.

Luke looks around and his eyes fall on one particular club to his right. "That's perfect! 'The Tunnel of Love'. That'll do us fine. (Luke looks to his left). What luck, the other perfect club we need, the 'Bikes 'n' Beer' club. And so close to Sir Marcus' house too. Tina, my darling, here's what we're going to do. I'm going into 'The Tunnel of Love' and I want you to go into the 'Bikes 'n' Beer' club. This is what we're going to say to the punters in there—"

The two emerge sometime later and meet up.

"Well, I did—well more, told them in there exactly what you told me to say, Luke darling. It needed a bit of persuasion but once I locked onto the right sort, it was a doddle. I gave them the written address and time and—I would just like to say that your cunning plan might just work," confessed Tina.

"OUR plan, Tina my sweetest of hearts, it is our joint plan. I too, came out with a positive vibe, something that never happened at my final exams at school (he laughs, Tina smiles), so phase two—or is it phase two? Yes, it is as phase one happened back at the house. Phase two is now complete. Onto phase three, let us make haste back to Bainbridge's house because I feel like in a bit of an arts and crafts mood. Tina, I hope you are still good at art like you were in school?"

"Of course! Otherwise I wouldn't have got a spectacular grade C in it. I went from an E to a C. Sheer genius. What do you want me to knock out?"

"Signs! I'll explain what on when we've sorted out the materials. Oh! Do you reckon toffs, like Sir Marcus dabble in arts and crafts and such like?"

"Yeah, everybody always has stuff like that in their houses. Usually it's left to rot after the short lived art phase everyone gets, then gets over, like DIYing or other temporary hobbies."

"Good, 'cause I really don't want to use the lucky charm over such trivial little things."

Tina looks at Luke a bit deeply. "Right, now I'm wondering—more regretting, I bought the damn thing. I believe in it but the same as any normal person out there, maybe a bit more. You're taking it to the next level, you're just not snapping out of it. But I don't know, I don't want to be a doom monger or bring any bad luck, so I'll just shut up."

"I'm not taking it to the next level. And don't worry about it, sweet cheeks, you can't doom anything, you're not holding the lucky charm in your hand! (Luke holds the lucky charm in his hand). Now, I just said I didn't want to use it for little things but I could really do with a road sign just lying about that reads—
"

Chapter 31
Justice – The People's Way

As the bright lights of London shine away, they light up two unlikely, polar opposite lines of people walking towards Sir Marcus' house. One contingent is from the 'The Tunnel of Love' club and looking like they are on a Pride march, the other contingent is from 'Bikes and Beer' club and looking like they are leftover fans of a recent heavy metal concert from the seventies complete with beer cans in hand. Needless to say, both groups are composed entirely of men—even if they are at either end of the male spectrum chart.

As they approach the outside of the house, there is a large hand drawn sign stuck over the grand front door. It reads, 'Tunnel of Lovers—upstairs, turn right to the master bedroom. Bikes 'n' Beer boys—upstairs, turn left to the marked smaller bedroom. One requirement only for all who choose to enter—do enjoy! All free, my gee'.

Surprisingly, throughout the journey here of both groups, it had been a peaceful, in as accepting kind of way, affair. Hey-ho to modern times, eh? Why be a fighter when you can be a lover? Sorry!

The 'Bikes 'n' Beer' boys heavy foot step their way up to the smaller bedroom on the left that had a sign reading, 'In here boys' and the advance guard open the door. It swings away to reveal Sophia tied in a bent over position almost fully naked, at the end of the bed. She seems to be in a careless, stoned mood, like being high on drugs. She has a standard public highway road sign taped over her posterior that originally read, 'DO NOT ENTER' but the word 'NOT' has been crossed out so that it now reads, 'DO ENTER' if you were to not read the crossed out middle word.

"Mary, mother of Jesus, boys, we have been blessed! These rich twonks certainly know how to throw a great party!" said one of the lead bikers with great joy.

"Amen to that, brother Barry. It's about time we ate cake instead of bread, real silver platter lobster instead of mangy processed crabsticks. Come right in lads, desserts all served up, plenty for all!" said another.

They all give out a massive cheer as they pile in and the door closes loudly.

Over at the master bedroom, the 'Tunnel of Love' boys open the door, to see Sir Marcus also bent over and tied to the end of the large master bed. He is also really groggy, as a result of him too having a 'consultation' and the injection treatment by 'Dr Woam'.

Besides him, taking up the remaining space of the bed end is his loyal servant Benson, in the same positional predicament and state of awareness as his master. Sir Marcus has an A3 paper sign stuck to his royal posterior as well, which reads, 'THE Love Tunnel! Warning—Deep bore drilling in progress soon'. On Benson, the attached A3 paper sign reads, 'Notice—service tunnel and emergency overflow'. The art work lettering makes the two A3 signs look quite professional—hurrah for Tina and her spectacular grade C.

"Oooh bugger me sideways and upside down! Would you Adam and Eve it Pimple, my sugar plum, even when they're giving it away free, you still get two for one! I didn't know the rich and straight cared, it's making me all teary eyed," said one to another next to him.

"I don't know about you but I want a bite out of both cherries, my fluffy honey bunny. Move over rough and ready buttock sarnies, it's time to nibble and feast on some fine caviar peachy titbits?" commented Pimple.

"Get ready for some rough stuff sweethearts, we're storming the castle, it's ramming time!" shouted another from the crowd. "Let's put the nob into nobility."

Many cram into the room and the master bedroom door shuts with a bang too.

Chapter 32
Case Closed?

Luke, Tina and Isabelle and Mr Haversham are in the reception room, Mrs Haversham and their son Archie are also present.

The Haversham's are finishing their hugging of each other. All four then find seats to sit down as Luke and Tina look on, they are standing up.

"I can't thank you enough, you two. You—took your time and—one has to say, a fair amount of daily expenses on top of the initial fee—"

"My dear, we got our daughter back without any harm done to her, that is the most important thing," interrupted Mrs Haversham much to the delight of Luke and Tina.

"You're absolutely right, my darling, I was just about to say that myself. You two have returned our lovely daughter Isabelle to us unharmed. Serious harm would have happened to her, I'm sure, if you hadn't found her in time. We will always be grateful."

"No need to be, Mr Haversham, Mrs Haversham, we too are happy that we were able do our job of rescuing your beautiful daughter from a very real danger and a life of daily beatings and torture and probably a painful death due to—" Luke began saying but he too is interrupted by his other half Tina as she sees the looks on the Haversham's faces and senses unease and decides a quick intervention is needed.

"Luke! We all get the picture. (Looks at the Havershams). We are only too glad to have helped. If you ever need our services again, hopefully never, you know where you can reach us," said Tina with a bit more soothing words. She then adds, "We engrossed your business philosophy and are into fully advertising our firm now."

"Yeah! One could say, we're like doctors at the hospital or firemen or prison wardens—it's been nice meeting you but let's not meet again," chipped in Luke and only he and Archie chuckle at this.

"We'll see ourselves out, Mrs and Mrs Haversham. Have a good day," said Tina as she beckons Luke to follow her out of the door.

"See you la—ooh, I nearly said later but we hope that doesn't happen. I'll just say, have a good day from me as well, folks. So, that only leaves one final thing to say from the two of us, well maybe two things, have a very merry united Christmas all of you and my partner and I have to flowcha!" added Luke as he follows Tina out.

Once outside, the two missing person finders reminisce on the very recent events.

"That's it! We've done it, our first case concluded. I guess its case closed as they say in the business," proudly announced Tina.

"Not quite, my dear. There's just one more thing I'd like to sort out, put to bed before I call it a day," replied Luke, Tina looks at him with a bit of wondering.

"This ending, it hasn't got anything to do with sex, has it, I'm ever so tired with the journey back here?" asked a slightly weary and worried Tina.

It is night time in their home town Bolton's city centre streets, a bit different from the night time streets of the big city down south they have been used to. Luke and Tina are watching the same group of boys that had harassed them and half beaten Luke and Tina a while back, before their London adventure.

"I recognise them, it's those lager lout batty boys that banged us on our night out," said Tina. "Not to mention also being extremely offensive to me beforehand."

"Ruffled, Tina, not banged," replied Luke.

"If that's what you want to call it, fine! What have you got in mind, solving one case don't make you a super hero. They'll still ba—ruffle us to God knows what state!"

"I know, to both of those statements. I ain't exactly planning on challenging them in open combat shoot-out, no mano a mano macho shit. I—am going to use this again, my secret weapon. (Luke shows the lucky charm to Tina). Come on, let's finish this, finish what they started."

Luke walks off hotly followed by Tina, they both go towards the five drunken youths they had met that unfortunate night. "Tina, be ready to run when I say,

OK?" Tina just looks at Luke but says nothing. Running—not again, pretty please!

The five lads are doing what they do best, drinking, being loud, offensive to each other, laughing for no reason. They all see Luke and Tina very near them and getting closer.

"Hey! Some fat bird and her twiglet boyfriend coming our way. How about having some fun, let's bang 'em right out?" suggested one.

"Yeah! Why not! Flipping boring night anyways," said another.

"I'll piss on 'em," said a third. All five make a rather lame effort to be ready for a physical encounter but how good a preparation can a bunch of very drunk lads make? Obviously, none of them have the slightest memory that they had met these two previously. The mind altering effects of binge drinking and maybe cannabis spliffs?

Luke and Tina get to the five lads and before the young boys can fire off any verbal abuse, let alone physical abuse, Luke enacts his own plan. "Look here, Tina, five gay boys about to bum each other with their matchstick-sized dicks! (Looks at Tina). Run!"

So, Luke and Tina do what they so often did in London, run like crazy from their foe, only this was planned. As the two run, Luke grabs the charm in his hand and smiles. He says to himself, "Come on baby, one more time, for daddy!"

The chasing fivesome run after Luke and Tina. Even being inebriated and having set off many seconds after them, being young lads, they are catching up well—too well. It can only be a matter of time before Luke and Tina get— 'ruffled' again.

Tina looks back whilst running and comes to the same conclusion anyone would if they were observers to this incident. "I don't know what you got planned Luke but if it's us getting banged, battered and bruised, then I'd say your brilliant plan is going to work."

"Have faith, Tina my dear doubtful darling," replied Luke. Again, Tina looks at Luke in a funny way but says nothing more. The two run into a sheltered housing complex grounds.

The five youths run with—well youthful energy, with a smile or two appearing on their faces, maybe they foresee a victory shortly. They too enter the sheltered housing grounds. Suddenly, the ground gives way underneath them and they fall into a large void created by this sink hole. They disappear from street level view. Luke and Tina witness all this and now turn around and run towards their vanished enemy. They look down into the sink hole and burst out laughing.

The five youths had the misfortune of falling into the complex's broken concrete cesspit tank. They are all covered in human faeces/urine and one of them even has a turd half in and half out of his mouth. It is one hell of a disgusting site, even for the on-lookers Luke and Tina. The five monsters from the brown lagoon shout and scream and cry like toddlers, whilst squirming about in this brown hole from hell itself. At least the contents of the brown sludge soup are all organic and natural colours—no artificial stuff!

Luke looks at Tina.

"THEY do say that eating and drinking at these night time fast food joints is like eating shit and drinking piss. I think THEY might be right my dear. Saves them buying a donner kebab later on, don't it?"

Luke, whilst laughing, sees a ladder nearby and puts it down into the hole. Oh! He has a heart, even to lager lout scum like these. He says loudly to Tina, "Let's get the heck out of here before they climb out!"

"You don't have to tell me twice, dearest."

Luke has a last look at the wriggling poo brigade down below. "Hope not to see you later guys, we've got to flowcha!"

The two happily semi-run off, then after a while, slow to a comfort walk a safe distance away.

"Now, I trust this really is the end?" asked Tina.

"Yep! But if we ever find all the doors closing on us, we can always open another expensive but lucrative door in London. (Luke produces and shows Tina the little black book that once belonged to Pops). Sir Marcus was just one of many clients in this book!"

They both laugh, then celebrate by jumping up in the air and doing a high five together. Once back on the ground, they put their arms around each other and walk off into the moonlit night time.

THE END

CPSIA information can be obtained
at www.ICGtesting.com
Printed in the USA
BVHW050114070223
657977BV00011B/395